I0608077

Poisoned Patchwork

A Quilt Shop Mystery

DIANE QUAIL & BARBARA MILLS

Copyright ©2022 Barbara Tenney Mills
and Diane Quail

This is a work of fiction. Names, characters, businesses, events and incidents are the products of the authors' imaginations. Any resemblance to actual persons, living or dead, or actual events is purely coincidental.

All rights reserved. No part of this publication may be reproduced or transmitted in any form or by any means, electronic or otherwise, without written permission from the authors.

ISBN: 978-0-9905412-9-5

QUILTING FACTOID: A quilt is a warm bed covering made of two layers of fabric with batting sandwiched between them. The three layers are stitched together using a decorative design.

DEDICATION:

For quilters who give from their hearts to their hands to you.

Table of Contents

QUILTING FACTOID: A shop hop is a pre-planned shopping route between quilt stores where participants 'hop' from shop to shop. They often receive a free quilt pattern designed especially for them, as well as meals, snacks, and prizes. Sometimes the individual quilt shops offer the option of traveling by chartered bus.

CHAPTER ONE

Grace Meadows stood, her hand on the door of the quilt shop. She didn't want to do this; it seemed demeaning for a woman her age to be begging for her money back on a no-refund bus trip. But she had to start economizing somewhere.

She took a deep breath. It wasn't like she was going to starve. There was money, just not as much as there should have been. After years teaching students to think, using algebra and geometry as her mantra, she'd run the numbers only to find the wonderful retirement she'd planned snatched from her just as she was ready to enjoy life.

Through the large front window she could see the display proclaiming the countdown to the shop hop — One Day to Go!

Gift bags, cleverly arranged around Lego figures and a child's toy bus, promised fun and prizes. Lovely fabrics from the newest Moda line created a collage of colors and patterns in a vintage red wagon. The jellyrolls of pre-cut 2 ½ inch strips and nickel packs of 5 by 5 squares in coordinating red and blue prints made her fingers itch to touch the fabric—glossy, smooth, top of the line cotton fiber that felt like silk. Nothing like the greige goods of coarse textured, slightly off shade material that you found at the discount store between the crafts and cleaning products.

"Are you going to just stand there?"

"What?"

Regional quilt designer, Camille Christianson, impatiently stood behind her. Her perfectly styled hair not moving, as frozen in place as Grace was frozen in the doorway. "Some of us have things to do today."

Grace moved aside and let Camille steamroll past her. For an instant, the reflection she glimpsed in the glass startled her. Threads of gray ran through her deep brown hair. Wrinkles made a cross stitch pattern around her eyes. Well, she wasn't getting any younger. Best to get this over with. Darcy Duncan, the quilt shop owner, had always seemed friendly. She would understand.

As she entered, the smell of cotton fabric, like the scent of warm towels fresh out of the dryer, welcomed her. She quickly glanced around for Darcy but didn't see anyone. A shipment of new fabric sitting next to the counter, waiting to be placed on the shelves, called to her. Grace resisted. She had enough fabric to last a lifetime. Even if she spent hours quilting every day of her retirement, she would never deplete the substantial fabric stash she had curated over the years.

She headed to the back wall display of notions and quilting tools. The last time that she'd cut her quilt fabric, it had frayed, the rotary tool had made a ripping sound as it ran through the fabric instead of a clean slicing noise. Before she started another project, she needed to purchase a new blade for her rotary cutter. Once in front of the pegboard display, she dallied. Should she buy the more expensive, though supposedly more economical, blade sharpener instead of a package of rotary blades? Was it the good deal they said it was? How many blades would it need to sharpen to offset the cost? Perhaps when she got home, she'd do the math.

From the back office area, indistinct voices grew in volume. Although too distant to make sense, the meaning of the words was clear—a heated disagreement was in progress.

"Just try to do something about it." One of the voices declared.

A moment later, Camille brushed past. She gave Grace an oversweet smile and lifted a dark green travel cup with the Farmers Bounty Fabric logo on the side in a snide salute before she slammed out the door.

A few moments later, Meg came from the back. Although normally well composed, her pale skin had a flush, and her long red-blonde ponytail swished between her shoulder blades in an angry bounce. Obviously the two had been arguing and Meg hadn't won.

One of her former students, Grace caught herself thinking of Meg as a girl even though she was now all grown up. When had Meg graduated? Ten? Fifteen years ago? There had been so many students during her teaching career. Grace remembered that Meg had gone away to a large university. But, unlike most, had returned to Lake City. Something about her parents having health issues. It must be a struggle for her to settle back into the quiet of a small town after experiencing a real city.

Grace was glad that Meg had returned. She was perfect for her job — not only did she love quilts and quilting she also had a gifted eye for coordinating colors and fabrics.

When she noticed Grace, Meg forced a smile. "Mrs. Meadows, good to see you. I bet you're excited about the bus trip tomorrow."

Grace swallowed. It was now or never. "Actually, I've decided not to go. I'd like a refund."

"Oh?" Meg turned her attention to stacking bolts of fabric onto the cutting table. "You'll have to talk to Darcy about that."

"Is she in?"

As if on cue, the shop owner came through the door carrying two to-go coffee cups. Her short, dark hair was freshly done and her make-up understated. She'd subtly accessorized her slim cut slacks and silky white blouse with a delicate gold chain bracelet and matching necklace that flashed a small diamond pendant, all giving her an air of good taste and authority.

"Camille left." Meg told her.

Darcy hesitated. "But I brought her coffee. Just the way she likes it. Even though I had to wait for decaf."

"Mrs. Meadows would like to talk to you about the shop hop."

Darcy glanced over at Grace, a curious lift of her eyebrows. "Grace, good to see you. Are you excited about the bus trip? You'll have so much fun."

Grace swallowed. "Actually, you see..."

Darcy's back noticeably stiffened.

"I need to cancel and would like to get my money back." Grace finished in one burst.

The smile dropped from Darcy's lips. "That's not possible."

"Normally, I wouldn't ask, but with James," Grace couldn't say it, and yet she had to get used to saying it and having people ask. "With James going to the care center," there, she'd said it, "I find money is a little tight."

Darcy's lips formed a straight line of disapproval without an ounce of understanding. "I had heard that he was having issues."

Issues? Wasn't that like saying being a quarter yard short of fabric was a minor inconvenience when your quilt was already half pieced? "Yes, I've had to place him in the memory care unit."

"I'm sorry about your misfortune, but you've made a commitment."

"Surely, considering—"

Darcy cut her short. "If I let you cancel, what's keeping the next person from thinking they can use any excuse to change their mind?" She made the mildest shake of her head. "No, my contract calls for thirty people to be on that bus or I'll be cut from the next hop. Then you'll have to drive an hour to the closest bus pickup point. Think of how inconvenient that would be. Leaving your car all day in a strange town. Exhausted after a day of shopping and still having to drive home. So tired that you get into an accident. None of us want that to happen."

For an instant, Darcy's eyes hardened. "I have expenses to cover. Goodie bags. Prizes. Display models. No, if you can't sell your seat to someone else, you'll have to come yourself. The ticket plainly states no refunds."

"But you refunded Barbara."

"That was a mistake and it won't happen again." Her gaze flicked across the room to where Meg was cutting fat quarters. "See how being nice snowballs?"

The bell over the door jingled and a new customer entered, giving Darcy the opportunity to leave Grace standing.

Well, just because she had a ticket didn't mean that she had to go. It wasn't her problem if Darcy was alienating her customers with the snippy attitude she'd developed over the past few months.

Meg gave Grace a reassuring smile before she began folding the cut fabric into fat quarters.

"Meg, leave that. Show these ladies the goodie bag for the trip tomorrow?" Darcy's tone clearly said it was an order and not a request.

Although her jaw tightened, Meg left her project and went to the back of the shop where a long, folding table had been set up. Broadcloth bags with the shop logo stamped on them were stacked and waiting to be filled with the numerous give-away items spread across the table. A pen, notepad, and assorted patterns, most of which Grace already owned, so she knew the selections were older and weren't selling. Fat quarters cut from orphaned bolts of dated fabric lines or just plain ugly colors.

But among those less exciting offerings were true prizes — charm packs of 20 to 30 two and ½ - inch squares cut from yet to be released fabric collections, a coupon for discounted long arm quilting, one for a free class, and another for a free massage to soothe aching necks and backs after a long day of sewing. Even a signed copy of Camille's latest book. Grace didn't own one but would like to since Camille was a regional designer.

"There'll be brownies as well. Darcy knows how everyone likes them." Meg informed the women who were examining the offerings. "I'm baking them right now."

Grace wasn't overly fond of Meg's brownies. Unlike normal brownies, Meg used gourmet recipes that added savory ingredients, something she must have learned during her years in the city. But the women studying the shop prizes told her they were looking forward to the treats.

Arms loaded with bolts of colorful fabric, another shopper stepped over to the cutting table. Meg hurried over to help, leaving Grace by herself.

On top of a wastebasket full of discarded packing material, Grace noticed a newer mixer. Now why would someone throw that out? Studying it closer, she got her answer — the cord had been cut through exposing the wires inside, otherwise it was like new. It was certainly in much better shape than her worn out appliance at home. If she switched cords, she wouldn't have to buy a replacement.

Maybe Kevin would be willing to help her. After James went to the care center, he'd come by several times asking if she needed anything.

On her way to the kitchenette and back office area, Darcy breezed past. Grace stopped her. "Are you throwing this away? All it needs is a new cord."

Darcy's eyebrows knit for an instant. "Meg ran over that with a rotary cutter this morning. Sometimes I wonder where her head is. If you think you can fix it, go ahead and take it. It's of no use to me."

Without buying anything, Grace left the shop. After tossing the appliance into the trunk, she headed to the care center. She always spent the evening with James. Once parked, she studied the one story brick complex. The front entrance was inviting with urns of plants on either side of the door giving it a homey feel. But before going in you had to punch in a code, or ring for an attendant. That it was necessary made her heart tighten.

James had settled into his new life better than she had. As they sat in front of the television, watching car chases race across the screen, for a little while it felt like they were at home — her with her hand piecing and him engrossed in his show.

The nurses said that he was a dear, but Grace could have told them that. Except when he got agitated, then he wasn't. At precisely eight an aide came by and let her know it was time for James to get ready for bed.

Grace gathered up her fabrics. "The quilt shop hop is tomorrow." She said, not knowing if James understood. "You remember we take a bus and go from quilt shop to quilt shop."

James kept watching the flickering of the television.

"I've already paid, but I don't think that I should go."

In the past, they would have discussed the pros and cons of her going. By asking the right questions he would have resolved her indecision. Instead he sat there locked in his own world.

"I wouldn't get home until late, so I wouldn't be able to see you." She blinked away a film of tears.

When she went to give him a kiss goodnight, he pulled away. "We'll have none of that. I'm a married man."

~ ~ ~

Once home, the night seemed to drag on and the shop hop monopolized Grace's thoughts. She had signed up months ago. She'd actually been the first one to put her name on the list. But that had been before she'd recognized the downward turn of James' mental state. With both of them working — his odd hours as a county deputy, her with teaching responsibilities and school activities — it seemed they'd hardly seen each other over the last few years. When James' co-worker Kevin Oleson had approached her with his concerns, Grace had been offended. But the more she took note, the more she realized James was no longer the man she had married. His slow smile and dry sense of humor were gone.

At first, she'd made excuses. He was working too hard. The rotating hours wore him out now that he was getting older. With all his responsibilities at work, keeping up with routine tasks at home became more and more difficult. When he'd been assigned to a desk, she'd been relieved. His hours were regular, and they spent more time together. It had helped for a while.

She worried the edge of her blanket, clutching the soft fabric with her fingers, remembering how quickly James had changed. Almost overnight he'd become surly with everyone. Including Kevin. Even with her. His supervisor had given James the choice: to retire or be fired. Grace hadn't known what to think. After devoting his life to the force, to be pushed out like that seemed unfair.

To keep him from moping around the house, Grace had taken early retirement as well. They were savers, so she had thought they would have enough money to live comfortably. Even have extra to take the trips that they'd never made time for. James' brother suggested a men-only fishing weekend. The shop hop was on the same weekend and she'd signed up for it so she wouldn't be home alone.

Thinking they would travel, she excitedly began gathering brochures about all the faraway locations she'd dreamt they'd visit together. At first that helped. He'd looked at the itineraries with her and seemed himself most of the time. But when he'd begun listening to the police scanner and thinking he should go out on calls, she knew something was wrong.

One day after replanting bulbs in their yard, she went inside and James was gone. She still didn't know how she had missed seeing or hearing him leave. Hours later, Kevin found a confused James wandering around the lake and brought him home. Although rumpled and exhausted, thankfully, James hadn't come to any harm. At first Grace had been relieved. Then the worry it would happen again nagged at her. What if James slipped away in the stifling heat and humidity of the lake summer? Or during winter with its snow and bone-chilling winds?

She was thankful Kevin was the one who had found James. During their years working together, James had taken Kevin under his wing. Kevin was more than just a fellow deputy and seemed to understand what Grace was going through.

After that, James' condition unwound like thread off a runaway spool. Although the doctors put him on medications, he refused to take them. Even accused her of trying to poison him. Eventually, she had no choice. Well, she had options, but the only choice to her was a very expensive care center with therapy and activities, rather than one where he sat alone in a room staring out at the world he was no longer welcome in.

It didn't feel like she'd slept at all when she heard the neighbors head out with their dog for its early morning walk. Sunlight reaching across the bed seemed to highlight the fact she was the only one sleeping in it. With a sigh, Grace went downstairs and started coffee. Before it began to perk, she turned it off. The milk was sour and the last egg in the carton cracked. If she wanted to eat, she needed to go to the store.

On her way, she drove past the Quilters Playground. It was only 7:30, but a crowd of women had already gathered in front of the shop. They formed a sloppy line as they waited for the bus to arrive. Grace slowed down and peered at the women. Although there were a few faces she didn't recognize, Grace knew most of them from the local quilt guild, or from taking a workshop or quilting class together. As with any hobby, if you stayed at it long enough, you got to know the regulars. And Grace had been quilting for many years. She'd started back when you did everything by hand. With rotary cutters and long arm machine quilting, what used to take months now only takes days.

Several ladies standing along the sidewalk held cups of carry-out coffee and napkins with pastries. Grace's stomach rumbled. Wasn't breakfast included? She'd paid for the trip, even if she didn't go, she could eat breakfast and not have the money she'd paid be a total waste.

Grace pulled into the parking lot. With a determined stride, she entered the shop. The morning sun had energized the shoppers, and despite the early hour, the shop was abuzz with activity. In the back, a crowd of woman were gathered around a breakfast buffet. Joining them, Grace studied the array of food. Besides coffee, tea, and bottled water there was an assortment of pastries and breads, along with two egg bakes — one with bacon, the other gluten-free.

To be polite, Grace reached for a brownie, but Meg pointed to the tray of quick breads. "If I know you, you'll love the banana peach bread."

Although she was trying to watch her waistline, Grace loved peaches and took a slice. Instead of nuts, the bread had chunks of peaches and a peach glaze. The combination worked surprisingly well. But then Meg was known for her baking.

While Grace made herself a plate, Camille came from the back office area. "Meg." She called loud enough that several women turned to look. "My coffee's gotten cold." She held up a dark green travel cup. "Could you be a dear and make me a new pot?"

Camille set her cup on the edge of the table where Meg was refreshing trays of food. Despite being busy at the register, Darcy glanced over. From the disapproving look on her face, Grace expected her to say something. Instead, Darcy turned to her next customer. Meg set her lips as if biting back a rude reply before she disappeared to the backroom kitchenette.

After a moment, Darcy breezed over, carrying several totes for the bus trip participants. "I'm glad you've decided to come. I know you'll have a great time." As Darcy set the totes down, she nudged Camille's travel cup a safer distance from the table edge. Then casually tilted it so she could read the logo. Her eyes narrowed into a scowl, and she turned the face of the cup to the wall.

Taking one of the canvas totes off the stack, Darcy focused her attention on Grace. "Here's your goodie bag." Darcy gave Grace a smile as she handed her one of the shop hop totes.

Her mouth full of the delicious peach banana bread, Grace wasn't able to respond that she was only there for breakfast. She still hadn't decided if she was going.

"Meg made brownies especially for the trip. Wasn't that sweet of her? And I've put one in each tote to make sure everyone gets one and there's no complaining there weren't enough."

Grace took the cloth shopping bag and peered inside. Besides a plastic wrapped brownie, there were more snacks, both store bought and homemade, as well as a bottle of water, a free pattern, a free fat quarter, pen, notepad, and a number for the prize drawing.

"Don't forget to pick up your free block at each stop. And for every $20 you spend, you'll get a free fat quarter." Darcy kept emphasizing the word free, as if Grace hadn't paid for her bus ticket.

When Meg returned with a fresh pan of egg bake, Darcy handed her Camille's cup. "Would you take this to the kitchen?"

Camille reappeared from the office area. "Is my coffee done yet?"

"No, not yet." Meg replied, forcing a smile.

"Well, hurry up. The bus will be leaving soon. Not without me, of course." Camille took a brownie off the tray. "I'll take one to tide me over until lunch." Then she headed back to her office. Meg's gaze followed her, a look of unconcealed dislike on her face.

Grace swallowed down her last bite of banana bread. "Lunch is included?"

"At the Lakeside Marketplace and Spa."

The Marketplace featured an amazing deli with seating on a dock overlooking the lake. She hadn't been there in years. Not since her twentieth anniversary when James had surprised her with a leisurely sunset dinner there. Afterwards they'd gone dancing and on their way home stopped at the ice cream shop for hot fudge sundaes.

"And then supper back here." Meg looked back at Grace. "Didn't you read your information sheet?"

Grace had to admit with her concerns for James she hadn't. Or perhaps she had forgotten.

"We're taking care of everything, all you have to do is enjoy yourself." Meg smiled.

"And shop, of course." Darcy chimed in as she went past.

It was so tempting. A day without worries. Someone else doing the cooking. And she'd get a block pattern from each shop with directions at the final shop on how to assemble them into a quilt. Shop hop quilts were always fun projects and pieced together into stunning quilts. She used the one she made after last year's trip on her guest bed.

"I think you'll have a wonderful time, but I better get this filled up." Meg lifted Camille's travel cup in a resolute gesture and headed to the back.

Still undecided, Grace stepped outside just as the bus arrived. The cluster of women straightened into a line. Quilt guild president, Julia, stood at the front, followed by her ever present best friend, Elaine. Unexpectedly, Grace found herself falling into step and moving along with the others.

At the door, the bus driver admonished the woman directly in front of Grace. "Sorry, no food on the bus. Only water. We don't want any spills on the fabric seats."

A slice of quick bread still in her hand, focused on her cell phone, Aaliyah began boarding the bus,

"Excuse me, Miss. No food on the bus." His voice increased in volume, and he pointed at the food. "Miss. Please, no food."

The young woman realized he was talking to her and quickly removed one of her earbuds. "What did you say?"

"For the fourth time. I don't allow any food on the bus."

"Oh, okay." Aaliyah folded her slice of quick bread into its napkin and stowed it in her tote.

It made Grace uncomfortable that he'd singled out Aaliyah. Several others carrying the last of their breakfast had boarded before her. She doubted he cared about the fabric seats. He just didn't want any messes to clean up after the trip.

Grace hesitated before taking that first step onto the bus. Mentally she listed why she shouldn't go: She shouldn't spend any money. Heaven knows she didn't need more fabric. But she couldn't get her money back. The trip was already paid for and meals were included. She'd also get a free block pattern at every shop.

But she'd be apart from James all day.

Then again, maybe it was time for her to trust the care center to take care of James. She couldn't stop doing the things she enjoyed, or she would begin to resent giving them up. The grocery store could wait. Giving the driver a grimace, Grace climbed the steep steps onto the bus.

QUILTING FACTOID: In the 1920s, magazines such as McCall's and Good Housekeeping prominently featured quilt patterns and quilt making tips. Newspapers also printed serialized quilt patterns.

CHAPTER TWO

At the top of the bus steps, Julia stood with a clipboard of paperwork that she wielded like a scepter and designated her as the one in charge. The woman enjoyed being at the center of things and knowing all the right people. She belonged to every community group and served on every committee; her mini-me Elaine always at her side.

For a casual bus trip, Julia had taken great care with her appearance—wearing slacks that coordinated perfectly with a light sweater and strappy sandals. The highlights and lowlights added to the artful layering of her hair must have taken forever to achieve. Her make-up was freshly applied, down to a shiny gloss over red lipstick. With the hours it took for her to get ready, Grace wondered how Julia ever had time to quilt. But then Grace couldn't recall ever seeing any quilts Julia had made.

Like a mini-Julia, when you saw one you saw the other, Elaine stood close by in a similar, complementing outfit. She even wore a tiny string of pearls. The fashionable pair made Grace feel dowdy in the clothes she'd thrown on when she'd thought she was merely dashing to the grocery store for eggs and milk. Like a turnip in a rose garden.

As she walked past them, they glanced right over at her. She felt like a nobody. Then she reminded herself she had a loving marriage with James and had helped hundreds of students during her teaching career. To her those things meant so much more than knowing the town's movers and shakers or being fashionably dressed.

The first two rows of seats were blocked off with ribbons and had little reserved place cards on them. The first row, of course, was for Camille, and the second was for Julia and Elaine. Grace kept going down the double rows of soft velvety seats with high headrests. Above the seats were compartments for stowing luggage. From her previous shop hop bus trips, Grace knew by the time they returned to the Quilters Playground later that evening, the compartments would be crammed full of packages as some women used the hop as a tit-for-tat spree, spending on their hobby what their husbands spent on their fishing equipment, hunting gear, or sports tickets.

Grace hadn't understood how much that could be until after James had moved to the care center. She'd realized the days of his treasured fishing trips were over, so hoping that he'd get the same enjoyment from it as James had, she'd offered Kevin his fishing gear. The young deputy had reluctantly accepted, only to return weeks later with the money he'd made selling much of it online. The amount Kevin had given her was equivalent to yards and yards of fabric, possibly even a new sewing machine. No wonder some quilters felt a shop hop was a guilt free excursion.

Although it was close to departure time, there were plenty of seats to choose from. The bus could hold forty and if Darcy had contracted for thirty, she was several shoppers short. It looked as if there was going to be room enough to spread out. Most people would get two seats to use, so Grace wouldn't have to ask to sit with anyone.

When she went past Aaliyah, the woman was busily texting on her cell phone. Not wanting to disturb her, Grace kept moving toward the back, stopping when she reached Connie. Although Grace always thought of her as a bit of a gossip, Connie was another long time quilter. She was dressed for comfort in sensible shoes, leggings, and a long dress shirt that reached mid-thigh.

At the last guild meeting, Connie had excitedly talked about buying fabric to make Christmas gifts for her children. Knowing she would enjoy telling Grace more about her projects, Grace took a seat across the aisle from her.

After several minutes Camille entered, another brownie in her hand. She glanced at the half full bus and scoffed. With a disapproving snort, she sat, and the bus doors closed. Julia immediately leaned over the seat and said something to Camille. The designer reached into her large designer tote, pulled out a bound purple notebook, and pretended to be too busy to respond. After a moment, Julia sat back in her seat, glancing around to see if anyone had noticed the snub before flipping through the papers on her clipboard.

Connie stopped investigating her shop hop tote bag and leaned over to Grace. "I wouldn't be surprised to hear that she's leaving."

"Leaving? Who?"

"Camille. Didn't you notice her mug? She's been flashing it around with that smug smile on her face ever since she came back from market."

"Her mug?" Did Connie mean the thermal travel cup that Camille was using?

"It has a Farmers Bounty Fabrics logo. Darcy and the sales rep had a disagreement two years ago, and she hasn't bought from them since then. If Camille's signed on with them, she'll leave the shop for sure." She waited for Grace's reaction.

Seemingly satisfied by the little gasp of surprise Grace hadn't been able to contain, Connie continued. "All Farmers Bounty designers do podcasts. Camille called over to the high school asking the speech teacher if she'd meet with her and give her some pointers on giving presentations. Camille got mighty upset when the teacher told her she was too busy with the school play and didn't have time to help. Then Camille tried getting our computer guy to help her with the tech stuff, but he didn't seem to be available either. Guess sometimes you reap what you sow."

Connie pursed her lips in a superior smile and gave a slight nod with her head. "Still, she'd be a fool not to sign with them, she'd have her own series of books as well as patterns."

Grace blinked in disbelief. That sounded like a great opportunity for Camille, but what about Darcy?

"Darcy will not be thrilled about it." Connie added.

No, Grace didn't suppose she would be. Quilt shops were destination stores, and having a designer in residence drew serious quilters who spent hundreds of dollars on their hobby.

"Are you sure? Darcy gave Camille her break into the business." Grace recalled the design contest Darcy had sponsored when she opened the Quilters Playground. Grace had even entered a pattern herself—an uninspired layout of nine-patch blocks set on point. Camille had won. Then she'd designed another quilt, and Darcy had promoted it in the shop. It didn't take long before Camille was producing pattern after pattern, and the Quilters Playground was only carrying fabric that showed Camille's work to the best advantage.

But Camille's use of bold prints and focus fabrics didn't seem to match with Farmers Bounty's muted color palette and tiny patterned repeat designs. Certainly Camille would feel a sense of loyalty to Darcy.

Connie gave a lift to her shoulders. "Maybe it's only a rumor, but Laura got here early and she heard Meg and Camille arguing. If the shop goes under, where does that leave Meg? The poor girl's papered the town with resumes and has gotten nothing."

Grace had heard Camille and Meg arguing as well. But that didn't mean Camille was leaving. Before she could ask any questions, another woman shuffled down the aisle.

"Oh, Judy, I didn't know you'd be on the trip." Connie got up, taking her possessions with her, and followed Judy down the aisle. "We haven't talked in forever. How is your son doing? Does he like military life?" They stopped a few rows back and sat across from each other.

Grace would have been offended at being abandoned, but Connie and Judy both belonged to the School Marm Quilters, an informal group of teachers and retired teachers who periodically sewed together—sharing snacks, recipes and all the latest news around town. The group had invited Grace to join them, but she had always been busy and now with caring for James, she could never find the time. Even if she could, she wasn't sure if she wanted to commit herself. Or if she really belonged.

She glanced out the window at the sun, now well above the lake's shimmering waters. The line in front of the bus was gone, and Judy seemed to be the last of the shoppers. Grace hoped they would depart soon.

The feeling of dread in her stomach at leaving James kept growing. Certainly eating breakfast had made up for some of the ticket cost. She didn't need to go. One of the girls from the guild would share the patterns with her. Just as she was gathering up her tote and purse, the hydraulic brakes groaned and Grace sat back down. It was too late to change her mind now.

Before the bus could move, a loud banging on the door stopped the driver. Hiding a frown, he opened the door. "You almost got left behind."

A disheveled woman gasping for air climbed into the bus. Although Grace knew most of the area quilters, she'd never seen this woman before. Taller than average and a little on the heavy side, she wore an enormous hat with fake flowers, carried the shop hop tote, as well as one of her own, and a large notebook. With a great plop, she sat next to Camille in one of the designer's claimed front seats.

Camille glared at the woman. "That seat's not available." Either the woman didn't hear her, which didn't seem possible as the entire bus could, or she was too tired to move after scrambling to board the bus.

The ladies watched to see if a scene would unfold.

"Oh, it isn't?" The late arrival fanned herself. "Well, just let me catch my breath."

She didn't move, but the bus did.

As soon as they left Lake City and were out on the highway, the driver got on the PA. "Welcome ladies, don't think I saw any gentlemen on this trip."

He gave a quick overview of the bus, bathroom in the back, luggage compartments overhead, and stressed that everyone was responsible for their own packages. He gave an estimate of the time to their first stop and then the stop thereafter, and when they would have lunch and dinner. "So just sit back and enjoy the ride."

Recalling how he'd chastised Aaliyah about not allowing food on the bus, Grace wondered why he didn't announce it to everyone, and if Aaliyah noticed as well.

Grace looked over her fellow passengers and was happy to see Violet and Rose near the front. Their heads together, Vi and Rose studied a quilt magazine. Violet's fine gray hair and pale white cheeks contrasted with Rose's dark tightly coiled curls and bronze skin, but the love between grandmother and granddaughter glowed between them. After her initial resistance to her daughter marrying a black man, Vi had melted at the birth of her first grandchild.

Someone told Grace this was Rose's first shop hop. Violet was passing along the family tradition of quilting, just as her mother had to her. She was introducing Rose to the specialty fabrics, magazines, blogs, podcasts, and the star designers who had turned quilting into a multi-million dollar business so different from the hand pieced, hand quilted heirlooms made by previous generations.

Leaving home as she had, Grace hadn't brought anything to read or do on the bus, and it was a good hour to the first stop. Maybe Vi would loan her the magazine to glance through. Before she could move forward to ask, the woman who had gotten on at the last minute came down the aisle. She openly stared at the occupants as she went, swaying right and left with the unsteady rocking the moving vehicle, her bags banging against first her legs, then the arm rests. Grace could only guess that at last Camille had succeeded in giving her the heave-ho.

The woman made eye contact with Grace. Before Grace could look away, she plopped down in the aisle seat across from her. Grace didn't have enough energy to be friendly, and making small talk made her feel awkward. Without a book to bury her nose in, she could only hope the woman had been so badly burned by Camille she would leave her alone.

"Hi, I'm Bea. This is my first shop hop."

QUILTING FACTOID: Applique is a quilting technique where pieces of fabric in different shapes are sewn onto a larger piece of fabric or quilt block to create a picture or design.

CHAPTER THREE

Grace's heart sank. Bea kept talking and didn't give Grace a chance to introduce herself. "Might be my first, but it won't be my last. Nope, I'm going to be a designer. I just stopped for a moment up front there to get some pointers from Mrs. Christianson. I understand she's a big name around here."

Never having gotten past her Midwestern politeness, Grace nodded in agreement. "Yes. I've made quilts from several of her patterns."

"Really? Which ones?" Bea rummaged through her totes and pulled out a stack of quilting books. "That lady in the shop let me have these at half price." She fanned the books open.

They were all Camille's. Why would Darcy sell Camille's books at half price? Even so, the total had to have been over a hundred dollars.

"Where do you think I should start?" Before Grace could answer, the woman plucked a book out of the stack. "Now I hate the colors she used in this one, so it's a no go." She tossed the book onto the seat beside her.

Grace blinked. "You don't have to use the same colors."

"I don't?" Bea gave Grace a puzzled look. "Then why did she put them in the book?"

"That's just to show how you might want to arrange the fabrics."

"I do like that fabric there." Bea pointed to the large border of the quilt pictured on the cover. "I think I'll buy myself some of that."

Obviously the woman was new to quilting. "Yes, it is a lovely fabric. But you won't be able to find it. It's years old."

"What? I thought all these stores had all the fabrics."

"No, there are dozens of fabric manufacturers and they put out multiple lines of fabric every year, like car makers put out new car models. So most stores specialize in certain kinds of fabrics. The Quilters Playground carries lots of bold fabrics in primary colors."

"That's the store we just left?"

"Yes. Now the Hummingbird, the one we're going to next, specializes in botanicals: florals, greens, and softer tones."

"Not for me. I like bright bold colors."

From the way the woman dressed in the big hat and a flashy floral print top with hot pink leggings and neon yellow flats, Grace had no doubt Bea would prefer bolder fabrics and quilts.

"So what kind of quilts do you design?" the woman asked.

Grace did a double take. "I'm not a designer."

"You're not? Why not? Doesn't look that hard to me. Slap some fabrics together and print them into a book, then wait to rake in the money."

"That's not actually how it works."

"Why don't you tell me about it?"

Grace was certain she didn't want to. She wasn't an authority, just had picked up bits and pieces of knowledge. If Camille wasn't forthcoming with information, then Darcy, or Meg, or even Julia, the quilt guild president, would be the people to talk to.

Bea dug into her shop hop tote. Grace expected her to pull out a notepad and pen. Instead Bea retrieved the frosted brownie. "That Camille thought these were the best. She ate two while I was sitting there."

That would be three she'd eaten, Grace thought, but who was counting.

Unwrapping the brownie, Bea took a large bite. After one chew, she spit it back into the wrapper. "That's awful. Tastes like someone put leaves in it."

Grace hadn't tried hers yet. Sometimes Meg got adventurous in her baking and would add savory to her brownies. Mostly rosemary, but once she'd even used onion. Although Camille loved it, most of the other quilters weren't as excited about the gourmet additions.

Rose came down the aisle and stopped, hanging onto the back of the seat in front of Grace. "Grandma wanted to know if you've seen the new American Patchwork issue."

Relief swept through Grace. Count on Violet to notice her situation. "No, I haven't."

"Here." Rose thrust the magazine at her, "I'm going to make the one on page thirty." Then scurried back to her grandmother.

Although Bea made several more attempts at conversation, Grace kept her nose in the quilt magazine, not looking up until they stopped at the Hummingbird Quilt Shop and Tearoom. Nestled between fields of corn and soybean, and a good half hour from any major roadway, it was a favorite stop for travelers.

The shop owner, Fern, was originally from England, or across the pond, as she loved to say. Missing the exquisite cottage gardens of her English home, she had laid out over an acre of vibrant flower beds and winding walkways. The bright flowers and bird feeders scattered about the gardens attracted colorful butterflies and glittering hummingbirds that darted from flower to flower, sipping their sweet nectar.

With the quilt shop at one end of the property and tearoom at the other, the gardens and their pathways connected them with a sea of flowers and greenery. Homegrown herbs and fresh flowers were available for purchase, along with imported teas, chocolates, pastries, table linens, and fine porcelain tea cups and saucers. Some people only stopped for the tearoom's delicious food and exotic teas. But there were always plenty of quilters.

The bus hadn't even come to a full stop when Camille leapt from her seat. As soon as the door opened, she raced to the quilt shop. "Well, that's what my late husband would call a potty emergency. She didn't even bother to take her purse with her."

Although there was a bathroom on the bus, many of the ladies didn't enjoy using the swaying, cramped facilities.

"Of course she didn't look none too good when I was sitting with her." Bea continued as they shuffled down the aisle and off the bus. "Kept slugging down whatever she had in that travel mug. She's not a drunk, is she? Of course it wouldn't matter to me. My second husband liked his liquor."

Grace wasn't sure if Bea was talking to her or just talking, or if the second husband and late husband were the same person, so she ignored the woman. As she waited at the top of the steps for one of the quilters to move stiffly down them and exit the bus, Grace glanced over at the empty front seat.

In her rush, Camille had left her things scattered across the cushions: her shop hop tote, a half-eaten brownie, along with her purse and a large designer bag. The contents of her bag: a quilt book, several patterns, and a thick stack of printed pages held together with a binder's clasp, had even spilled onto the floor.

Grace couldn't avoid following Bea into the shop, but when Bea turned left, Grace turned right. After a quick scan, she spotted Vi and Rose at the snack table and hurried over to return the quilt magazine.

"Thanks for letting me borrow your magazine. The quilt on page thirty is beautiful, Rose. You'll have fun making it and will have to bring in to show and tell when you finish."

Vi gave a half nod. "You looked like you could use a little diversion. Who is that woman?"

Both of them looked over at Bea who was pulling bolts of fabric off the shelves and inspecting them.

"I don't know. But she sure did seem to want to talk."

"Let me take a picture." Rose used her phone to snap a photo of Grace, then of Grace handing her grandmother the magazine, then of herself scooping up a handful of nut and cracker mix. Grace had seen Rose taking pictures at the Quilters Playground earlier in the morning. She'd heard Vi telling someone Rose had just gotten her first cell phone and was excited to try it out.

"Are you done looking around already?" Most of the quilters didn't stop at the snack table until the end, so they had clean hands when they touched the fabric and no one could resist touching the fabric. "Have you found what you need for your quilt?"

Rose shook her head. "Everything in here is too old lady."

Grace understood. Not everyone liked the graceful florals and soft colors the Hummingbird specialized in.

"We're going to get some tea and look at the gardens. Do you want to join us?"

"Thanks for asking, but no, I think that I'll look around. I haven't shopped here in quite a while."

After wandering through and wanting everything, Grace settled on a fat quarter from a bin of older fabrics. She had several of the companion pieces left over from an eight-point star quilt she'd made last fall. With the fat quarter, she should have enough to make a matching pillow. And if not, it was in her favorite color palette, and she could use it in a scrap quilt.

She loved the new line of river bend fabrics. With its background colorways of muted blues, greens, and gray, they reminded her of the fishing spots that James used to tell her about. Colorful wildflowers and shade trees bordering the riverbanks with red-winged blackbirds and goldfinches balancing on the tall wild grasses moving with the breeze. It wasn't the Hummingbird's or Grace's typical soft color choices, but they kept drawing her in and enticing her to make a wall hanging for James' room.

A wave of guilt struck her. She hadn't thought of James since she'd gotten on the bus. Had he had his breakfast? She didn't know. Of course they would have fed him. But what had he eaten? Maybe they'd forgotten to put just a tiny bit of sugar in his coffee, not a full teaspoonful, just a taste is all he needed.

Tears welled up in her eyes. Not wanting anyone to see her crying and know how distressed she was, she headed for the bathroom. At least there she could cry in private. But when she turned the door handle, it didn't budge.

"Occupied." A voice behind her said. "She's been in there since we got here."

"Who?" Grace choked out.

"Who else? Camille." Laurie, one of the School Marm Quilters, shook her head as if Camille was a third grader and should know better. "So rude. As if she doesn't know the shop has only one bathroom." She must have noticed the distress on Grace's face. "If you can't wait until we get back on the bus, the tearoom's bathroom is open."

Grace tried to wipe a tear discreetly from her cheek.

"Everyone's already been there to check out the decor. Fern took an antique dresser and re-did it into a sink vanity. Then she put an old chintz wallpaper on two walls and painted the other two sky blue with decoupage flowers from the chintz. It's absolutely charming."

At the moment Grace didn't care about Fern's new décor. She only cared about James and how he was doing without her. Laurie's calming voice steadied Grace and the earlier wave of emotions receded. "Yes, I'll do that."

The other quilter moved on and Grace turned back into the shop area. She would just pay for her fat quarter and wait on the bus. Maybe she should call the care center. She'd gotten to know several of the employees there and knew they wouldn't mind if she called to see how James was doing.

On her way to pay, she went past a bin that held discounted bolts of fabric. Right in the front was a teal and cream stripe that would be perfect as sashing or binding for the trip around the world quilt top she had half pieced on her work table. Most of the fabric had already been sold off the bolt, leaving only a yard or two, three at the most. Even though she didn't need much, if she bought it all she should get the usual 20% off for finishing a bolt. And didn't the shop hop have a skinny bolt special of 25% off?

At the cutting table, Bea stood ahead of her in line. "What ya got there?" Bea pointed at the neatly folded square of fabric Grace was holding. "I seen them all over. Lots of ladies have 'em."

"It's a fat quarter."

"A what?" Bea squinted at the fabric as if expecting to see coins hidden in the folds.

"It's a quarter yard of fabric, but instead of cutting nine inches off the bolt, they cut half a yard. Then cut it in half so you have two rectangles 18-inches by 20-inches instead of two at nine-inches by 40-inches. Same yardage, different shape." Grace had often used one to explain how the area of a rectangle could be the same, even if the length and width were changed.

"Well, why would you do that?" Bea asked.

Feeling like she was back in the classroom, Grace mentally put on her teaching hat. "People who applique like it so they have more choices in placing a design without buying a half yard of fabric and only using half of it."

"So you like to do this applique?"

Although Bea gave the word applique a slight inflection, as if she didn't know what it meant, Grace chose not to explain the technique to her. "No, not very often. But fat quarters also work well with scrappy quilts, and sometimes it's just fun to have a bit of a fabric that you like, even if you don't know what you're going to do with it right at the moment."

Bea nodded as if she understood. Before she could ask another question, the woman at the cutting table motioned Bea forward. The shop clerk expertly flipped the bolt Bea handed her, exposing a yard of fabric and straightening it along a green mat that was fixed to the table. Rotary cutter poised, she looked at Bea. "How much?"

Bea turned to Grace. "What do you think? How much of this do I want?"

"What are you going to make?" Grace asked her.

"A quilt." Bea's answer only underscored her inexperience.

"Yes, but what kind? A bed quilt? A throw for the couch? A table runner? A wall hanging? Do you have a pattern? How much does it suggest that you buy?"

"A pattern? No, I'm going to make my own pattern. Ya know that I'm going to be a designer."

The clerk smiled at them. "Perhaps you ladies wouldn't mind if I helped the next customer while you decide."

Not wanting to be rude, Grace stepped to the side. Bea followed, her arms loaded with bolts of mismatching fabric. Some bright, some subdued, mostly large scale prints.

"See, I want to make some old fashioned looking thing that people can see when they come over. Make them think it's a family heirloom, like my grandma made it. Impress them."

Grace's eyebrow lifted. None of the fabrics looked old fashioned. "Maybe you could start small. Say 16 x 24. If you chose fall fabrics, I'm sure you could be done by autumn. Do you have a space on your walls where you could hang something?"

"Oh, I got lots of spaces."

"About this big?" Grace leaned the bolt of fabric she'd been holding against a shelf and held out her hands to visually show the size of a wall hanging.

"No, now that's too small." With a shake of her head, Bea nudged Grace's arms much wider. "There now, that looks about right."

A project that size would be a challenge for anyone's first quilt. "That would be a small quilt. Like a throw for a couch." Grace doubted Bea could handle something so large without some serious help. But the woman was an adult and could make her own decisions. "Alright. About 50 by 50." A square quilt would be much easier to figure the math on. "What color is your couch?"

"Which one?"

Grace was confused. "You have more than one couch?"

"Well, sure, there's one in the formal living room and another in the family room. I was thinking about maybe putting a smaller one in the master bedroom, but haven't decided if I want a small couch or a chaise."

Grace hesitated, thinking about her only couch. She and James had bought it years ago to update their living room. Now it was worn and faded and the cushions had indentations where she always sat to sew or read while James relaxed in his recliner watching TV.

She used to hide the wear with pillows and throw quilts, but now she cherished the reminder of happy times spent together with James. With the cost of James' care, she couldn't imagine having a new couch, let alone more than one.

"What colors are in the room?"

"Well, right now it's pale colors like a spa or the beach. It's pretty but too boring for me. I'm wanting to change things up."

This wasn't getting Grace anywhere. "How about, what's your favorite color?"

"Hmm, I can never decide on only one. Red seems to be catching my eye and making me happy today, but I like fuchsia and bright pink too. Any of those colors work for me."

Of course. Grace should have known even Bea's favorite color wouldn't be a simple thing. She fumbled through the bolts Bea was holding until she found a fabric with a large floral print in reds and pinks, similar to Bea's flashy flowered top and hot pink leggings.

"What do you think of this? You could use it as a border and pull colors from it for the blocks."

"Whatever you say."

Without a pattern, Grace wasn't sure how much Bea should buy. Most of the time two yards would do for the border of a small quilt, but it was always good to have extra. "How much do you want to spend?" That would give Grace some idea of how much extra fabric could be bought.

"Why, as much as I need to. I brought a thousand cash and spent somewhere around a hundred at that other lady's shop. But we can put some on the old credit card if we need to. I get an allowance and living here is way cheaper than the city, so I have lots to spend."

"Well, that's certainly more than enough to make a nice quilt." Grace set aside most of the fabrics Bea had already picked out and chose some companion fabrics for the blocks. Grace made some mental calculations. Finally, they returned to the cutting table where Grace directed the clerk on what yardage to cut.

As they stood in line to pay, the woman ahead of them paid for her fat quarter and asked if they had any caffeine tablets. "They have those here? Why does she need them?" Bea asked. "Do you think she's a drug addict?" Bea scrutinized the woman, Susan. "Looks mighty nice to be a drug addict."

Grace felt like rolling her eyes. "She's not a drug addict." Grace knew Susan was working two jobs so her husband could complete his master's degree and this quilting trip had been a birthday gift.

Even so, she only held one fat quarter, just enough of a purchase to get the free pattern. "She might have worked last night and wants something to help keep her awake."

"What's wrong with coffee?"

"After a while, it can upset your stomach. Besides shop hops, some quilt stores have all night quilting parties, and occasionally someone will want an energy boost."

"So it's a service?"

Grace guessed that it was. As if understanding, Bea pursed her lips and nodded her head. Finished with her purchases, Susan moved out of the way and the line shuffled forward.

When they reached the front and paid, the clerk added a sheet of colored paper and a stamped card to Bea's sack. "What's this?" Bea held up the paper. Puzzled by the line drawing of an applique flower and cutting instructions on the front.

"That's your free block. When you buy something at each store, you get a block pattern and they stamp your card. When we get back to the Quilters Playground, you show them your fully stamped card and you'll get the instructions to put together a quilt with the blocks." Grace gestured toward an exquisite quilt displayed at the entry. "That's the quilt design for this shop hop. Fern has made it up in fabrics from her shop. You can buy a kit to make one just like it."

"Nah, too prissy for me."

Personally, Grace thought it was beautiful and wished she could afford the kit for herself.

"Well, I'll see you on the bus. I'm just going to make a little pit stop." Grace stepped over to the bathroom, only to find it occupied.

One of the School Marm Quilters, she wasn't sure if it was the same one as before, glanced up from the discount bin she was rifling through. "Camille, ever the diva, is still in there. Everyone has had to use the bathroom in the tearoom."

With a sense of urgency, Grace headed through the gardens at a quick pace. Bea followed, right on her heels. "Say, why don't you let me buy you a cup of coffee. As thanks for helping me."

"I don't think there's time. Our hour here is almost up." Grace finished up in the bathroom and took a few minutes to admire the elegant decor.

She came out to find Julia informing everyone it was time to get on the bus. "We have a schedule, ladies. Please make your last purchases. The bus leaves in five minutes. I'd hate for anyone to be left behind."

En masse, the women went back to the quilt shop. Julia stopped to knock on the door of the restroom. "Camille, it's time to leave." No answer.

"Are you alright in there?"

Still no answer.

After frowning at the door, Julia turned to Elaine. "You better go find Fern." As Elaine sped off to obey, Julia tapped her toe and spoke to no one in particular. "I hope she's alright. Camille has been under a lot of pressure lately."

After a brief delay, long enough for a curious crowd to form, Fern appeared with the key. "Maybe she left and pulled the door shut with the lock on."

Grace hadn't seen Camille since they'd arrived, so it didn't seem likely.

When the door opened, the sickening sweet smell of chocolate and stomach acid wafted outward. Camille lay on the floor, curled up in a little ball, her head near the toilet.

Vi was the first to react. "Go get Aaliyah." She told Rose. "I saw her waiting to get on the bus."

Everyone except Bea backed away. The large woman pushed her way into the bathroom and flushed the toilet, waving her hand to dissipate the smell. "Someone needs to light one of those fancy candles. It's going to take hours to get rid of that stink. Reminds me of my first husband. Boy, he could smell up a bathroom."

Over her shock, Julia took command. "Everyone step back. There's no reason to stare. We need to make some room here."

Aaliyah came running from the parking lot, Rose close behind. Several ladies hustled along behind them, wanting to see what was going on.

"What is she doing here?" Julia cast a suspicious eye on Aaliyah's arrival.

"She was pre-med before her and her husband moved to Lake City. I thought she could help." Violet said.

"Fine. Has someone called 911?"

Elaine nodded, her cell to her ear. "It's too noisy in here. I'll go outside and make the call."

Grace noticed an unspoken exchange between Elaine and Julia. What was that about?

"And take care of things." Elaine added.

Aaliyah bent over Camille. Her normally smiling lips fell into a straight line. "How long has she been in here?"

After much murmuring, everyone agreed they hadn't seen Camille since she hurried off the bus. Aaliyah peered into the toilet bowl. "Was she feeling sick? Earlier?" She sniffed the air. "Did someone flush the toilet?"

"Really, who cares about the toilet, why aren't you doing something for her? Mouth to mouth, or something." Julia put her hands on her hips, making her diminutive frame larger.

"I'm sorry. It wouldn't do any good. You should all wait outside and watch for the EMT's."

Julia let out a half-snort, the most a woman of her breeding could produce to show her displeasure.

"Is she dead?" Rose's tiny voice sounded loud in the silent shop.

QUILTING FACTOID: Funeral quilts were made from the deceased's favorite clothing. Designs characterizing their personality and interests were often used. Sometimes the deceased contributed to the quilt before their passing.

CHAPTER FOUR

Grace was close enough to the front to see the body. Not Camille, the body. A shiver went through her. Camille's bright lipstick had rubbed off, making a smear of red across her cheek.

Aaliyah caught Grace's eye and with a slight twist of her head motioned her to come closer. In a soft whisper intended to go unnoticed in the shuffling of women headed outside, "I think you should call that friend of your husband's. That younger deputy he worked with."

"Kevin?"

"I don't remember his name. Looks like a Viking. All muscle." Grace nodded her head. That would be Kevin.

"He'll want to take charge as soon as he can." Aaliyah glanced around the room, seemingly uncomfortable meeting Grace's eye. "I wish someone hadn't flushed the toilet. It would have told them the last contents of her stomach."

"You think she was poisoned."

"No, no. It would just have helped them find out why she was vomiting."

Grace touched her hand to her heart. Both women stared down at the body. More than once James had investigated an unattended death. Usually it was nothing, but they had to be investigated as if a crime had been committed. Grace hastily found her phone and called the county sheriff's office asking them to transfer her to Kevin. "Grace, what can I do for you? Is James all right?"

Just the sound of his voice calmed her. "Yes, he's fine." At least she had to trust he was. "I'm on a quilt shop hop and…" How should she put this? "One of the ladies has died."

"Where are you? I'll be right there." Although she couldn't see it, she knew he had stood and was reaching for his deputy hat, just like she'd seen James do hundreds of times.

"We're at the Hummingbird Quilt Shop."

Julia appeared in the bathroom doorway. "Everyone's on the bus except you two. The next shop's bus of quilters radioed that they are turning off the highway. There isn't enough room in this parking lot, our bus is blocking the entrance. We need to get out of the way."

When Grace didn't move, Julia added. "We're already running late. If we don't leave now, we'll miss lunch." Her voice had taken on the tone one used with a wayward child.

Grace looked from Julia back to Aaliyah as she tried to decide whether she should stay or go.

Then Kevin's strong voice came through her phone. "Grace, are you still there? The call just came in. I'm on my way. This kind of thing happens. Usually an unknown heart condition, or a stroke. Everything will be fine. You go on with your quilt trip." Before she said goodbye, Kevin ended the call.

"I need to stay." Aaliyah told Grace. "I'll be required to talk to the EMTs and the police."

"See, Grace, Aaliyah will stay behind. You're not needed here. Let's get back on the bus with the other ladies." Arms crossed, Julia waited for Grace to move.

"I guess you're right." Grace said.

"There's nothing that any of us can do for Camille now." Aaliyah looked up at Grace. "If the police need anything, Darcy has a list of who's on the trip."

Aaliyah's expression told Grace she agreed. It felt wrong to be leaving, but Kevin had told her not to worry about it and continue on the shop hop. When she turned to leave, Julia moved along with her like a chaperone on a school field trip, making sure she boarded the bus.

No sooner had Grace sat down when Bea leaned across the aisle of the bus. "I knew she was dead."

As if she could escape the unwanted intrusion, Grace straightened, pressing her back against the bus seat.

"You can't always tell. My fourth husband, he went in his sleep. There's me, snoring right next to him."

Grace's eyes widened with horror. The more that woman opened her mouth, the more she stuck her foot in it.

Bea nodded her head in wisdom and to Grace's relief settled back in her seat. Everyone was strangely quiet, as if they were in shock from Camille's unexpected death or perhaps were afraid they might say the wrong thing. No one pulled out their packages to share the fabrics they'd bought or dreams of the quilts they would make.

Several watched as Rose snuggled against her grandmother and sniffled back her tears. Poor child, likely never seen a dead body. And how sad, on her first quilting bus trip. At least her grandmother was there for her.

Vi looked back and motioned Grace to come forward. As if Grace hadn't noticed, Bea leaned across the aisle and nudged Grace's arm. "That woman's trying to get your attention." She pointed toward the front of the bus.

Sidestepping through the narrow aisle, Grace made her way to Vi's seat.

Vi looked up at Grace. "I've called Stan. He's going to come pick us up. Do you mind asking the driver if he would drop us off when we turn back onto the main highway?" Rose shivered and pressed closer to her grandmother. Vi smoothed the girl's unruly curls only to have them bounce back. "Shh."

"Isn't she feeling well?" Grace asked. Could something in the breakfast buffet have spoiled? How long had the egg bake sat out?

"Oh, I think she's fine, just overwhelmed. All the excitement and then this." Vi pursed her lips and shook her head. "Poor Camille."

Grace nodded. Vi always saw the best in people. Although the driver grumbled that it was against company policy, he agreed to stop and let Vi and Rose off. While talking to the driver, Grace couldn't help but stare at where Camille had been sitting. Her designer bag leaned against the back of the seat, with her books and patterns stacked in a neat pile next to it.

Maybe Camille had a contact name in her purse. "Have you called Darcy?" Grace asked Julia. It seemed logical Julia would take it upon herself to call. As she spoke, Julia slid something under the tote bag on her seat.

Full of self-importance, Julia straightened her shoulders. "She was busy. I left a message with Meg."

"Did she give you someone to call? A family member or emergency number for Camille?"

"Oh, I hadn't thought to ask."

"Perhaps in her purse?" Grace glanced around Camille's seat, looking for the oversized leather purse Camille always carried.

"Really, Grace, we can't go snooping through someone's purse. Besides, it isn't here."

How did Julia know that so emphatically without even looking? Returning to her seat, Grace was relieved to see Bea focused on her phone. But it was only a second later that the woman leaned across the aisle and nudged Grace's shoulder. "How do you spell Christianson? With an e or an o?"

"An o. Why?"

"I want to get this right. Last pictures of famous quilt designer."

Grace's eyes opened in horror. "Are you posting online?"

Bea's thumbs stopped moving, and she looked up at Grace. "Shouldn't I? I took the last pictures of her on this here bus."

"But what if her family doesn't know yet?"

After a moment, understanding crossed Bea's face. "Oh, I guess you're right. I should just keep these and wait before I share them." Bea shoved her phone in her purse and was surprisingly quiet.

The bus travelled down the gravel road in a cloud of dust. When they reached the highway, the bus came to an abrupt halt. Everything that had been placed on the floor shifted forward. Grace watched as Vi and Rose gathered together the few purchases they had made so far and hurried to the front.

Ever polite and considerate, Vi stopped to thank the bus driver. Next to her, Rose stood on the top step fidgeting and playing around with her shop hop tote until her grandma finished.

Vi and Rose were only part way to the waiting pick up when the bus driver sped up to merge back onto the main road. Everyone was thrown backwards, purses and totes scraped along the floor beneath the seats. Several of the women bent down to settle their packages.

Bea picked something dark green off the floor and stared at it for a moment. With a shrug, she shoved it into her tote bag, then turned to Grace. "Hope that little one's doing all right."

Grace nodded, her throat tightening.

Now that Rose was off the bus, the hushed whispers grew in volume. Connie came up the aisle and stopped behind Grace, hanging on the seat back. "Looked like a heart attack to me. What do you think?"

Grace had wondered the same thing. Between the stresses of coming up with new quilt designs and promoting herself, plus the extra pounds Camille tried to hide, it wasn't unreasonable to think she might be in poor health.

"Someone told me she had a bad heart. I think it was Meg." Connie said.

Grace doubted Meg would share that kind of information. It seemed more gossip than fact. Her expression must have conveyed her displeasure because Connie gave a shrug of her shoulders, "I guess we'll have to wait and see." She continued to move forward.

From the back, Tamara asked if anyone knew how many grandchildren Camille had. "Was it one? Or two? Maybe someone could arrange for quilts to be made for them."

Of course, Tamara would think of doing something for Camille's family. She organized benefit quilts at any hint of need. And always donated the most quilts for the guild's charity causes.

The woman in front of Bea answered Tamara's question, "One. Camille's son, Charles, but everyone calls him Charlie. He has a little boy."

"Doesn't he live in the city? I rarely see him visiting and it isn't that far."

"Only reason he visits is to get money from his mom." The woman gave a little snivel of disapproval.

Grace didn't know how anyone could know that for a fact.

Connie came back down the aisle. "Her daughter's the same way. Flunked out of that fancy school she went to."

With her seat being in the center of the bus, Grace could hear every word said. Any attempt at being discreet was forgotten. Instead, all the women leaned in to listen.

"She lives with her dad now and goes to community college." Connie wrinkled her nose in displeasure.

Grace had to agree that Camille's family didn't sound very close.

"Still, the little grandson should have something to remember his grandmother by." When no one leapt in to volunteer to help, Tamara added. "Maybe Darcy will give us a discount on fabric."

"If Meg and Camille were still getting along, I'd bet Meg would help."

"But everyone gets along with Meg, she's so sweet." Tamara said. "And after living in the city and working at an ad agency, she has some wonderful ideas about blending fabrics and colors."

Grace hadn't known Meg had worked for an ad agency in the city. What a change working in a quiet little quilt shop must be for her.

"Well, I overheard Meg accuse Camille of taking her notebook, seemed plenty put out by it. Camille just laughed like it was some kind of joke."

"Oh, that would explain why Meg hardly even looked at Camille this morning."

"Did you see the face she made when Camille ordered her to make a fresh pot of coffee? If looks could kill."

"I heard that Camille was leaving the shop." Judy said.

"Where did you hear that?"

"Well, I don't remember, but she'd been carrying around that Farmers Bounty Fabric mug since she got back from market."

"Oh, she's just doing that to tick-off Darcy." Susan said.

"She certainly hadn't been attempting to get along with anyone lately."

"Not since her divorce." The woman who had known Charlie's name said.

"Whatever the reason, she certainly seemed to be burning her bridges behind her."

Bea leaned across the aisle and loudly whispered to Grace, "And maybe making a few enemies."

~ ~ ~

It was well after eleven when they reached their next stop, the Lakeside Marketplace and Spa. Fortunately, an extra-long stay had been scheduled, but now their hour for shopping and a second hour for lunch had shrunk to just over half an hour for each. As if nothing had happened earlier, Julia took charge.

After reminding the ladies that their time was cut short so not to dawdle, she split the group in half, sending some to the merchandise area and others to claim their box lunches at the deli after.

Grace had always enjoyed the Lakeside Marketplace and Spa. The fabric wasn't to her taste, too many character motifs that were hard to work into a quilt other than as a border or large panel, but the food was delicious and the setting was ideal. The shoreline fingered out into the lake and you could sit dockside and eat under umbrella covered tables. Or walk along the shore, either on the beach, if you didn't mind a little sand, or the paved walkway of small flagstone lined with native flowers.

After purchasing a fat quarter in a neutral beige so she got her free pattern and her card stamped, Grace strolled the area admiring the lake until it was time to get her box lunch. She'd chosen the ham and cheese croissant with a tangy mayo and honey mustard dressing, a sweet broccoli salad for her side, and a lemon mud cookie for dessert. The shortbread cookie layered with a lemon custard then drizzled with a dark chocolate was a particular favorite.

She deliberately chose a spot away from the others where the sound of the gentle waves helped her momentarily forget her worries. The gulls swooped over the water, cawing out as they hunted for food, while a family of ducks paddled along the shoreline, bobbing their heads under water. Just as she'd opened her box lunch and took a bite of the thick sandwich, Bea appeared, pulling a chair along.

"Now, ain't this nice out here." Bea sat.

When Bea didn't pull a box lunch from her large tote, Grace put her sandwich down. After their uneasy exchange on the bus, she was surprised Bea had joined her. "Did you need something?"

"Nope, just enjoying the pretty lake."

"I was going to eat."

"Go right ahead. I had mine first off. Not bad, could have eaten a dozen of those lemon cookies. Then I went shopping. Bought something called a kit to make into a pillow case." Bea rummaged through her totes and pulled out a bright fabric montage of construction workers, their rolled-up shirt sleeves showing bulging muscles and their handsome faces smiling suggestively.

Grace had no idea what she would do with such a fabric, certainly not make a pillowcase. She could only imagine the expression on James' face if he saw that kind of fabric covering her pillow. With his dry sense of humor, she was sure he would have made a few suggestive comments about it as well. Thinking about it made her cheeks warm.

"I do miss having a husband." Bea said.

Grace nodded. She missed James. Missed his head next to hers. She ate slowly while Bea stared out at the water.

"See, that's why I want to be a quilt designer."

Obviously Grace had missed some steps in Bea's train of thought. "Excuse me?"

"Well, Orlando always said that I had a head for business and was creative to boot. And I'm good with numbers, better than with people. I like all the pretty colors and touching the fabrics. I like how they make me feel happy." Bea let out a quiet breath. "I like people good enough, they just don't always take to me. But I'd like to give people a little bit of happy. Isn't that why you quilt? For the happy?"

Grace swallowed. She'd never thought about it. She enjoyed working with fabric, and the math was easy for her. There was a certain thrill in giving someone a quilt that you'd made yourself and watching their face light up with delight. Or making a quilt together with someone like Vi and Rose were doing. "I guess you could say that."

Grace was about to bite into her cookie when she noticed Kevin striding along the lakeside pathway. He could have been one of the construction workers from Bea's pillowcase fabric kit. Even without his shirtsleeves rolled up you could tell his arms were all muscles and he moved with the natural confidence people in great physical shape have. Tall with blond hair, Aaliyah was right, he did look like a Viking.

He stopped to talk to the cluster of School Marm Quilters who had commandeered a large table close to the dock. One of them pointed in her direction. Grace realized he must be looking for her and her breath caught in her throat.

She leapt from her chair before Kevin reached her. "Is James all right?"

"He's fine." He stopped and nodded to Bea. "I just wanted to talk to you for a moment." He glanced again at Bea, who didn't take the hint. "Grace could you help me with Mrs. Christianson's belongings?"

"I could help." Bea said. "I sat right next to her."

Kevin evaluated Bea with his eyes. After a moment, he gave the woman a touch of a smile. "Thanks for the offer, but I'd like to talk to Grace. Alone."

Bea accepted his refusal of her help and waved her phone. "I'll be fine here if you need me. This baby gets the internet."

Grace and Kevin strolled out of earshot before he cleared his throat. "Are you doing all right?"

"Yes, yes, I'm fine."

Kevin nodded his head approvingly. They crested the hill before he spoke again. "How well did you know Mrs. Christianson?"

"Camille?" What an odd thing for Kevin to ask. "Not very well. I had her youngest in a remedial math class a few years back. She didn't need to be there but wouldn't do the work."

"Do you know if she took any," he paused, "drugs?"

"Rachel? No, just a bad attitude."

"I meant Mrs. Christianson."

Surprise made Grace stop walking. "Oh, goodness, no."

"Sometimes people forget prescription drugs, when used improperly, can be dangerous."

"I don't know anything about any medications she might have been taking." Grace had never heard any talk that Camille was taking anything. Unless maybe she took something for her rumored heart condition.

Kevin nodded without expression. "I understand that Mrs. Christianson made quilts. Since all you ladies know each other, could you tell me if she was well liked?"

Grace pulled in her lip. She did that sometimes when she didn't know what to say. James would tease her about it. How could she answer Kevin's question without seeming petty? Although many of the women made Camille's patterns and followed her blog, they would also make less than complimentary comments behind Camille's back.

Instead of spreading gossip, Grace censored herself. "Camille actually designed quilts."

Kevin's expression told her he had no idea how that was different from making quilts. "She made patterns for people to buy and use to help them make their own quilts."

"I thought everyone made their own patterns."

"A lot of people would like to." Bea came to mind. "It seems easy. But even after you come up with something original, you need an eye for selecting fabrics that play well together—mixing the right prints and colors and hues. Then it takes time and money to test the patterns. And there's no guarantee that anyone will like the result, so you don't always make back your money."

"And Mrs. Christianson could support herself doing that?"

"I guess so. I don't know if she had any other job."

"Husband? Boyfriend?"

"She was divorced. No boyfriend that I'm aware of." After all the gossip flying on the bus, if Camille had had a boyfriend someone would have mentioned it.

Kevin nodded like he already knew that. "So alimony?"

"I doubt it, probably just child support." Alimony seemed like such a quaint idea but she also knew money was status and seemed important to Camille. "Darcy might know more about that. Camille worked out of Darcy's shop."

"Could you clarify that? Do you mean she rented space at the quilt shop or was she an employee?"

"I'm not sure what the arrangement was, but Camille had an office there and Darcy would feature Camille's quilt patterns."

"Meaning?"

"Oh, make quilts from the patterns and put them in the window for people to see. Promote them at quilt guild meetings. Even took them to quilt market so they'd get wider exposure."

"Sounds like Darcy did a lot for Camille's career?"

"Well, yes, it always helps to have a shop behind you."

"And Darcy and Camille were on good terms?"

Instead of answering, Grace stared at Kevin. Why was he asking such odd questions? It seemed obvious Camille had died from a heart attack. Did Kevin think her death hadn't happened naturally? "Why all these questions?"

"Unattended death, has to be investigated."

He avoided her eyes, and Grace knew it was more than that. They resumed walking in silence.

She was relieved when they'd reached the bus. The door was closed, but they could see the driver napping in the driver's seat. A sharp rap on the glass woke him, and he opened the door.

"No one's allowed on the bus during stops." He began, and then noticed Kevin standing behind Grace. "Oh, Deputy. How can I help?"

"I need to collect the deceased woman's belongings. Where was she sitting?"

The driver turned and looked at the first row. "Right here behind me."

Kevin took photos of the neat stack of Camille's possessions, then the surrounding area, even under the seat. "Did she use the overhead bin?" he asked as he reached up and opened it.

The driver looked confused, so Grace answered for him. "No, she kept everything in her big tote, or her purse. Camille rarely bought much on these trips."

Satisfied that the bin was empty, Kevin closed it.

"Do you mind getting her things together while I talk to the driver?" He asked Grace before the two men stepped outside. As Grace put Camille's things into her designer tote, she could hear Kevin ask about when Camille had gotten on the bus. What she had acted like? Who she had talked to? How she had seemed?

"Brownies?" Kevin asked.

"Well, she didn't like that other lady sitting next to her. I can tell you that. Kept telling her the seat wasn't available. Finally told her to shove off or else." The driver rubbed his chin. "Can't say as I liked Ms. Christianson much. For being an important person and all, she didn't think she had to follow the rules. You're not supposed to have food on the bus. But she kept pulling out those brownies. I bet she ate two. And she just dropped the wrappers on the floor. I have to clean that up, you know. Can't take a dirty bus back to the garage."

"She had one in her hand when she got on. Had another in her bag. Then Julia gave her another one."

Again Kevin prompted the driver. "And where did Julia get the brownie?"

"Everyone had one." The driver stopped, thinking for a moment. "I guess they were in their shop bags."

"And everyone was eating them?"

"Well, not everyone. Most people know you aren't supposed to eat on the bus, and they don't. Sure, sometimes I have to give a little reminder, but because Ms. Camille is such a big name designer, I look the other way."

"No one else got sick?"

Without hesitating, the driver replied that they hadn't. Now Grace was certain that Kevin wasn't just asking idle questions. She knew from living with James questions were often open-ended, which made them likely to get more information. And Kevin definitely seemed to want additional information.

"And who is Julia?" Kevin asked.

"Oh, she's the lady in charge."

Although the driver's tone was emphatic, Grace bit back that it wasn't actually true. Officially, there wasn't anyone in charge. But Julia always appointed herself leader. Somehow she always had a list of quilters to make sure no one was left behind.

"Do these bus trips happen often? Do you always drive?"

"My wife's a quilter and regular shopper at Darcy's shop, so she asked for me. Normally there's three shop hops a year. Spring, summer, and fall. Sometimes in the summer they'll also go to the big quilt convention in Minneapolis. We just got back from that about a week ago."

"The owner of the quilt shop hires you?"

"That's the way it works. Each shop sends around their own bus. But since Meg's been working at the shop, I've mostly dealt with her. Sweet girl. Makes the brownies, so that's why I don't get after the women for bringing them on board."

"Meg?"

"The go-to girl. She works at the Quilters Playground. So what happened to Ms. Camille? She have a heart attack?"

When Kevin didn't answer, the driver kept talking. "The way her face was all flushed, and she kept fanning herself, I thought she was having a hot flash. My wife does that sometimes, I didn't think anything of it."

Grace had to agree. A hot flash was entirely possible. Camille liked to hide her age, but with her daughter in college, and her son already married and with a child of his own, Camille was likely approaching menopause.

Grace stared at Camille's possessions. Camille rarely bought anything on these trips, just smiled in front of displays of her quilt patterns and the sample quilts made from them. Even so, her fancy designer tote didn't seem very full.

"Do you know how her things got stacked up like this?" Grace asked the driver.

He shook his head. "No, I didn't see anybody messing with her stuff. But you should ask Julia. She always sits right behind Camille, so she might have noticed."

"Do you have everything ready?" Kevin asked Grace.

Grace looked up at Kevin. "I seem to remember she had a purse. She usually carried one, but there isn't one here."

The driver, Joe, got a worried look. "You don't think that pair that got off before we got back on the highway could have taken it?"

"Vi?" Grace couldn't think of a reason Violet would take Camille's purse. Although Vi had tested a few patterns for Camille, lately the friendship had cooled.

"Or that girl?" Joe said. "She was fidgeting around when they got off."

Grace tensed, a ripple of anger rising through her. Why did he suspect Rose?

"Someone got off the bus between stops?" Kevin asked.

"Older woman, and I guess the girl is her granddaughter. It's against the rules to leave the bus between destinations."

"I'll need their names."

The driver shook his head. "You'll have to ask Julia. She has the list of attendees."

Grace gave Kevin their names. He jotted them down in his notebook. "Thanks, Grace, you've been a big help."

With a nod he took Camille's big leather bag and disappeared to his waiting police car. After years of living with James, Grace knew there was more going on than Kevin was saying.

QUILTING FACTOID: Unlike seamstresses who use a ⅝ inch seam allowance, quilters use a ¼ inch allowance. This reduces the number of layers of fabric that have to be quilted through when there are many small pieces.

CHAPTER FIVE

After depositing Camille's bag in the trunk of his cruiser, Kevin radioed the station. Grace moved closer and heard him request that a deputy go to the Quilters Playground to secure Camille's office and belongings. He signed off and turned to her. "Could you point out Julia to me?"

"She's sitting over there at one of the umbrella-ed tables. I can introduce you."

Grace could feel everyone's eyes tracking them as they approached the tables. When they arrived at Julia's table, conversation faded. Everyone continued eating while listening in to hear as much as they could.

Grace intended to introduce Julia to Kevin. But before she had a chance to say excuse me or hello, Julia started talking to him.

"Why, Deputy Oleson, what can I do for you? We met at one of the city council meetings a while back."

Grace moved slightly off to Kevin's side, feeling like a ladybug brushed off his sleeve.

"I've made reports at a lot of meetings and met quite a few people at them." Kevin politely let Julia know he didn't recall meeting her. Julia's smile dimmed ever so slightly.

"I understand you're in charge of this group and that you sat behind the deceased. How did Mrs. Christianson seem to you?"

"Well, she seemed to be in a mood. Of course, a shop hop is such a stressful time for a designer. And I'm sure that loud woman who brazenly sat in the reserved seat with her didn't help. Camille told her repeatedly that the seat was unavailable before she moved."

"What do you mean by 'in a mood'?"

"She seemed stressed, or maybe even a bit angry? I hate to speak ill of Camille, but she was being rather abrupt and quite impolite. She had been acting that way at the Quilters Playground even before we got on the bus."

"Any idea why?" Kevin asked.

"I heard that she had words with Meg before we ate breakfast at the shop. After we got on the bus, Camille wasn't very friendly with the other ladies and she started looking through her bag for something. I imagine so she wouldn't have to talk to people. She was muttering about how no one appreciated her or her designs, or knew how hard it is to be a designer. On top of that she had to get pretty pushy with that rude woman that I mentioned before."

Grace thought it was interesting Julia only mentioned Camille was being inconsiderate to everyone else and failed to mention Camille had snubbed her too.

"And what was her name?"

Julia had a blank look on her face.

"Who?"

"The rude woman who sat next to her."

"Why, I don't know, and I know most everyone in town. She must have been the late addition. I'd never heard of her before. But I could check my list for you."

"Bea." Grace supplied quietly. "She was the gal down by the lake with me when you got here."

Kevin nodded at Grace, and then turned his attention back to Julia.

"Did Mrs. Christianson say or do anything else?"

"I know, sorry, knew Camille well, and when she was stressed or upset she turned to food, especially chocolate. She couldn't seem to find a snack in any of her bags so I offered her my brownie from the quilt shop."

"Did she eat the brownie?"

"Why yes, she ate it down in just a few bites. That's how I knew she must be extremely upset."

Grace tried to count how many brownies Camille had eaten. Was it four or five now?

Kevin pressed for more information about the events of Camille's morning. "You mentioned her bags and some notebooks. Tell me more about them."

"When that obnoxious lady sat down, Camille pulled one of her design notebooks out of her tote. I imagine she didn't want to talk to that woman. She started looking through the pages and writing on them. That woman, Bea, did you say her name was, still wouldn't quit talking. Camille was trying to ignore her and kept telling her that she needed to move."

"Did the woman move?"

"She didn't seem to get the message and started taking pictures with her phone. That annoyed Camille even more, and she became quite angry and threatening. Finally, that woman got the message and moved to the back."

"Did you notice what Mrs. Christianson did after the woman moved?" Kevin asked.

"I believe she went back to drawing in her notebook. She mumbled something about hating selfies and how people didn't understand celebrities needed their space. Her blood pressure had to have been through the roof."

"Why do you say that?"

"She kept fanning herself. And she drank down all her coffee, then all her water. I couldn't help but notice that her face was all flushed."

With a nod, Kevin jotted something down in his notebook. "What happened when the bus got to the shop?"

"Camille jumped up and ran off the bus before it had barely stopped. I thought she might not be feeling well. Maybe carsick or something."

"Did she take anything with her?"

Elaine, who had been standing silently behind Julia during the entire conversation, spoke up to support her friend. "I think Camille left everything on her seat. When we returned to the bus, I helped Julia stack Camille's things next to her tote bag. We noticed her purse was missing then."

Grace saw Julia glance toward Elaine and slightly purse her lips together. She didn't appear to appreciate Elaine's contribution to the conversation.

Kevin turned to Elaine and asked her to identify herself. Julia quickly introduced Elaine to Kevin. "This is my dear friend and guild vice president, Elaine Butler. She has been sitting with me on the bus and assisting me with the shop hop."

"Did either of you ladies notice anyone near Mrs. Christianson's seat or handling her things?"

Elaine shook her head no, and Julia spoke for the two of them. "No, not really. Maybe the bus driver noticed something?" She lifted her eyebrows as if waiting for Kevin to say more.

When he didn't, she helpfully added. "You should talk to Darcy. I understand that she and Camille had a falling out. Or maybe that lady that Grace met today. The one who made Camille so upset."

"Well, thank you for your help. I will look into it." He tipped his head and motioned for Grace to join him as he started back to his patrol car. Grace could feel Julia and Elaine's eyes piercing into her back.

She couldn't stop thinking about Julia's comments, especially about Darcy. Julia didn't share any specific details, just enough information to make it appear Darcy had serious issues with Camille.

When they had walked out of hearing range of the rest of the group, Kevin stopped. "What do you know about this Bea person?"

"Well, I just met her on the bus this morning. She must be new to town. I've never seen or heard of her before. We've mostly been talking about quilting. She does seem like a bit of a character though." That was an understatement, but Grace didn't feel it was fair to judge Bea based on the brief time they'd known each other.

She noticed Kevin frown just a bit and recalled Bea not wanting to leave when Kevin arrived. "I think she means well but at times she doesn't seem to have much of a filter." Grace clarified.

"Where did you ladies first board the bus?"

"We started at the Quilters Playground. Darcy owns the shop." Grace thought back to when Darcy first moved to Lake City and opened the quilt shop. No one knew much about her except that she'd managed a chain store in the city and when quilting was at the height of its current popularity, she moved to Lake City and opened the Quilters Playground. It had seemed to do well at first, but now, with the interest in quilting fading from what it once was, she spent most of her time in her office and let Meg run the place.

"The driver said he dealt with a Meg? What do you know about her?"

"Meg? Meg Reynolds. You might have been in the same class in high school. She used to live here until she went off to college."

"I think I remember her. Don't her folks live down by the school?"

"Yes. In the little yellow house on the north side."

"They're getting up in age. Is that why she moved back?"

Grace hesitated, she'd heard talk that Meg's fiancé had passed away shortly before their wedding and that was one reason Meg had moved back to Lake City, but she didn't know it for a fact. "Possibly, but I couldn't say for sure."

Grace could only imagine the heartache of having the one you loved so abruptly snatched away. Even though she and James were going through a challenging time now, Grace felt very lucky to have been given so many good years together and hoped to make the most of the years to come.

They took several steps before Kevin spoke again. "What can you tell me about those brownies that Camille was eating?" The words had barely left his mouth when Grace heard Bea calling her name. Grace stopped walking and looked toward Bea's voice. Hanging onto her floppy hat, she charged toward them.

"Oh, Grace. You're not hitching a ride home with Deputy Kevin here, are ya?" Bea screeched to a stop within feet of them. "I saw ya heading toward his car and thought ya might be leaving us."

For all her brashness, Bea looked nervous about possibly being left without a shopping buddy.

"Of course not. I'm staying with the shop hop. Kevin just had a few questions I've been trying to answer for him."

Bea looked relieved to hear Grace was still shop hopping and turned her attention to Kevin. "Well, ya know, Deputy Kevin, I might be able to help ya with the answers to some of your questions, if ya give me a chance." She straightened her hat and gazed at him.

Kevin must have decided as long as Bea was offering, he might as well take her up on it. "What can you tell me about the brownies that were in your bags?"

"Disgusting things." Bea answered. "Full of weeds."

"Weeds?"

Grace tightened her lips. "She means herbs. Meg likes to experiment with different flavors by adding savory to sweet."

"Is that usual?"

"Well, not around here. But yes, it's a style of baking. Camille loved them."

"Disgusting style if you ask me." Bea said.

No one had asked her.

"So Camille ate one?"

"Ate two or three." Bea said.

"You know that for sure?" Kevin asked.

"Well, yeah. While I sat next to her, she snarfed down two. Chomp, chomp, you'd think the lady hadn't eaten in a week."

Grace hesitated for a moment. "She had one at the quilt shop before we left. And another one right after getting on the bus."

"Do you know what kind of," Kevin glanced at Bea. "Weeds, she put in them?"

"St John's wort." Bea answered.

"You're sure?"

"Well, I can't be 100% sure. I spit it out as soon as I tasted it. But after I divorced my third husband, I got into a depression and I tried it. They say it helps with depression, but I didn't think it helped me much. So the doctor gave me a prescription for something, but I didn't know to stop taking that St. John's wort and got myself pretty sick."

Grace was embarrassed for Bea. One didn't talk about such things. And to someone you hardly knew. Then a pang of guilt shot through her. One shouldn't be ashamed of their mental health. And certainly shouldn't hide it. But they'd only met that morning, and she already knew far more about Bea than she wanted.

"I'm sorry to hear that. Are you better now?"

The look of concern on Kevin's face seemed genuine. How was it he was so in tune with and understanding of other's moods and feelings? He'd been one of the first to notice the changes in James' behavior and personality, even before Grace had admitted or accepted it. And now he was asking Bea how her depression was. As close as she felt to him, she realized how little she knew about Kevin. James probably knew more about him. If only he could remember and tell her.

"Why, that's so kind of you to ask. Yes, I take a little something to keep me on the even, and then when I married my Orlando, I got much better. The man knew how to make a woman feel wonderful. You know what I mean?" Bea winked.

Grace felt her cheeks flame red. There she goes again. Did she have a filter or any social graces?

Kevin tried to maintain a professional expression, but a dimple flashed in his cheek and a slight blush moved up his neck before he regained his serious deputy's demeanor.

"You don't have a brownie left, do you?"

Bea shook her head. "Threw mine away."

Grace dug to the bottom of her tote and pulled out the clear plastic wrapped brownie. "Here it is."

"Do you mind if I take it?"

"No, no, of course not, but...?" Grace was going to ask why and then realized it must have something to do with Camille.

Kevin must want one of Meg's brownies for testing. But if Camille had died from a heart attack, why would they be checking on what she'd eaten? Then she remembered Bea rushing past everyone to flush the toilet at the Hummingbird and Aaliyah telling her she wished the toilet hadn't been flushed. Something about it would have told investigators the contents of Camille's stomach. Bea claimed she'd flushed it to get rid of the odor, or did she have another reason for flushing the toilet so quickly?

Of course, Bea wasn't the type to keep quiet about the brownies and blurted out. "So do you think there's a problem with them brownies? Boy, am I glad I only took a small bite and spit it right out. Maybe the other ladies should know if they're off or something isn't right about them?"

Bea's comments made Grace's jaw drop. Kevin didn't answer. Perhaps he was trying to formulate a diplomatic, professional reply. She wondered if he was thinking about what James would say in a situation like this. She could imagine James advising Kevin not to give away information about a case while still needing to keep the public safe and calm.

"No, ma'am, we don't believe the brownies are harmful to anyone. You don't need to worry. I'll take care of this. Just go on and enjoy your outing." He tipped his hat and headed toward his patrol vehicle.

Grace wasn't sure he was even out of hearing range when Bea remarked. "Well, that deputy is mighty fine to look at, but he sure isn't very talkative, now is he?"

Grace knew that Kevin was doing his job and Bea was being a little too pushy. Perhaps she should have told Kevin about Meg's interactions with Camille. But she didn't have the complete story behind what she'd seen and needed to find out more before she shared anything. She remembered James telling her how people, thinking they had it all figured out, shared their insights on a crime. Sometimes, listening to them gave him clues about the people involved.

None of the quilters she knew would commit murder; it must have been a heart attack due to all the stress Camille had been under. But why was Kevin continuing to gather information?

QUILTING FACTOID: During the Civil War era, Jane A. Stickle made a famous sampler quilt that can still be seen today. Hand stitched with 169 quilt blocks, pieced corners, border triangles, and a scalloped outer edge, it contains a total of 5,602 pieces.

CHAPTER SIX

Grace and Bea watched Kevin walk toward his Lakeland County SUV. It wasn't just the uniform, but at over six feet tall with broad shoulders and an athletic build even she had to admit Kevin could make a woman's heart flutter.

"Attractive fella. Is he married?"

Grace nearly dropped her purse. Why on earth would Bea want to know? Certainly the woman was twice his age. And she'd been married several times. "No, he isn't. Why do you ask?"

"Oh, I just like to know these things. Never know when some eligible lady is going to come along and I can fix the two up."

Grace doubted that Kevin needed or wanted any fixing up. Let alone being fixed up with Bea's help.

"A police officer. So, how do you know him?"

A flicker of discomfort narrowed Grace's eyes. Why was Bea asking? "He's a family friend."

"Thought it might have something to do with that dead woman."

The bluntness of Bea's comment surprised Grace. Only hours ago Camille had been a living, breathing person and it felt disconcerting to call her a "dead woman" so soon.

Before she could respond, Bea quipped, "Must be nice to have family friends like that fella."

With every comment Bea made, Grace was understanding more and more how Camille must have felt about Bea's unwanted company on the bus. What was it Julia had said about Bea annoying Camille when she planted herself in Camille's seat? Something about Bea taking pictures with her cell phone. And Camille had to threaten Bea before she finally got the message and moved to another seat.

"He worked closely with my husband before James retired."

A slight shadow crossed Bea's face. "Your husband was a cop?"

"James was a deputy with the sheriff's office for many years before he retired."

People had differing reactions when Grace shared her husband was, had been, in law enforcement. Some were impressed, some intrigued, others, like Bea, became a little stand-offish. She wasn't sure if they did so because of some sort of guilt, or wariness that they should be on their best behavior around him and also her.

Bea seemed to have become a little less boisterous, but given the morning's events and Kevin's visit, everyone was less talkative. Grace wondered if Bea felt guilty about something, maybe about what had happened between her and Camille.

"Your husband must have run into some pretty interesting investigations. Did he talk about them much? One of my husbands was what ya call a venture capitalist. I couldn't get him to stop talking about all his fancy-pantsy investments. Why he'd go on and on about contracts and insurance, and below the line expenses versus above the line. Bored me to tears."

"Actually, Lake City is a pretty quiet place to live. James wasn't involved in many major investigations while he was a deputy. He had to respect confidentiality, so he didn't say much, if anything, about his cases. He did go to a lot of trainings and seminars. If I asked, he talked about some of the things he learned at them."

"Did he teach you any self-defense techniques? Bet that was interesting. I wouldn't mind your friend giving me some self-defense lessons."

Thankfully, Grace heard Julia and Elaine announce their departure. The ladies boarded the bus for their next stop.

~ ~ ~

While Bea struggled to get settled into her seat, Grace reflected on the events of the morning. How could something like this happen on a shop hop, of all things? Grace scanned up and down the rows of seats, looking at the ladies on the bus. She knew most of them. Had quilted with many of them for years. That one of them might have done something to harm Camille didn't seem possible.

But then a cloud of doubt floated through her mind. People and situations weren't always what they seemed. If she had learned anything from teaching all those years, it was that there's usually more going on with people than what's on the surface. Once you started digging, it explained a lot of things, for better or worse.

Grace wondered what it was like for Kevin working without James now. James had been Kevin's mentor, and they often worked closely together. James said Kevin was a quick learner and quite a fine deputy for someone still learning the job. He was proud of Kevin, like a father would be of a son. Sometimes she forgot she wasn't the only one learning to live with James' illness. There were others, like Kevin who were also adjusting to being without James.

They sped along the highway until they turned onto a gravel road. After a few miles, the bus turned again, then crawled down the bumpy drive of The Willow Grove Quilt Shop.

The shop was housed in a large, red barn that had been on the property for years and years. The barn, saved from demolition and painted traditional red, was remodeled in such a way that it retained a rustic farm feeling. A grove of berry bushes, vines, and older trees grew along one side. The long, dangling branches of several large weeping willow trees moved gracefully back and forth. Grace always found the somber trees peaceful.

After Bea held up the line, handing something to the bus driver, the ladies spilled out of the bus and strolled toward the barn. Flowers bloomed along a wide gravel pathway which lead to the shop. Inside, warm light seemed to stream through holes in the rafters, but on closer inspection Grace could see that sun tubes had been installed in the ceiling to magnify the sunlight and create a warm, sunny space.

The shop specialized in reproduction fabrics of all kinds: the Civil War era, feed sacks from the depression, and the psychedelic flower power designs from the sixties and seventies. Quilts hanging from the ceiling sectioned off the different historical display areas.

Like a student charging out of the classroom when the recess bell rings, Bea headed straight for the brightly colored, psychedelic 60s and 70s fabrics. With a sigh of relief, Grace made her way to the Civil War reproductions.

Grace had always promised herself she would make a Dear Jane quilt, but all those tiny pieces and small blocks seemed daunting. Maybe it was time to look seriously at it. She could take the hand piecing to the nursing home with her when she visited James.

Once in the Civil War area, she discovered much more than she'd imagined. Along with deep browns and blacks, there were bottle greens—a yellowy green that on its own was garish but when placed next to other colors made the block design pop. A reddish orange did the same. And then a cerulean blue grabbed her attention. As she touched the fabric, the smooth finish soothing to her fingers, she noticed that besides Dear Jane there were other pattern books of Civil War and pioneer quilts. So much to choose from.

She took several books from a bin and sat in a wooden rocking chair in the corner where two hanging quilts intersected. Voices, muffled by the quilted fabric, moved closer.

"Can't say as I'm sad about Camille. The old witch. Someone should have killed her years ago."

Grace froze, trying to place the voice.

"She's lucky it wasn't me." Finally Grace recognized the second voice as Judy, one of the School Marm Quilters.

The two women came around the corner. "I wouldn't have told anyone." Connie laughed until her gaze stopped where Grace was sitting in the corner. For a moment both women tensed, then relief washed over Connie's face.

"Oh, Grace, it's you." Connie said.

Grace stood up, unsure of what to say. "Hi, Connie, Judy. I love these Civil War reproduction fabrics." At least they didn't scurry off and leave, but there was a strained silence.

"Boy, this has certainly been a different shop hop, hasn't it? So unexpected Camille having a heart attack like that." If she kept the women talking about

Camille, maybe she'd learn something that would help Kevin. "But she did seem to be under a lot of pressure."

Judy nodded in agreement, vaguely adding, "Heart attacks do happen unexpectedly when people are under stress."

But Connie vented. "It's not like Camille didn't cause tremendous stress for other people." She emphasized the word stress as if it wasn't what she had wanted to say.

"I did notice she seemed to be causing Meg and Darcy quite a bit of tension at the shop." Grace couldn't stop herself. "And before I retired I thought I'd heard rumors that she might have caused someone a problem at school?"

"You bet she did." Connie's face tightened in anger. "I'm not going to name any names, but she cost a teacher their job."

Grace was grateful Connie didn't give a name. It told her the School Marm Quilters were loyal to each other and followed an unspoken rule that what happened when the School Marms met wasn't shared with others. But knowing about Camille causing someone to be fired might be important for Kevin's investigation. "What was that all about?" Grace nudged the ladies for more information.

"It was about a teacher's word against Camille's daughter's." Connie's voice was irate. "Even when the teacher had proof that the little cheater was plagiarizing, Camille wouldn't let it go." Connie ranted, her anger full blown. "She said that no one could prove it was deliberate. Then Camille went to the school board. Called in her lawyer. Threatened to take it to court."

Judy patted Connie's arm. She turned to Grace. "I know you'll understand. I wanted to stick to my principles, but what was the point? I knew she would drag my name through the mud, implying things that weren't true. Everyone would talk about it. It was my reputation on the line. For her, it would just be more publicity. It wasn't worth it. I was close enough to retirement, so I resigned."

Connie shook her head. "It was so unfair. You try to help kids and teach them right from wrong and that there are consequences for their actions. Instead parents like Camille get them off the hook. What does that teach them?"

Grace nodded her head in agreement. "I know what you mean. I'd heard the rumors and felt so badly for the teacher involved. Judy, I'm so sorry that happened to you." Grace was truly sad about the whole situation.

"It's not just me, I wasn't her only victim. Look at what she was doing to Darcy. Flashing that Farmers Bounty mug around. She certainly made it clear that she could leave if she wanted to. Well, she's gone now."

"I wonder where that leaves the Quilters Playground." Connie said. "Could it go under without Camille drawing in customers?"

Grace took a deep breath. She hadn't thought about that. "I would hate to lose the quilt store."

"We all would, but Camille didn't care. It was always about her. Look how she treated Meg this morning. Told her to make a special batch of decaf just for her. Now it's too hot, put an ice cube in it. Now it's too cold. Make another batch. She was worse than Goldilocks." Judy mimicked Camille's nasal voice.

"And I know for a fact that Meg spent all day yesterday baking those brownies that Camille loves. In between helping customers and getting things ready for the hop, and for the dinner tonight. But did Camille or Darcy so much as say thank you? No, it was Meg do this and Meg do that. If I was that girl, I would have shoved a brownie down Camille's throat and hoped she choked on it."

"I heard that Meg's papered the town with job applications. Even interviewed for a job down at the grocery store. Seems a waste of her college education. And her folks worked so hard to put her through art school."

Before anything else was said, Grace's phone rang. Judy and Connie used it as a signal to move along and exited the space while Grace fumbled for her phone. When the number read the care center, her throat tightened. James!

"Mrs. Meadows?"

"Yes. James? Is he all right?"

"Oh, I'm sorry to have frightened you. Yes, he's fine. Better than fine. I just wanted to let you know how well he's doing today. The activities director brought in a group of musicians. I didn't know that Jim could play the drums. He did a set with them, then danced with all the ladies. Twirled us round and round."

Grace had to blink away the tears. When they were courting, James would take her dancing. For a large man, he had a quick step. And he was so strong. He'd tease her and pretend he was going to drop her when the music called for a dip. She would grab his arms and he'd pull her tight. Why hadn't she been there? She could have danced with him.

"Grace, are you all right?"

"Yes, yes I'm fine."

"Perhaps, I shouldn't have called. It's so wonderful that you're doing something for yourself. It's important to recharge when you can. How is the shop hop going?"

Obviously, the woman didn't know about Camille. How was Grace going to tell her? Should she tell? Grace didn't even know if Kevin had notified the next of kin yet.

"Are you finding any pretty fabric?"

"Yes. Yes. One or two things."

"Well, I'll let you go. I just thought you'd like to know that James was all right. That he's having a good time today."

"Yes, thank you." Grace ended the call. She sat in the little alcove. The curtain of quilts offered arms of comfort as she wondered why she was on this silly bus trip instead of with James?

The blue and white star quilt next to her jerked and swung from its spot. Instead of using the entryway, Bea pushed it aside and bulldozed her way through the wall of quilts. "Why, there you are. I've been looking all over for you."

Inwardly, Grace groaned. She had so hoped Bea would find a new shopping buddy. "Would you mind helping me out again, this quilt designing being so new to me? I'm thinking I like some of those bright colored fabrics with the mod flower power prints. What about making one of those scrappy quilts you mentioned with a bunch of those fat quarter things?"

Bright mod prints were definitely not Grace's style, but she couldn't think of a way to politely disengage herself from Bea. Then again, maybe helping Bea would take her mind off the thoughts swirling around in her mind about being away from James, and what she'd just learned from the School Marm Quilters.

Grace followed Bea over to the retro prints from the 60s and 70s. She felt like she had walked back into a flower child, hippie world of psychedelic colors and prints. She could see how these would appeal to Bea. Most of the prints were too large and bold for a traditional scrappy quilt. Grace didn't even know if Bea could thread a sewing machine, let alone piece things together accurately. What Bea needed was a simple beginner project, something that could work for the large prints she enjoyed and would give her practice sewing a straight quarter inch seam. "How about making a strip quilt?" Grace suggested.

"What in tarnation is a strip quilt? I don't have to be naked, do I? Not that I mind, but that wind off the lake can be mighty cool." Bea must have read

Grace's look of disbelief. "Does it have strippers on it or something naked?"

My word, this woman really doesn't have a clue. Grace explained, "No strippers. It's made of strips of fabric."

"That's a relief. This body ain't what it used to be."

Grace continued quickly before Bea said something more about strippers or strip clubs. "You use several fabrics that are cut into strips of different widths. Then you arrange and sew the strips together. You can add a border if you want to frame it in. It makes a quick easy quilt that's great for someone learning to quilt."

"That sounds pretty basic for someone like me wanting to be a designer." Bea's tone said she didn't approve of the idea.

"It is basic, but quilters of all different skill levels buy a designer's patterns. Having some easier patterns can be a good thing. Sometimes even experienced quilters like a quick, easy project for a change of pace – to use up their stash or for a quick gift."

"Well, I guess I have to start somewhere. So, I'll give it a try if you think it's a good idea. I like this big pink, neon green, and orange flower power print. Could I use that?"

"Sure, that could be your wider main strip or border or both. We'll find some smaller flowered or paisley prints or stripes for the other strips and maybe a mottled solid too."

"Isn't having a solid color going to make it boring?"

With such limited knowledge of both quilting and design, how was Bea ever going to be a designer? "Sometimes you need a solid or less busy print so that your eye has a place to rest as it wanders over your quilt. Mottled solids have some light and dark variations so they're not as boring as a regular solid. I like using them to give some dimension and to frame in parts of a quilt."

"If you say so. I guess that kind of makes sense. I just want to be sure it's bright and pretty, so it will impress people. How much of this stuff am I going to need?"

Grace sighed. Here we go again. At least the math for this quilt would be straightforward. They found a mottled neon green to use for small strips on each side of the large flower power print, and for the binding. A bright orange and pink small paisley print seemed to work for the medium-sized strips in between the neon green on each side of the flower power print. Grace had Bea decide on her border fabric and Bea chose to use the flower power print there again. Not a big surprise. After all, Bea liked to go big and bold.

"You better write this stuff down for me or I'll forget."

Bea pulled a spiral-bound notebook out of one of her huge totes and handed it to Grace. Opening it to the first page she saw Bea's name, address, and phone number, Grace guessed that was so the notebook could be returned if lost. She flipped through several pages and didn't see writing on any of them. If this was Bea's design notebook, she hadn't even started.

After drawing a quick diagram of the strip quilt, Grace labeled the strips so Bea would know where each fabric went and how wide to cut the strips. Then she made a notation for how much yardage of each fabric was needed.

Grace helped Bea carry the bolts of fabric to the cutting table. She watched Bea referring to the sketch in her notebook to get the correct amounts of fabric, but her mind kept drifting back to what Connie and Judy had said. There'd been a closed-door session of the school board the year Judy resigned. And Judy's name had been mentioned in the rumors. That all made sense, but would she have been angry enough to kill Camille?

QUILTING FACTOID: Seams are pressed toward the darker fabric to keep its shadow from appearing beneath the lighter fabric.

CHAPTER SEVEN

Grace checked her watch; it wasn't quite time to board the bus. A few minutes to herself would be nice. She left Bea at the cutting table and wandered outside, sitting at a wooden picnic table under one of the tall willow trees. The breeze felt so cool and refreshing. It reminded her of how James enjoyed being outdoors fishing and how much he must miss it. He would enjoy spending time outside, relaxing in the fresh air at the care center or going for a drive around the lake together. The sound and view of the water was always so calming. She would have to ask about the care center's guidelines.

"Didn't see where you'd gotten yourself off to. Then I saw you sitting over here by yourself. Thought maybe you could use some company."

With James at the care center, Grace was getting used to being home alone. She didn't need any company now, but what could she say. The only one Grace truly wanted to spend time with was James, and here she was off on this shop hop. But as long as Bea was there, maybe they could chat and she could find out more about what had happened between Bea and Camille on the bus.

"That's kind of you. I was just trying to get some fresh air and decide what I should buy here. It's nice to have someone else doing the driving on these shop hops, but the trip can get long, especially depending on who you're sitting with. I think I saw you sitting with Camille earlier. How did that go?"

"Well, that Camille wasn't very friendly. When I tried talking to her, she stuck her nose in some notebook and started doodling in it. So I pulled out my phone and started taking selfies. You know this quilt stuff is all new to me and I wanted to record the experience. Especially sitting with a big name designer like Mrs. Christianson."

"I heard Camille got pretty upset about you and your phone."

"It turns out Mrs. Christianson doesn't like having her picture taken by just anyone. But that wasn't going to stop me. I took a few photos. She dug around in her purse and took out an envelope she had stuffed in there. She started fanning herself with it like she's all hot. Then all of a sudden she stuck it in her book and slammed it shut. Next thing I know she's ordering me to leave, or she'd have me removed from the bus."

"That seems a bit extreme. Are you sure it was just being in your selfies that upset her?"

"Who knows? That woman was already upset and awfully unhappy from the moment I sat down. I would have thought designing pretty quilts that make people happy would have made her happy too."

"Maybe she thought you were taking pictures of her design notebook."

Bea looked shocked and gasped. "Why would you say something like that?"

"Some people don't realize how competitive the quilting business is. If you took her designs and published them before she could, she'd lose a whole season. That could be a lot of money."

"Why, I never thought of that. I might have taken a picture or two of her book. Accidentally, of course. But I wasn't stealing her designs. I was just thinking of looking at them to see how this whole designing thing works. She might have noticed the camera wasn't just on her. That's when she told me to move or else. I didn't want to make a big scene, so I moved."

Grace was a bit surprised Bea would worry about what people thought of her. There was nothing quiet or subtle about Bea. She must realize wherever she went, people couldn't help but notice her flamboyant personality.

"I never would have taken the pictures if she'd been nice to me when I asked her for advice. Instead she grumbled everyone thinks they can be a designer, and that no one appreciates the talent or skill that it takes. Since she wouldn't talk to me, I got out my phone thinking I could sneak some pictures of her notebook while making it look like I was taking selfies."

Grace wondered if Bea realized that she'd just admitted her wrong doing.

Bea rambled on. "I wasn't going to use the pictures for my own designs. But studying them might help me figure out how quilt designers do things."

"Then when she asked to see your selfies, you knew she suspected you were taking photos of her designs. That's why you figured you better get up and move before she accused you outright of stealing them."

"Okay, you've got me. I was going to delete them, but first I wanted to learn more about designing. Only I couldn't figure out what all the numbers and notes meant, especially with them being so blurry. I thought maybe after I studied them some more, I would figure things out and be able to design my own stuff. Then I was going to delete the pictures, I swear."

Maybe Bea wasn't going to claim Camille's work as her own, but copying someone else's designs without permission was still wrong. Bea probably thought those photos were a shortcut to her becoming a quilt designer and if she eventually deleted them, it wouldn't hurt Camille. Grace had students over the years who had copied others' work and didn't think it hurt anyone, either.

"I guess I believe you, but copying another's work without their permission is never appropriate." But those photos could be important information for

Kevin's investigation. "Normally, I would say confess and apologize to the owner. Then delete the photos while they watch you do it, but that's not possible in this situation and besides I think you need to keep those photos."

"I would never have passed the designs off as my own. I was only going to keep them for a little while. I was hoping you might help me sew one together, or show me how to draw up a pattern with notes and numbers so that can I understand how it's done. You know, just enough to give me the feeling of being a designer like Camille. Sort of like you did for the strip quilt in my notebook. Then I was going to delete them for sure."

"Now you need to save them. I think the sheriff's office might want to talk to you and take a look at those photos."

"I guess you're right. Could we call that good-looking deputy friend of yours? I wouldn't mind talking to him and showing him my pictures."

Of course Bea wouldn't mind talking to Kevin. Grace was surprised Bea didn't wink at her when she asked to talk to him. Didn't the woman realize what Kevin would think about how she'd gotten those pictures?

Bea's admission about what had happened when she sat with Camille made Grace wonder what else the woman might have done. Could Bea have picked up Camille's design notebook and purse and be hiding them in one of those totes she was carrying around? She had the blurry photos on her phone, but maybe she wanted all the designs in Camille's notebook. Perhaps Bea's colorful personality was hiding someone who was more clever and driven than Grace had given her credit for. After all, there had to be a reason she had gone through so many husbands and had so much money. If that was the case, Kevin should talk to Bea.

Julia came patrolling through the shop. "Five minutes, ladies."

Bea looked at her watch. "Bossy, isn't she? We got eight minutes."

Oh, dear, between talking to the School Marms and Bea, Grace had forgotten to make a purchase. If she didn't buy something, she would miss getting the free block. Of course, one of the other ladies would be happy to share, but that always felt like cheating. She remembered the books about Dear Jane quilts. There was just enough time to scoot back to the Civil War section and pick one up.

"Bea, I need to buy something so I can get my free pattern and my card stamped."

A woman on a mission, Grace dashed back into the shop with Bea trailing behind her like a duckling waddling after its mother. Grace grabbed one of the books she'd paged through and hurried to pay for it. At the cash register there was a basket of fat quarters.

"One free for every twenty dollars spent." The clerk ringing her out cheerfully reminded her as she overspent for the book. While Bea watched, Grace took a moment to consider her choices, sorting through the basket for something more neutral. She didn't have any plans, and she hated having that odd piece of fabric. At last she found a white on white that would go with everything and completed her purchase. Once they were outside, Bea stopped her.

"Here, you'll like these." Bea pulled a pretty tan fat quarter with little flowers from her bag of purchases. Then she scooped out two more — one blue, the other dark brown and handed them to Grace. "I thought you might like them."

They were softer, traditional prints that Grace loved. "But I couldn't take yours." Along with the neutral fat quarter Grace had just chosen, they would work together beautifully to test a block or two from the Dear Jane book she'd purchased.

"I don't know what to do with them fat quarter things yet so you might as well get some use out of them and make something real pretty."

Grace hesitated.

"You take them for helping me." Bea said.

The anxious look on Bea's face told Grace if she didn't accept them, Bea would be hurt. She smiled. "Why, thank you."

Bea's face lit up.

Maybe she wasn't all that bad, everyone deserves a second chance. Many people didn't understand how designing is a job and taking a designer's work without paying for it was like taking someone's paycheck.

Julia's saccharine voice sounded through the shop, announcing the bus was getting ready to leave. While Julia herded several women onto the bus, Elaine rushed a few stragglers along. Most of the shop hoppers stowed their packages in the overhead compartments, but here and there ladies pulled out purchases to share their excitement about future projects. There was more chatter on the bus than earlier in the morning. The trip was starting to feel and sound like a typical shop hop, but Grace couldn't seem to enjoy herself. She wasn't sure whether it was being away from James, or Camille's death, or both.

Although seating wasn't assigned, most of the women went back to the same spot they'd sat in since they'd left the Quilters Playground. Bea and Grace again sat across the aisle from each other. Grace tried to study the Dear Jane book she'd purchased. Unfortunately, Bea wasn't able to occupy herself and started quizzing her about the next shop.

"I can't find my shop hop flyer. Where are we headed to next? Do ya know what kind of fabrics they have there? I hope they'll have snacks and something to drink. I'm getting mighty hungry."

My word, was this woman ever quiet? Grace felt like she was on a road trip with a small child.

"We're headed to the Old Windmill Quilt Shop. It's in an old farmhouse. Each room of the house has a different colorway or style of fabrics. They have lots of cute, rustic and seasonal decorations. It's a fun shop to wander through and get not just quilting ideas, but also great decorating ideas."

"It sounds a little too folksy for me. I like things bright and cheery that make me happy."

"I'm sure you'll find something there that's bright and cheery. It's sort of a smorgasbord of beautiful fabrics. They have a little of just about everything."

"I hope so. They say variety is the spice of life. I like variety and definitely love some spice in my life, if ya know what I mean."

Grace tried not to blush at Bea's need for spice in her life and attempted to refocus the woman back on fabrics and quilting.

"You might think about making a seasonal project for fall or Halloween. They always have fun kits for small wall hangings or table runners. It would be a great way to learn more about quilting and designing."

"I don't want another kit telling me what to do. I only bought that pillowcase kit because I liked the fabric and I could use a fun, sexy pillowcase. Kits might be good for some people, but I like to let my creative juices flow and do my own thing."

Bea might call herself creative, but so far she'd definitely needed a good deal of help with choosing fabrics for her projects. Like most people, Bea thought making a quilt was just sewing a bunch of pretty fabrics together. There was much more to it if you wanted to make a beautiful quilt that was attention grabbing and pleasing to the eye.

Without taking a breath, Bea continued talking. "What about snacks?"

Grace was relieved to change the subject to food. "Have you already eaten the snacks in your shop hop tote bag?"

"Why sure. I ate everything except that dusty old brownie. I took a taste and then I threw it out. My water is gone too. This shop hopping is work and makes a gal like me awfully hungry. I need to keep up my energy level if I'm going to keep on shopping and get what I need to be a designer."

"Well, hopefully they'll have drinks and a light snack to tide us over until dinner back at The Quilters Playground." Grace had to admit her stomach was feeling a little empty, too.

Eventually, the bus turned down the long lane to The Old Windmill Quilt Shop. At the head of the driveway was a small painted sign announcing it as a century farm. The farm had been owned and worked by the same family for over a hundred years.

Two farm houses, one old and one modern, sat on opposite sides of the lane. The quilt shop was in the old white farmhouse with wooden rocking chairs and porch swings on its wraparound front porch. Quilts were draped over the porch railings and on rungs of old ladders leaning against the walls of the house. The gentle fragrance of the lilac and bridal wreath bushes growing near the house wafted through the open bus windows.

The two-story house on the other side of the lane was the updated home where the family lived. A driveway extended further back from the home to the barn, machine sheds, and grain bins. Beyond were the green fields of the farm operations. Grace couldn't help but think that this farm seemed to have one foot in the past and the other stepping into the future.

The other ladies left and strolled toward the shop, even the bus driver stepped off the bus to stretch his legs. Grace sighed and leaned back in her seat to gaze out the window. She loved the classic charm of the older farm house.

"Are you coming?" Bea asked before leaving.

"Just give me a minute to get my thoughts organized. I'll catch up with you inside." She watched Bea walk sideways down the aisle, her oversize purse and tote bags thumping against the seats.

It was calm sitting alone on the empty bus. She watched the blades of the old wood and metal windmill spinning. It was a pleasant nod to past times when life moved at a slower pace.

In contrast, off in the distance, behind the newer home, she could see huge wind turbines with their gigantic blades turning in the breeze, providing power for homes and families in the surrounding counties. The old windmill and wind turbines were signs of the changing times.

Grace's eyes blurred, thinking of James and how much he'd changed. She missed the strong yet gentle man she had married.

She was glad Bea hadn't pressured her to get off the bus with her. Maybe Bea had been in a hurry to find out if there were snacks. Or all that spending money she had was burning a hole in her pocket. Whatever the reason, Grace was glad to have this moment to herself.

Although Grace thought she was the only one on the bus, a voice from the front startled her.

"Camille's dead. We don't have to worry about her anymore."

It would have been polite to stand or somehow let the person know she was there, but before Grace could move, the woman's next words stopped her.

"Just the way we thought it would happen. From all appearances a heart attack."

Grace held her breath. The woman sounded so matter of fact, not at all surprised or upset. Grace slouched down in her seat to listen.

"In the bathroom. Yes, the bathroom. Seeing her there, all curled up around the toilet I wanted to laugh my head off."

Who could be saying such horrible things? The voice was familiar, but Grace couldn't quite place it. She peeked through the high head rests and saw the back of the woman's head. The perfectly styled hair, and the manicured nails of the hand holding the phone immediately told her who—Julia.

"I'm just glad that it's done."

What was done? Julia's voice had a snide edge, instead of her usual sugar-coated, overly sweet tone.

"Instead of ripping you apart for not getting her any alimony, like who gets alimony these days? She should have been grateful that you got her husband to cover her health insurance. What with her bad heart that was worth a bundle, more than the fees she claimed you overcharged. Not that she needs health insurance now." Julia chuckled at her little joke.

Grace couldn't believe her ears.

"Yes, I'll keep looking, but how much damage can a letter from a dead woman do?—Have you mailed that bill for looking at her contract with the Quilters Playground?—Well, tear it up and type up a new one. Double your fee. No one will know. Serve her right for the stink she was having over your last charges. After what you've put up with, you deserve a little off the books.—Yes, I know she had it. She kept waving it in front of my face with that arrogant smirk of hers.—I'll find it and we'll celebrate after I get finished babysitting these quilting busybodies. Thank goodness they only have three shop hops a year they are so-o-o tedious."

What a phony. If that was the way Julia honestly felt, she sure put on a good act around town. Maybe some quilters loved to chat, and knew everyone's life story, but they were also some of the most kind-hearted and generous women in town. Grace would never look at Julia the same after hearing the way she spoke about them.

Grace heard Julia shuffling things around in her seat, then the click of her sandals down the steps and off the bus.

Julia must have been talking to her husband. He had handled Camille's divorce, something Julia had used to buddy up with Camille. Until the pendulum swung the other way and then Camille would barely look at Julia, let alone talk to her. This explained why Camille shunned Julia. And maybe her grievance with Julia's husband was a legitimate one.

As her anger subsided, Grace wondered if Kevin knew Camille had a heart condition. Certainly he would have talked to Camille's doctor. But he might be interested to know that Julia and her husband knew about it. And that Camille was sending a letter complaining about his fees to his partners because those fees didn't seem on the up and up. Or that Camille was having him look at her contract with the Quilters Playground. What could that be about? Grace reached for her phone then stopped herself. Better to get off the bus before the driver returned.

Slouched in her seat, Grace waited until she saw Julia marching up the farmhouse steps with her clipboard in the crook of her arm. The coast clear, Grace got up to leave.

As Grace hurried down the bus steps and walked toward the farm house, the driver came down the porch stairs with a cup of snack mix in one hand and a bottle of water in the other.

He looked at her disapprovingly. "You know you're not supposed to be on the bus unsupervised."

Grace stretched her shoulders and yawned. "So sorry, I must have dozed off in the back."

"Don't let it happen again." He sternly warned her and plodded back to the bus. She was tempted to remind him food wasn't allowed, but thought better of doing so. She didn't want to call more attention to herself than she already had.

Grace scanned the property for a private spot to call Kevin. But before she could, Bea's voice called her name from the front yard. How was it that this woman always seemed to find her? Grace felt like Bea had put a tracking device on her.

"Grace, over here. I thought I'd lost you for sure this time. Was waiting for you to catch up with me. Started looking in all those little rooms in that quilt house and didn't see hide nor tail of ya. What ya been doing all this time?"

Grace repeated what she'd told the bus driver. "So sorry, I must've dozed off after you left. Just woke up and now I need to get my shopping done so I get my free block pattern and my card stamped."

"I saw ya staring out the window when I left, and ya looked a little preoccupied. Didn't think you'd fall asleep though."

Leave it to Bea to notice how long she'd been on the bus. The woman sure didn't miss much of anything going on around her. "So, did you find some snacks here? When the bus driver walked by me it looked like he was eating something." Hopefully talking about food would distract Bea and Grace wouldn't have to explain herself any further.

"You bet your lucky stars there are snacks here. They've got something salty, something sweet, and even something healthy for ya to munch on. I'll help ya check it out."

Contacting Kevin would have to wait until she could talk privately. With the way her stomach was growling, a snack would help tide her over until dinner.

As they walked toward the porch, Grace slowed. Her gaze roamed over the numerous quilts hanging on the porch railings and ladder rungs. She wanted to stop and take in the gorgeous array of colors, fabrics, and designs, but Bea grabbed her arm and pulled her forward.

On the porch, a scrappy quilt covered an old paint-splattered wooden table. Three large speckled ceramic bowls held snacks. One had a salty cracker combination, another a colorful candy mix, while the third held an assortment of fresh fruit, including grapes, watermelon, cantaloupe, and strawberries. Cups, napkins and forks were arranged on the side of the table, along with a small tin bucket of packaged moist towelettes for cleaning hands and fingers before shopping inside. Off to one side was an old wash tub filled with ice and bottles of water, ice tea, and lemonade.

"See what I mean," Bea declared. "Fill up a cup and stop that growling coming from your stomach."

There was no sense arguing with Bea about the noise from her stomach. Grace filled a cup with fruit and grabbed an ice tea from the wash tub. Hoping that the caffeine would recharge her tired brain cells, she sat down in a rocking chair. Bea settled into the rocker next to her, munching on a cup of candy mix. Grace couldn't stop thinking that she needed a few minutes away from Bea to contact Kevin. But once Bea was with her, it was hard to shake her.

"I was looking at some more of them kits you were talking about. You might be right. They could be a good way for me to learn about choosing fabrics that work together and how designers write patterns.

Let me show you the ones that I'm liking and you can tell me what you think."

"Sure, I'd love to see what you found." Grace was pleasantly surprised that Bea was considering the idea of kits. Yet Grace hoped it wouldn't take long to give Bea her thoughts on them. She wanted to get free so that she could call Kevin.

"All righty, come this way." Bea said.

But first Grace carried their garbage to the trash can around the corner. When she turned to catch up with Bea, she saw Julia and Elaine across the porch. Their heads were bowed toward each other. While one of them watched her, the other whispered something in her ear. They took turns staring her way and whispering to each other as Grace walked across the porch and entered the house.

QUILTING FACTOID: The log cabin is one of many traditional quilt blocks. Made by arranging several rectangular pieces known as logs around a center square which is often red and represents the hearth.

CHAPTER EIGHT

Grace found herself in the main sitting room of the house, but she couldn't enjoy the cozy farmhouse decor and beautiful quilts and fabrics. Julia's and Elaine's behavior on the porch was so strange. Unless Julia had discovered she'd been on the bus and had overheard her phone conversation.

Grace checked the view out the window. Then it dawned on her. She should have realized it sooner. Elaine must have glanced out a window and saw her leaving the bus after Julia. Of course, she would have told Julia about it.

That was what those intense looks and whispers on the porch were about. If Julia and Elaine were so concerned about what Grace heard on the bus, perhaps there was more going on with Julia and Camille than Grace realized. She needed to talk to Kevin. Julia hadn't sounded at all surprised Camille was dead. But did she know something about how

Camille had died? Kevin should know Camille had a heart condition that Julia knew about, and that something was going on with Julia's husband. Something about a contract he'd looked at for Camille. And why was Julia looking for a letter? Grace's heart pounded. Could Julia have killed Camille?

"Grace, I'm over here." Bea's voice carried through the house.

Stop being melodramatic, Grace told herself and walked toward the sound of Bea's voice into a small room filled with fabrics and decorations for fall and Halloween.

Sample quilts made with the warm, rich colors of autumn were displayed on the walls above the shelving. Smaller runners and table toppers were rolled up and placed like scrolls in bushel baskets on the floor. Along one side of the room, garlands of colorful fall leaves were draped around the shelves and doorways. On the other side were fabrics in the typical Halloween colors of black, orange, yellow, purple, and witchy green. Jack-o'-lanterns, spiders, ghosts, bats, and black cat figurines accented the shelves along with strings of lights, some shaped like candy corn and some like skulls, lighting up the top display shelves.

"About time you got here. Look at this kit I found. It looks like pieces of candy corn. Ain't that sweet."

"That is very cute. It would be a great table runner. Candy corn works for the entire fall season. You'd get a lot of use from it."

It was a good find for Bea. The table runner used strips of white, orange, and yellow print autumn fabric sewn together into a strip set. Then the strip set was cut into triangles and the triangles were turned to alternate points. Its two short ends were angled making the table runner the wacky shape of a parallelogram. It would give Bea practice sewing a straight quarter inch seam. Although sewing on the bias edges and binding would be a little tricky, it could be done. Bea was going to need someone to help her with the projects she'd found and Grace figured she was probably the top, and only, candidate for the job.

"That's what I was thinking. I'll get one of these. I found another kit. Take a looks-y over here."

Bea led Grace to the Christmas room. Deep shades of red and green fabric, along with miniature pine trees, candy canes, reindeer, and Santa figurines, gave her that special feeling of Christmas. In one corner a small Christmas tree with a flannel tree skirt was decorated with a frayed fabric garland, crocheted snowflake ornaments, and paper pieced Christmas quilt ornaments. A diffuser released the scent of sugar cookies throughout the room. Grace thought back to happy Christmas times with James. Now she could only hope James would still recognize her when this Christmas came. She turned away from Bea to blink the tears from her eyes.

"What do ya think about this kit? It's for a Christmas tree skirt. The label says it's a rag quilt. So I was looking for rags in it, but only found this pretty flannel fabric. Confusing ain't it?"

The mist clearing from her eyes, Grace turned back to Bea. "Rag quilts aren't made of rags. They have raggy edge seams. After you sew the quilt together, instead of machine quilting it, you snip along the seam allowances. Then you wash and dry the quilt. That makes the seams fray and creates that raggy, shaggy look." Grace felt like she was teaching Bea a crash course in Quilting 101 and although it was a bit exasperating that wonderful feeling of helping another learn something new made up for it.

"I'm glad there aren't any rags in it. That sure would make a cheap looking tree skirt. I can handle raggy seams. If frayed edges are good enough for them pricey blue jeans with all the slits and holes in them, then they're good enough for a Christmas tree skirt. Ya know, after looking around here I'm starting to like this farmhouse country decor stuff so I'm going to do that for one of my Christmas trees. This raggy tree skirt would work perfect."

"Yes, they are fun. Just pick the colorway that will go with the decorations you're going to use." Grace was skeptical about Bea putting up several Christmas trees. But then she remembered Bea had multiple couches. Why not multiple trees? She wouldn't be surprised if every room in Bea's house had a Christmas tree—even the bathroom. How different from her and James. There were years when they were working such long hours she struggled to find time to decorate the single Christmas tree in the corner of their living room.

Bea stood, a kit in each hand, staring at them. "Here's the problem. I like the gold in this one and the burgundy in that one. I'll just switch them." Bea started to open the package and pull out the fabric.

Hastily, Grace stopped her. "Sorry Bea. You can't do that. You have to take the kit as it's done up. Maybe we can find the pattern and fabrics you like and buy everything separately."

Bea studied the two kits before tucking them under her arm. "I'll just take both and use what I like."

There was no reason Bea couldn't do that, and she certainly could afford it. Kits were cheaper than buying each fabric separately and you knew when you finished everything would go together perfectly. Besides, any fabrics Bea didn't use for the tree skirt could be the start of her fabric stash. Collecting a stash of fabrics was one of the most enjoyable parts of quilting and considered a necessity by most quilters.

"You've made some nice selections. These smaller projects finish pretty quickly so you get the fun of seeing how your quilt turns out much sooner."

"I'm liking these kits. While I'm still learning this quilt designing stuff, they take the guesswork out of things for a newbie like me. I might start by designing and selling some of these kits myself."

"Kits are a good way to learn quilting techniques and how to coordinate fabrics. You'll learn and practice some of the skills that you need to use along with your own creativity to make pretty quilts." Grace was glad Bea was starting to pick projects that more closely matched her skill level so she would be successful.

Grace wondered how much time they had left here. She still needed to make a purchase so she could get her card stamped and get the free block pattern.

"I need to take a few minutes and find something to buy. Go ahead and pay for your things and I'll catch up with you. I promise." Grace didn't just need to shop, she wanted to call Kevin too.

"We probably are running short on time, so I'll get this stuff paid for and see ya on the bus. Don't ya take too long now. I'll be watching for ya."

Grace nodded her head and hurried into the next room. It was filled with neutrals. The shelves were arranged in an ombre of shades of cream, ivory, white, tan, and gray. There were small and large prints, vines, florals, stripes, plaids, geometrics, solids, and more. It reminded Grace of a log cabin quilt she'd made using shades of tan, cream, and ivory back when Darcy first opened the Quilters Playground.

When she got to class and took out her fabrics, Darcy ever so slightly shook her head back and forth in disapproval. Grace knew most people thought the shades of creamy neutrals would make a bland, nondescript quilt, but she liked giving the unexpected a try every once in a while. When she completed the quilt top, Darcy and even Grace herself had been awed at how striking it was.

A cream on cream striped fabric caught Grace's eye. She liked using stripes for inner borders, sashing, and bindings. A yard of this would come in handy. She pulled the bolt off the shelf and carried it over to the cutting table. Other ladies were also scrambling to complete their purchases before Julia and Elaine made the announcement to board the bus.

There it was, Elaine declared they had ten minutes before the bus would leave. Grace hurriedly paid for her purchase and got her stamp and free block pattern. She made her way out the back door of the farmhouse and down the steps to a sidewalk leading to a small white gardening shed. Grace walked around the side of the shed where she could see the bus, so she didn't miss it, but where she didn't think anyone could see or hear her.

She quickly pulled out her phone and tried calling Kevin's personal number. The phone rang, but he didn't pick up. Her call went to Kevin's voice mail, and she quickly had to decide whether to leave a voice message. With Bea following her everywhere, who knew when she'd have a chance to get free and call again? But she hated leaving messages. Sometimes they made sense only to her.

"Kevin, this is Grace. I heard one of the ladies on the bus talking about Camille. She said that Camille appeared to have died of a heart attack, just like she thought, as if she knew in advance. And that she was looking for something but hadn't found it yet." Grace didn't think it was wise to include Julia's name in the message. "And that Camille had some sort of contract with Darcy." She wasn't sure if he'd remember who Darcy was. "She owns the Quilters Playground." It would be better to tell Kevin the details of Julia's phone call when she saw him in person.

Julia's voice announced the bus was almost ready to leave. When Grace looked toward the parking lot, the last of the line of women was getting on board. She needed to hustle, or they'd be leaving without her.

Julia stood near the bus door, checking her clipboard to be sure everyone was on board. "Why Grace, it would have been a shame if you'd missed the bus."

Grace could hear a bit of that snide, arrogant tone Julia used during her phone conversation with her husband. It didn't sound like it would bother Julia one bit if Grace missed the bus. She felt like Julia would have liked nothing better than to leave her behind. Heart pounding, Grace ignored Julia and trotted up the bus steps without saying a word.

Grace hurried down the narrow aisle toward her seat across from Bea. Her anxiety lessened when she saw Bea waiting there for her. She had to admit it was reassuring knowing someone was watching and looking out for her.

"Girl, you sure took your sweet old time. I was beginning to think I might have to hunt you down."

"Sorry, you know how I lose track of time when I'm looking at quilts and fabrics." Grace thought that certainly was true and just left out the part about calling Kevin.

"Don't I know it, and we only just met. What's with that Julia woman getting all snooty with you? She looked like she was itching to leave you behind. But you know I never would have let that happen."

Grace was impressed by how Bea seemed to pick up on things going on around her. If she always noticed and remembered everything that happened, being married to her must have been a challenge. Divorcing Bea had to have been a no-win situation for her exes. That might explain why she had no shortage of cash.

"It's been a difficult day. Julia's probably getting tired of herding all of us around. I just happened to be the last one this time, and she took it out on me."

"It sounded like more than that to me, but who am I to say being so new to these parts."

Come to think of it, Grace didn't know much about Bea. Maybe it was time to give the quilting lessons a rest and get to know her. It was better than worrying about those looks Julia and Elaine had given her, or if Kevin had gotten her message.

"I don't think that I've seen you around Lake City before today. Have you lived here long?" If Bea had been in town for a while, Grace couldn't figure out how she could have missed her or hearing about her. With Bea's loud and vibrant personality, people were bound to notice her and talk about the new gal in town. Then again, Grace didn't get out as much as she used to. She spent most of her time at the care center with James or at home quilting, reading, or gardening.

"Well, it's kind of a long story, but in a nutshell, after Orlando, my last husband, died, I got tired of spending all my time in the city. Nobody talks to anybody there. It's real impersonal and not real friendly. Even I can only shop and spend money for so long before I get bored. So I did some traveling. Went to all those foreign places—London, Paris, Prague, Hong Kong. I met some mighty nice people on my trips, but then you meet 'em, travel with 'em, and go back home. Ya say you'll email or call or visit, but it never seems to happen or if it does, it's not the same and doesn't last for very long."

Grace felt a little sad for Bea. She might have lots of money, but it didn't sound like she had steady people in her life. People who cared about her and spent time with her. Grace knew she was fortunate to have James and live in her friendly, small town. Even if everyone seemed to know your business, there was something comforting about knowing and chatting with most everyone you met as you shopped or walked around town.

"So how did you end up here after living in the city and traveling around the world?"

"Well, it was a friend of a friend of my last husband's lawyer. He told me about this place called Lake City where everybody knows everybody and people care about each other and help each other out in their time of need. After all that penthouse life and traveling around the world, I decided maybe I needed a change and should check out this little place and see if I could find some happy there."

"So are you just visiting, or do you think that you'll buy a home here?"

"Well, right now, I've just been renting a place on the lake. It's furnished and everything, so all I had to do was bring my suitcases. It's got an option to buy, so if I like it here I just might do that. I'm still thinking about what I should do. Nothing's definite, but at my age I'd like to settle down where I feel like I belong. "

Grace wondered where on the lake. Even the smaller houses the summer vacationers rented were luxurious by Grace's standards. She and James used to drive by and wonder what the homes looked like on the inside. And she'd heard the lake sides were even more beautiful than the street side of homes, with gorgeous landscaping, decks, and patios, along with the sound of the water right outside your door.

Grace fell into a fantasy of seeing inside one of the large houses that dominated the shoreline, of sitting on one of the decks and gazing out at the lake. A sound broke her daydream. Bea had kept talking.

"So, I have a lady who comes in and does the cleaning. She's been filling me in on some places to go and things to do around these parts. I was telling her I needed a hobby to keep me busy and help me meet people. She thought quilting would fit the bill and told me about the Quilters Playground."

Grace wondered who Bea's cleaning lady was, but decided to ask another time. She was glad Bea had met a local who truly knew and loved the area to help her learn more about it. Even if the cleaning lady spent more time chatting with Bea than cleaning, it was probably well worth the money Bea paid her.

"Then how did you find out about the shop hop?" Grace had heard about the shop hop at a quilt guild meeting. She'd also seen signs around town with Camille's name prominently displayed on them to entice quilters to sign up and rub shoulders with a famous designer.

"After she told me the quilt shop's name, I looked up Quilters Playground on the internet. They have a website. It's got a few pictures and tells about the shop. Could do a lot better job though. It's not that easy to navigate and needs more visual interest. Like maybe a video or virtual tour. But I found the information about the shop hop, so I said to myself, why not? And signed right up."

"I'm so old school. I forget about websites and online things." Grace wasn't comfortable using the computer. She knew just enough about computers to record grades and take attendance on them, as she'd been required to do at school. Paper and pencil and hard copies of things were still much more natural for her.

"After I signed up for this here shop hop, I tried learning stuff about quilting on the internet and watched some of them teaching videos. But I think I need someone right beside me telling me how to do it and then watching me to be sure that I do it like they told me. Sort of like you've been teaching me about all this quilting and designing stuff today. Maybe in return, I could show you how to use some of this technology and web stuff, if you'd like to learn more about it, that is."

It was kind of Bea to offer Grace help with her technology skills, but she didn't use the computer much these days and she was just fine with that. Besides, most of her time was spent with James, quilting, or in her garden. She didn't need a computer to do those things.

"I'm glad you found the shop online and signed up for the shop hop. Although this has been a pretty unusual one." Having a quilter die on a shop hop was definitely not the norm. It made the trip quite memorable, but not in a good way.

After listening to Bea, Grace realized spending time together with her had been nice. In spite of Bea talking too much, without her it would have been a very different day. She would have questioned every penny she spent and been even more worried and anxious about being away from James. The trip would have been much lonelier for both of them.

"I'm glad too. It's not every day that you meet a new friend, and find a dead body to boot." Bea grinned and Grace scowled at her. The moment Bea noticed, her smile dropped. "Not that I like finding dead bodies. But I figure it makes this place a little more interesting than most small towns. I might even end up becoming a permanent resident." Bea patted Grace's arm and smiled.

Grace couldn't help herself, and smiled back. It felt good to have something positive come out of a day that had started in such a terrible way.

QUILTING FACTOID: Machine quilting is using a sewing machine to stitch rows or patterns through layers of fabric and batting in the manner of old-style hand-quilting. Some quilt shops provide custom quilting using long arm sewing machines some with computer programs that stitch customized designs on quilts.

CHAPTER NINE

When the bus pulled up in front of the Quilters Playground, Grace sighed with relief. A shop hop was always exhausting, but today's had been even more so. She just wanted to go home. Or rather to the care center. She had known that she would miss James, but hadn't realized how much until she had spent the entire day away from him. As the bus coasted to a stop, she collected her things, hoping to take off as quickly as possible. When she reached the bus steps, she glanced toward the quilt shop and saw the front door open.

From the doorway, Meg waved at them. "If you could all come in before you leave." While several of the ladies went into the building, others headed for their cars. "Please, this will only take a moment. If you could please come inside. We need everyone to come inside for an announcement."

After a moment's hesitation, Grace tossed her purchases into the trunk of her car alongside the mixer that Darcy had given her the other day and hurried into the building. Across the street, Bea threw her numerous bags and totes into the trunk of a bright red convertible with personalized license plates: BHAPPY1.

After the long, eventful day on the bus and time spent worrying about James, a slight headache was beginning to gnaw at Grace's forehead. Her headaches usually meant she needed to eat something healthy or get some sleep as soon as she could.

Since sleep wasn't an option now, Grace knew she needed to eat before her headache got any worse. She might as well go inside and grab something before visiting James. Meg continued motioning the stragglers in. What could be so important? The ladies heading for their cars must have been wondering the same thing because they turned and walked back to the shop.

Unexpectedly, Kevin was inside, his blond head towering above the ladies. He stood near Darcy at the cutting table, waiting for everyone. As the ladies gathered around, they spoke to each other in hushed whispers.

While Grace waited with the others, she noticed Julia and Elaine coming out of the hallway and casually inserting themselves into the group. They were acting a little guilty, but of what? Grace watched them whispering to the gals next to them, trying a little too hard to blend in. Then again, maybe she was being paranoid, and they'd just been using the restroom.

After calling for quiet, Darcy introduced Deputy Oleson.

Kevin cleared his throat to be sure he had their attention. "I'm sorry to intrude on your day out. As you know, Mrs. Christianson died today while on your shop hop. We will be contacting each of you over the next few days."

A wave of murmurs went around the room.

"Ms. Duncan has agreed to gather your contact information. Please be sure to leave it with her or Ms. Reynolds. If you have any pertinent information and would like to talk to me right now, I'll be outside by my patrol car till after your dinner. Otherwise, you may call the sheriff's department." Kevin repeated the number several times.

That set the group abuzz. Connie lifted her hand as if in a classroom. "But Camille died of a heart attack. Why does the sheriff's office want to talk to us?"

"There are some inconsistencies that require further investigation."

"Such as?" Judy demanded.

"I'm not at liberty to say. We would just like to retrace Mrs. Christianson's activities over the last few days." That brought the room to dead silence. "I'll let you get on with your dinner. Again, if anyone would like to talk, I'll be right outside." He thanked Meg and the group for their help.

Before Kevin left, his gaze caught Grace's eye. "I went by the care center and checked on James for you. He's been having a good day. I'm sure he'll be happy to see you later." It was going to be hard to say anything more with all the women milling about. From the corner of her eye, Grace noticed Bea had approached and stopped to listen.

"I got your message. I'll stop by tomorrow morning to talk about it." He whispered.

Grace was relieved to hear that Kevin had received her message about Julia's phone call. It impressed her that he'd been able to let her know by making it sound like it was about James.

"That sure is nice the way you look out for Grace and her hubby. Not many fellows would take the time to do that for someone who's not their own family." Bea said.

"Grace and James are like family to me." He informed her.

It warmed Grace's heart to hear Kevin say that. She and James had always felt like Kevin was part of their family. Since their family lived so far away, they treated Kevin like one of their own. Hearing Kevin's comment confirmed that he felt the same. When she told James later what Kevin had said, she hoped he would understand.

Grace watched Kevin stride through the shop toward the door. She couldn't help but notice she wasn't the only one watching him leave. Few men ventured into the quilt shop, and those who did were usually much older and with their wives. Having someone as young and attractive as Kevin there, even under these circumstances, was unusual. Several women had pleasant smiles. Bea's grin definitely said she enjoyed the view. Even Darcy's eyes were locked on him over the top of a display. When she noticed Grace watching her, she straightened a bolt of fabric and called to Meg. "We need to get the buffet going."

Bea took a deep sigh and fanned her face with her hand. "My, my, my. If that fella ain't one fine piece of eye candy. Who doesn't love a tall, handsome man in uniform? M-m-m, m-m-m."

Oh, my word, Grace thought. Bea could be Kevin's mother. She'd heard about older women who dated much, much younger men. What had James called them? Cougars. But she'd never pictured one looking or acting like Bea did around Kevin. A woman her age should know to be less obvious. It made Grace wonder about the ages, looks, and bank accounts of Bea's many husbands, but she was too polite to ask.

"Oh, to be young again. Even at my age it's fun to flirt with a good looking fella just for the heck of it." Bea gave Grace a friendly jab to the ribs and laughed. "You should see your face. You didn't really think I'd be interested in a young fella like him. A woman like me needs a man with a little more experience in life, if ya know what I mean." She winked, making her message abundantly clear.

Although Grace was relieved to hear that Bea was just flirting with Kevin for a bit of fun. It wasn't her kind of fun, and it didn't seem fair to Kevin. She felt a little ashamed for thinking Bea was only interested in men who were younger and good-looking, or maybe that's how she'd gotten such healthy bank accounts.

Exhausted and with her headache growing, Grace decided she better get some dinner and hurry on her way. It was nice to hear James had a good day while she was away on the shop hop. But it also made her feel like maybe he hadn't missed her and didn't need her, leaving her with a feeling of emptiness along with her headache. She hoped seeing James would help those feelings go away.

"Well, I've worked up an appetite. Let's go get something to eat." Bea exclaimed.

Grace thought Bea's appetite might be as big as the flowers on the fabric she seemed to gravitate toward. She followed her over to one of the tables and put her purse in a chair to save her place.

The smoky, sweet smell of barbeque sauce made Grace's mouth water. Bea pushed her way into the buffet line, budging in front of the bus driver. Grace tried to be more polite about finding a place in the line.

Two tables had been put together end to end and decorated with a variety of quilted table runners and clever layered cakes made from fabric. A milk glass platter held stacks of buns. Next to it was a heated roasting pan heaped with pulled pork. Meg manned the table and encouraged everyone to take as much as they wanted. She kept trying to catch Grace's attention, but Grace couldn't think of a reason why.

At the end of the buffet, Darcy helped with drinks and desserts. Between them, they kept the food line moving quickly. As the quilters stood in line, they chatted about how hungry they were and how good the food smelled after such a long day, noticeably avoiding any discussion of Camille or her death.

Grace dropped her ticket for the grand prize into a wicker basket. Then she started filling her plate. She loaded her whole wheat bun with pulled pork and a touch of the sweet smoky barbecue sauce. Hot and super-hot barbecue sauces were also available, but Grace didn't like spicy things. James used to tease her about not being able to eat fiery foods. It always amazed her how he could eat the spiciest foods when even the smallest taste of them burned her mouth like she was eating molten lava.

Next were bowls of potato salad, cole slaw, and potato chips. Grace loved potato salad and added a heaping spoonful to her plate. Last, of course, were Meg's specialties, the desserts. Tiny chocolate chip, and cherry cheesecakes were artfully displayed on one milk glass platter. Chewy, chocolate scotcheroos were piled on another. Grace wished she could take two, a cherry cheesecake for herself and a scotcheroo for James, but she didn't want to appear greedy so she chose a scotcheroo. It would be easy to cut a taste of it off for herself and then save the rest for James. She picked up a bottle of water and hurried to her chair.

Grace sat down and started eating her pulled pork sandwich as quickly as she could while still using her manners. Bea set her plate on the table and plopped down in her chair next to her. Grace couldn't believe the mound of food heaped on Bea's plate. She was surprised the heavy duty paper plate hadn't collapsed under the weight. To top it all off, Bea had a second plate with slices of chocolate chip cheesecake, cherry cheesecake, and a scotcheroo. Bea liked to push boundaries that was for sure.

"This sure is a nice way to finish the day. I love a spicy barbecue sandwich and sweet dessert to top it off." Bea started shoveling potato salad into her mouth with one hand and taking bites of her pork sandwich with the other. It looked like Bea was going to be pretty quiet while she was enjoying her meal with such huge mouthfuls. This was Grace's chance to finish her own meal and head out to see James before Bea could strike up a conversation and delay her.

Sure enough, Bea was absorbed in her food and definitely enjoying the meal. Light chatter floated around the room as the ladies talked about their purchases and how they were going to spend the rest of their weekend. Grace finished her sandwich and started on her potato salad. She wished she hadn't taken so much, but she had missed eating it. During the summer she used to make it quite often since James loved it almost as much as she did. She rushed through the rest of her meal like she used to at school when she needed the last few minutes of her lunch period for a quick restroom break before her next class.

Just as she finished and getting up to leave, Darcy clapped her hands together to get everyone's attention. "Ladies, I know today didn't go as planned. Camille's passing at the Hummingbird was a shocking and sad moment, especially for those of us who called her friend. Please, let's all take a moment of silence in Camille's memory." Darcy bowed her head and the other ladies followed her lead.

Grace noticed Meg had left when Darcy started talking to the group. She didn't seem interested in what Darcy was saying about Camille. Grace couldn't blame her if Camille had ordered Meg around the way that the School Marm Quilters had described.

Grace heard a soft mumble coming from Bea. "Oh, brother, the way she treated people, I doubt she had any friends." Bea whispered.

Grace turned her bowed head toward Bea and put her finger to her lips to shush her. Bea got the hint, rolled her eyes and zipped her lips together.

The moment of silence was a quick one. Darcy cleared her throat, and everyone looked up at her.

"I want to thank you ladies for sticking with the shop hop after the sad turn of events this morning. I hope you found some new projects and enjoyed yourselves as the trip continued. It would have made Camille happy to know you all carried on sharing time with fellow quilters and finding new projects for your quilting talents." Darcy sniffled and wiped her eyes as if drying a tear, then she continued.

"We still have the grand prize drawing, ladies. I hope everyone remembered to put their name on their ticket and drop it in the basket on the table here." Darcy looked around and everyone nodded their head, assuring her that the tickets were all there.

Grace saw Bea pause and stop eating as Darcy continued talking about the prize drawing.

"Our grand prize is a gift certificate for free batting and free custom machine quilting from the Quilters Playground. I hope it will inspire the winner to complete their shop hop quilt or another beautiful quilt project and allow us the honor of machine quilting it. Julia, as quilt guild president, will you assist me and draw the name of the winner for us?"

Grace was afraid to look at Bea. She knew she was probably rolling her eyes again and shaking her head in disgust at the mention of Julia's name.

"Why, of course, Darcy. It would be my pleasure." Julia smiled and joined her at the front of the room. Darcy held the basket aloft while Julia reached inside and pulled out the winning ticket.

"The grand prize winner is Bea Andrews Vargas! Congratulations Bea!" With a plastic smile on her face, Julia announced the name off the ticket.

Bea practically exploded out of her seat and rushed to join Darcy and Julia. She snatched the certificate out of Darcy's hand and grabbed the shop owner in a bear hug, rocking back and forth as the smaller woman tried to escape her grasp. She repeatedly thanked Darcy and totally ignored Julia.

"Oh, my stars! Thank you! I can't believe it! This is so exciting for a rookie quilter like me. Thank you! Thank you!" Bea waved the certificate in the air as she sashayed back to the table to show Grace and the other ladies sitting with them.

Julia tried to cover her exclusion from Bea's celebration by quietly clapping and returning to her seat.

Darcy smoothed her hair and straightened her blouse before speaking again. "I'm very happy our winner is so thrilled about her prize. Congratulations to Bea and we look forward to quilting your project at our shop. Now I know you ladies want to finish your meals, but I wanted to remind you to be sure to show Meg your completed, stamped card before you leave. Then she'll give you your free copy of the shop hop quilt pattern. She'll be waiting for you over by the cutting table. Thank you again for being a part of today's shop hop. On behalf of all the shop owners, I want to thank you for your participation."

A smattering of clapping and a few voices spoke up thanking Darcy. Grace heard Bea's voice whisper again. "I'll bet she appreciates it. I heard she needs all the business she can get or her shop might close. And just when I win this prize and am thinking I like this quilting thing."

Word had certainly gotten around fast. Of all times to say something like that, it shouldn't be openly discussed, especially here, now. She gave Bea her stern teacher look and hoped she'd stop talking.

While Bea went back to eating her desserts, Grace excused herself and cleared her area of the table.

Meg was cleaning up the buffet table but again caught her eye. As Grace moved near her, she wondered what she wanted. Meg slipped a zip lock baggie from her apron pocket and handed it to Grace.

"For James. I remember you saying how much he liked them."

How thoughtful of Meg to remember while she was so busy with the shop hop. Meg had always been a sweet girl.

Camille's death had to be difficult for Meg and Darcy, but Meg seemed to be the one most bothered by it. With the rumored financial condition of the shop and now Camille's passing Darcy was the one who should be having serious concerns about the shop's future, yet she appeared to be unfazed by it all. Meg was the one who seemed to be bothered.

"Thank you, Meg. Rather, James thanks you."

Meg smiled. "He let me sound the siren once. I'd fallen on my bike and he'd taken me home. I was crying, and he let me turn on the siren. He didn't have to do that."

No, he didn't, but it was so like James.

"I hate to ask," Meg merged the two plates of cheesecakes into one as she spoke, "after everything that happened, but did you notice if Camille had a purple notebook with her?" She looked up at Grace, her eyes hopeful. "You, see, it's mine, and she took it. Well, actually I gave it to her and she wouldn't give it back."

After giving herself a moment to think, Grace nodded. She remembered Camille having a purple notebook when she got on the bus. "Yes, I believe she did."

"I went out and looked on the bus, but it wasn't there."

"No, Deputy Oleson took Camille's things. It must be in her tote." But was it? Grace didn't remember seeing it when she gathered Camille's things for Kevin.

Meg pressed her lips together. "Do you think he'll give it back to me?"

"I couldn't say. You'll have to ask him." The crestfallen expression on Meg's face touched Grace. "If it's yours, I'm sure he'll give it back to you when his investigation is over."

Somewhat relieved, Meg focused on moving the last two scotcheroos to the cheesecake plate. "I hope you had a good time. I mean even with, in spite of…"

"Yes, I did."

Meg's lips turned up as she looked at Grace again. "I knew you would. Quilting is a good escape from the pressures and hardships of life. We all need that sometimes."

For someone so young, it was a much more understanding comment than Grace expected. "That's very true. Thanks again for the extra scotcheroos for James. Hope you aren't here too late cleaning up."

"I'll have things cleaned up and be out of here in no time. And if I get too tired, I have some caffeine pills or an energy drink. I learned that trick working at the ad agency." Meg continued busying herself by putting things away.

Grace was about to leave, but her good manners reminded her she had forgotten to tell Bea a quick goodbye. She returned to the table where Bea was enjoying her plate of desserts and moaning about how delicious they were.

"Bea, congratulations on winning the grand prize. It should motivate you to get a project done soon. I need to get going so I can spend what's left of the evening with James. It was good getting to know you today. If you need a little help with your kits, just let me know." Grace's offer of help surprised even herself. What was she thinking? Must be that teacher instinct of hers, always wanting to help others out with things.

"Why Grace, I enjoyed the day with you, too. It would be great if I could get some expert help from you. I definitely want to get a project done right away so I can use my prize. Let's exchange numbers." Bea seemed thrilled at the prospect of getting Grace's number.

She took her phone out of her bag and entered Bea's number as Bea recited it to her. Likewise, she told Bea her number and Bea added it to her phone.

"You'll be hearing from me soon. Have a nice evening with your hubby." The last was said with a hint of loneliness.

Grace put her phone back in her purse. What had she gotten herself into?

QUILTING FACTOID: A jelly roll is a coordinated collection of 2 ½ inch strips of fabric rolled together like cinnamon or jelly rolls. Having pre-cut strips saves the quilter time when making strip quilts such as trip around the world or log cabin.

CHAPTER TEN

Grace stopped at the cutting table and looked around. Meg was clearing the buffet, her back to the shop area. Before Grace could call out to her, Darcy hurried over.

"Hope I didn't interrupt what you were doing." Grace apologized, showing Darcy her fully stamped card. "I'd like to get my shop hop pattern, please."

"I was trying to get a head start taking down the shop hop display in the front window." Darcy handed Grace the quilt assembly instructions. "Did you and Deputy Oleson have a good discussion?" Darcy lifted her eyebrows inquisitively. "You're old friends, aren't you?"

"Yes, he worked with my husband."

"Oh, that's right. Well, customers have kept me so busy I haven't had time to think about everything that happened today, but it will probably hit me tomorrow. It will be a lot calmer around here now, that's for sure."

Darcy's words reminded Grace of the raised voices she'd heard at the shop. How often had that kind of thing been happening? Would things be calmer now that the bustle of the shop hop was over or because Camille was gone? Before she could say anything else, Judy came up to the cutting table and stood impatiently behind her.

Grace hustled out of the way, stuffing the pattern into her bag, and hurried out the door. After being away from James all day, she couldn't wait to see him. She hoped he would be the James who enjoyed talking about her day and loved to hear about any unusual things that had happened.

On the short drive to the care center, at the street intersections Grace caught brief glimpses of the sun setting over the lake. The incredible sunsets were one of the best things about living near the lake.

When James had worked evening hours, Grace would often walk the eight or nine blocks from their house to the beach to watch the sunset. She would marvel at the colors of the sun painting the sky and burning across the lake's surface. Even now, after her evening visits with James, she would sometimes stop at the beach on her way home and try to clear her mind.

Relieved that eating dinner had done the trick and alleviated her headache but afraid she would be too late to visit, Grace parked and sprinted to the care center entrance. Once inside, she could tell they were winding down their day. They had dimmed the hallway lights to mimic the sun going down. Nurses were dispensing evening medications and aides were gathering empty dinner trays from residents who'd eaten in their rooms rather than the dining center. Familiar faces smiled at Grace and said hello as she walked by. Grace quickened her pace, impatient to reach James' room.

From the doorway she saw him sitting in his recliner staring out the window, but the curtains were closed. This wasn't a good sign. When James didn't notice her entering the room, a wave of disappointment washed over her. Maybe he was just groggy from eating. He had a huge appetite and always ate his fill. After being away from him all day, she needed to find a way to reach him.

"Hey, deputy, how was your day?" Grace used to tease him that the only way she could be sure he was listening to her was if she called him deputy.

James slowly turned his head, a blank look on his face. Quickly it was replaced with one of confusion, then frustration. She knew that look. His mind was struggling to recognize her face and the sound of her voice. She hoped things would click and they could visit like they used to. Even if it lasted only a few minutes.

"Hello, young lady. Where have you been all day?"

Grace was cautious. She knew sometimes James' mind could be lost in time. He would think he was a young boy, or they were dating or newly married. Other times, it was just a vague welcome, like he was trying to cover up he had no idea who she was.

"Why, sir, I went on the quilt shop hop today. I had three nice meals and did a bit of shopping." She waited anxiously for James' reply. If he managed one, it would tell her what he was understanding.

"That sounds fun. It was all day long? How can anyone hop all day long?" His reply wasn't what she'd hoped for, but at least he'd answered.

Two-way conversations with James were happening less frequently. Much of the time he didn't respond, or his responses made little sense, or didn't connect with the topic of conversation. Grace felt more and more like she was conversing with herself.

"Oh, we managed somehow. We rode a bus to several quilt shops around the lake. It was interesting to see the different shops and the fabrics and designs at each one."

James' eyes glazed over like blinds being closed on a window and a blank, empty look came over his face. She waited for him to say something. When he didn't, still hoping she could reach him and they would connect with each other, she tried asking him about his day. Maybe he would remember the things the nurse had told her about.

"I heard you were dancing with the ladies today. Did you have a good time?"

"Dancing ... why yes. I think I might have taken a spin around the dance floor. Was that at The Ballroom ... with you ...?" He was trying so hard. It must be so frustrating thinking in bits and pieces, like the pieces of a jigsaw puzzle.

Grasping the fragments and assembling them into coherent thoughts was getting more difficult for him every day. And although he was sitting right next to her, she felt like she was losing him in a dense fog.

"We did go dancing at The Ballroom together back in the day. You twirled and dipped me around the floor." When they were younger, they would listen to the latest bands at The Ballroom. An unimaginative but descriptive name for a huge old building beside the lake with nothing more than a ballroom and a stage for bands to perform on. Large events were held there and many different styles of bands played concerts on its stage—from swing to rock to country to golden oldies. People came from all over the area to listen and dance.

Instead of answering, James picked up the remote and turned on the television, staring blankly at the screen. A wave of sadness hit Grace. It was as if he'd used the remote to not only turn the television on but to turn her off. She longed for the times when she'd share her day and he would be her sounding board. His dry humor always lightened a hard day. Sometimes he would listen to her vent until she ran out of steam. Then he'd offer his shoulder for her to lean against and wrap his arms around her. He always seemed to know how to make things better.

Someone tapped her shoulder. "Grace, so sorry to disturb you but it's time for James to get ready for bed."

Grace yawned and stretched. She must have dozed off in the chair. She looked over and saw James softly snoring in his recliner. It reminded her of the many nights at home when they would both fall asleep in front of the TV. "I'll get out of your way then."

She quietly tiptoed over and gave James a soft kiss on the cheek and whispered, "I love you, deputy."

As her lips left his skin, James turned his head. "Love you too, Gracie."

She felt a lump in her throat. She looked at James' handsome face and knew the man she loved was in there, somewhere.

Grace hurried to her car as if to outrun the tears rolling down her cheeks. Through blurry eyes, she made the short drive back to their dark, empty home. Parking in the garage, she sat sobbing until she couldn't cry any more.

Empty and drained, she dragged herself into the house and made her way to the living room. James' recliner beckoned her to its safe haven and she collapsed into its soft, worn leather. His familiar scent surrounded and comforted her. She took slow, steady breaths of his faint smell and felt herself gradually drifting off into a deep sleep.

~ ~ ~

The sun shining through the gap between the living room curtains woke her the next morning, curled up in James' recliner and still wearing the clothes from the day before. What time was it? She checked the clock and realized she'd overslept and needed to hurry if she wanted to get to the care center to catch even part of the church service with James.

She took a quick shower and dressed. There was no time for coffee or breakfast. She hadn't been to the grocery store yet, anyway. Sometimes the care center had coffee and donuts in the dining room for visitors on Sundays. She hoped there would still be something left by the time she got there.

As she drove, she savored the warm sunshine and the reflection of the topaz blue sky in the glassy water. What a gorgeous morning. She found her usual parking spot and hurried inside. When she got to James' room, he was sitting in his recliner listening to a televised church service. He turned and smiled when she entered. Grace smiled to see his smile.

She went over and gave him a kiss on the forehead. "Morning, honey. Sorry, I'm a bit late."

James winked at her and whispered, "Morning, Gracie."

Grace's heart sang when she heard him say her pet name again and saw the playful wink he used to flirt with her even after all their years together. She sat in the chair and listened to the end of the service with him. After the final prayer and blessing, James turned off the TV.

"So, deputy, how was breakfast today?" Grace waited to hear James' response to get an idea of how he was doing.

"Pancakes and sausage. Made me wish for those pancakes we used to get at the Goldfinch Cafe."

"I remember. I especially remember how long we had to wait for a booth or table. But the pancakes were definitely well worth it."

When James hadn't been on duty, they ate breakfast at the Goldfinch Cafe most every Sunday. Its light, fluffy pancakes and rich piping hot coffee were the talk of the county. People flocked there and enjoyed chatting with each other as they waited in the inevitably long line. For many, it was an after church ritual and one of the pleasures of small town life.

"What'd you have for breakfast, Gracie?"

"I was hoping to grab a cup of coffee and a donut here if there's anything left. I'm going to the dining room real quick to check, okay?"

She wasn't sure if he'd understood, but he nodded his head and motioned for her to go. In the dining room she discovered the coffee was cold and only crumbs were left in the tray where the donuts had been. She headed back and saw Kevin entering James' room. As she got closer, she could hear Kevin's baritone and James' lower bass.

When she walked in, Kevin was sitting in the chair closest to James. She smiled at seeing the two men in her life. "Good morning, Kevin. It seems like I just saw you. Nice of you to stop by to see James."

"I always enjoy seeing James, but I was looking for you. Remember we were going to talk this morning? I stopped by your place and you were gone so I figured you'd be with James."

"I'm so sorry. I forgot all about it." Grace felt awful that she'd wasted Kevin's time. It had completely slipped her mind after oversleeping.

"It was quite a day yesterday, James. Has Grace told you about it yet?" Kevin spoke with a slow, soothing voice.

"No, I haven't had a chance." Grace answered for James. She should have waited for him to answer, but she was eager to tell Kevin about the things she'd heard and seen.

"What's Kevin talking about, Gracie?" James had picked up on Kevin's comments.

James seemed to be doing pretty well this morning, especially now that Kevin had arrived. She started telling about the previous day, step by step, with the hope James would be able to follow along better than last night.

"I went on one of those quilt shop bus trips yesterday. You know where you ride on a bus to different shops and buy quilt fabric." Grace tried to keep it simple, hoping James would understand.

James looked at her, his forehead wrinkling before he weakly smiled "I'm thinking... I liked when you told me about the tasty food they fed you on those trips."

Grace had to laugh. "That's right. You liked to tease me that the shop owners must think the better they fed us the more fabric we'd buy."

"Well, James might have had a point. From what I saw, the ladies on your trip enjoyed some tasty looking food and they had plenty of shopping bags on the bus." Kevin grinned at Grace.

"Gentlemen, I'll have you know that I stayed on my budget." Grace teased back.

"It was good she took a day for herself, wasn't it, James?" Kevin asked him.

James looked a little lost. "Yes, why, yes. It was a good day."

Grace could tell James was catching only bits and pieces of the conversation now, like talking on your cell phone when you repeatedly lose the connection. James was echoing back his responses, repeating words and phrases he'd heard.

Grace was unsure how to tell him a death had occurred on the trip. "It was a different day because of what happened."

"A different day. Different how?" James echoed.

Grace hesitated and looked at Kevin.

Grace was relieved Kevin took the lead and told James. "Most of the town is talking about it. A lady on the shop hop died."

"Died?" James caught the last word and repeated it. "A lady died. We'll need to look into that."

"Oh, James, the lady had a heart attack. It was sad, but no one else was hurt or in danger." Grace wanted James to know she and the other ladies on the bus had been safe. When he was a deputy, the public's safety was always a priority for him.

"That's sad. Did she cry?" James said. He was starting to miss more of the conversation. Grace's heart always sank when this happened. He was drifting away from her again.

"Yes, it was sad." Grace didn't know what else to say.

"They called the EMTs and the sheriff's office and an investigation is now in progress." Kevin said.

Kevin had said it most likely was a heart attack. They knew Camille had a heart condition, so why would they need to continue to investigate? Then again, Kevin had taken her brownie to the lab for testing.

Grace couldn't stop herself. "I thought you said it was a heart attack and natural causes. So what else needs to be investigated?"

Kevin leaned over and whispered to Grace. "Mrs. Christianson was at the doctor's the day before to have an insurance physical and her heart checked out just fine. Her medicine was keeping her blood pressure under control so there was no natural reason for her to have a heart attack."

Grace could only imagine her expression. Someone had intentionally harmed Camille? No wonder the investigation was still in progress. There were some things that happened on the shop hop Grace definitely thought Kevin needed to know, especially now.

Grace heard voices on the TV. James was staring at the images on the screen. He was gone to her again. At least she'd had a few good moments with him this morning. She held onto these moments for all they were worth because she knew the time would come when those moments would be gone, forever.

Kevin checked his watch and told James he had to get back to work. He patted James on the back, perhaps thinking a little physical contact might help James remember he'd been there. Kevin, like Grace, had probably noticed that more and more frequently James failed to remember who'd visited him and when the visits had occurred.

Kevin motioned for Grace to come with him. First, she leaned over James and gave him a hug, telling him she'd be back later in the day. James patted her arm and waved goodbye as she moved towards the door.

She walked out with Kevin and strolled over to his patrol vehicle.

"Are you doing okay?" He asked. "Yesterday was a lot to take in and now the ME's findings make this a serious matter."

It was so like him to worry about her. He was the one with the tough job ahead. On top of it all, this was probably one of his first major investigations without James.

"Really, I'm fine. I think getting some rest last night helped. Since you're officially investigating Camille's death, there were some other things that happened on the shop hop that I think you might want to know about."

"That's what I figured from your phone message yesterday and is why I wanted us to talk this morning."

"I'm so sorry. I overslept and got in a rush to see James and forgot about talking with you this morning. I hope I didn't mess up your schedule too badly. Does it work to talk now? I could pick up coffee and we could talk by the sea wall. I'll be inside with James the rest of the day so it would be nice to spend some time by the lake. "

"I can make that work. You go on ahead and get coffee. I'll meet you at the seawall in fifteen minutes."

QUILTING FACTOID: Originating in the 1800s, a quilting bee is a social gathering where people who sew or quilt work on their own projects or together on a group project.

CHAPTER ELEVEN

Grace parked and walked over to sit on the seawall while she waited for Kevin. The sun's rays warmed her face, and the sound of the water washing up on the rocks below was hypnotic.

It was quiet now, the outdoor church service held in the city park every Sunday morning was over, but soon the area would be busy with boats parking at the city dock, jet skis zipping across the water, bicyclists pedaling by, people walking their dogs, and families strolling to the city beach just down the shore.

Kevin pulled into a parking spot and looked in her direction. She pointed to a picnic table under some trees where they could sit and talk while they drank coffee and munched on the jumbo muffins she'd picked up.

He walked over and removed his sunglasses, his crystal blue eyes scanning the area before he sat down. "I sure could use some coffee. And you picked up muffins too. You must have read my mind. Thank you." He picked up a muffin and saluted her with it before eating half of it in one huge bite.

"Now that this investigation is moving into high gear there isn't going to be much time to eat or sleep." He took a drink of coffee and finished the other half of the muffin. Grace hadn't thought to get a second one for him, so she gave him hers, telling him she'd had plenty of rich food the day before. He hesitated just a second, probably thinking about all the food he'd seen or heard about on the shop hop. Then he thanked her and downed the second one in short order.

"James used to say the same thing about investigations. It's just how the job is and he did love it." Grace remembered how hard James worked on those investigations, and how much he enjoyed working them with Kevin. He said Kevin wasn't afraid of long hours and hard work.

Kevin nodded his head as he took a drink of coffee. "A couple of the ladies told me there was a ruckus on the bus between Mrs. Christianson and another woman."

A ruckus? Grace thought for a moment. "I wonder if they meant when Bea got on the bus."

"Bea. That woman you were with last night?"

"Yes. We met on the bus and I ended up helping her with quite a bit of her shopping." A twinge of guilt hit Grace. She had enjoyed some of Bea's company. "When Bea got on the bus, she sat next to Camille but Camille told her to move."

"As I recall the whole front row of seats was reserved for Mrs. Christianson."

"Well, Camille did like her space."

"No one seems to have liked her much."

Grace didn't say anything.

"Or am I wrong there?"

"No, I'm afraid that you're right."

"Even Meg--" Kevin caught himself. "Ms. Reynolds had been arguing with her. Do you know what that was about?"

Oh dear, here she was gossiping again. "I can't be sure."

"I know it has to do with rumors about Mrs. Christianson signing a contract with some fabric company. Why would that cause trouble between them?"

"I don't know. Camille's leaving shouldn't affect Meg at all, or at least not directly. It's the Quilters Playground that would be hurt."

Kevin lifted an eyebrow.

"Instead of Darcy getting the patterns first, she'd have to wait until Farmers Bounty, the fabric company it's rumored that Camille was going to sign with, released them to everyone. It would also cost Darcy more money to buy the patterns from a distributor instead of directly from Camille. And then with Camille not working out of the shop, it would no longer be a destination shop for quilters."

"Being a destination shop, that's important?"

"Well, yes." How should Grace explain it? "A lot of quilters follow certain designers. They like the way they pick colors, or how the patterns are written.

Sometimes they will travel hundreds of miles just for the chance of meeting their favorite designer."

"Kind of like they're rock stars or professional athletes."

"Well, yes, I guess you could say that."

"So all these quilters are coming to the Quilters Playground hoping to see Mrs. Christianson."

"And to get patterns before they are released nationally."

"So Ms. Duncan is going to lose business." Kevin asked.

"Yes."

"How much business?"

"Could be a lot." Grace bit her lip. "Some of the quilters think the store might close."

"Which also means Ms. Reynolds would lose her job. My understanding is that everyone thinks she's overqualified for any employment that's available around town and that she needs the income from this job to help support herself and her elderly parents. That gives both women a reason to be arguing with Mrs. Christianson."

It did, but Grace didn't think either would go so far as killing Camille.

"Your phone message told me Camille had a heart condition. I knew that from the medical examiner's review of Camille's medical records. How did you find out about it?"

The investigator in Kevin was in top gear now, and Grace felt his focus on her. "I overheard Julia talking on her cell phone with her husband about it. It sounded like he had represented Camille in her divorce, and Camille was unhappy with the divorce terms that he negotiated for her. Camille thought she should have gotten big money for alimony, but she only got child support. Julia thought Camille should have been happy that her husband got the ex to give Camille health insurance coverage for what sounded like a serious heart condition."

"So Julia and her husband knew about Camille's heart condition and Camille was upset with Julia's husband about the terms of her divorce." Kevin said.

"Exactly. Julia also mentioned something about Camille sending nasty letters to her husband's law partners complaining about her husband and some discrepancies in his billing. That couldn't have been good for his job."

"Probably not. Do you think Julia told anyone else about Camille's heart condition?"

"I really don't know for sure, but if I had to guess, I would think she probably told Elaine about it. They're always together." Grace couldn't wait any longer to ask. "So if Camille's heart attack wasn't from natural causes what did the ME suspect caused it?"

"She thinks the combination of heart medications, the St. John's wort in the brownies, and an extremely high level of caffeine caused a heart attack. But the ME won't know for sure until the tox report comes in."

"Caffeine? But Camille only drank decaf."

"You're sure about that?" Kevin asked.

"Yes, a couple of the School Marm Quilters said Camille ordered Meg to make her some fresh decaf coffee that morning." Grace didn't know if sharing this kind of information was helpful or like sharing gossip. But she remembered James saying sometimes the most insignificant, silly piece of information could be important and help solve a case. The investigators were trained to figure out whether or not information was useful.

Something nagged at the back of Grace's brain. Something else about the coffee. Then it came to her. "Meg made two pots."

"Two?"

"Yes."

"And then Meg filled the travel cup for Camille from that second pot?"

"Well, I don't know for sure. I think so."

"And no one else drank decaf?"

"A few of the ladies do, but their cups were already full when Meg made the second pot."

Kevin nodded. "Could Ms. Reynolds have mixed up the coffee pots and given Mrs. Christianson regular coffee by mistake?"

Grace blinked in surprise. "I don't think so. Camille specifically asked Meg to make a fresh pot for her not long before the bus left. Besides, I think someone like Camille who drinks decaf all the time would probably taste the difference and notice if she'd been given regular coffee. She wouldn't have drank it and would have let Meg know it wasn't right."

"Maybe. I noticed packets of caffeine pills when I was in the store yesterday. That's one of the things that I wanted to talk to you about."

"Caffeine pills?" Grace felt like a parrot.

"Behind the counter. Why are those in a quilt store?"

It took a moment before she realized what he was talking about. "Oh, yes, those. Some of the classes go from early morning till evening. And there's even late night quilting parties. After too many cups of coffee, some women like to take the caffeine pills instead. Easier on the stomach."

"So who has access to them?"

"I imagine just the shop personnel. That's why they're behind the counter. Wouldn't the store be liable if someone took too many?"

"Or died from a caffeine overdose. Your friend Bea was right. According to the tests from the lab, those brownies did contain St. John's wort. Who did you say made them?"

"It was Meg. When she lived in the city, she learned about gourmet cooking." Grace remembered Meg seemed to be baking nonstop before the shop hop.

"Do you know anything about how Ms. Reynolds and Mrs. Christianson got along?"

Grace paused. Oh, dear, she didn't want to get Meg into trouble, but she had to tell Kevin. "I heard them arguing in the back the day before the shop hop." Grace chewed her lip. "And after the bus trip, Meg asked me if I'd noticed if Camille had a purple notebook. Meg said that it was hers and Camille had taken it. I told her to talk to you, that you had all of Camille's things."

"Is Ms. Reynolds also a designer?"

Grace did a double blink. "Not that I know of. She certainly has an eye for color. A lot of women ask for her help when they pick out fabrics for their quilts." And yet…? Before the thought caught hold, Grace's phone rang.

She read her caller ID aloud: "Bea." Why would she be calling on a Sunday morning? She couldn't need help on a quilt project already.

"Go ahead and answer it." Kevin prompted her.

Bea's loud, now familiar voice came through the phone. "Morning, Grace. Hope I'm not bothering you, but boy, did I get an earful after you skedaddled the dinner so early last night. A couple of those quilt ladies were mighty interested in you and I was thinking you might want to know about it."

"I can't imagine why anyone would be interested in me." She shrugged her shoulders at Kevin. Then the last stop on the trip flashed through her mind — Julia and Elaine.

"I was wondering if you'd like to come over to my house so I can tell ya all about what they said."

Grace noticed a hint of uncertainty in Bea's voice.

"If you're available now, we can sit out on the deck and talk and have some lemonade or tea."

"I really would like to hear your news, Bea, but I'm meeting with Kevin and–"

Before Grace could say another word Bea blurted out, "He's sure welcome to come along with you. He might want to hear this stuff, too."

Grace hesitated. She'd already missed one day with James and wanted to make up for it by spending the rest of the day with him. And after being with Bea most of yesterday, did she want to spend more time with her today?

To her dismay, Kevin nodded and gave her a thumbs up. Grace knew Kevin's investigation was the priority so time with James would have to wait, but the tug to be with James gripped her heart.

"Okay, we can come over for you to fill us in on things now. What's your address?" Grace wrote down the information and ended the call. She glanced uncertainly at Kevin, but he seemed energized by the invitation.

Although Grace knew Kevin needed to question Bea, and Bea had information he needed to know, her anxiety about being away from James continued.

Kevin must have noticed her hesitation and reassured her. "It will be fine, Grace. We'll make it a quick visit so you can get back to James."

He had the same look she'd seen on James' face when he was working an investigation—the tight set to his jaw, the thin line of his lips, his eyes narrowed in concentration. She knew how driven James became once an investigation started and how she'd tried to support him. She wanted to support Kevin in the same way. "Let me clear the table and I'll be ready to go."

"Thank you, Grace. This works. Now I can hear directly from Bea about the confrontation she had with Camille." Kevin put on his sunglasses. "You follow me in your car. That way, you can leave whenever you want, and if I get a call, you won't be stranded."

As Grace gave Kevin Bea's address, she realized it was on Shoreline Drive where all the most expensive Lake City homes were located. The broad street followed the curves of the lake and over the years wealthy families had built up their summer homes into fancy retreats. She'd never been in one, but always wondered what the interiors and lakefronts looked like. If only James was along to see it, too.

While she drove, she replayed her conversation with Kevin and kept going back to his question about Meg being a designer. She'd never seen or heard about her designing, but Meg had an art degree, something unnecessary, but helpful for a designer. If the purple design book was hers, it would explain why she wanted it back so badly. It could also have been the topic of the disagreement Grace had heard.

Grace couldn't help but wonder if it was just a coincidence Meg had put St. John's wort in the brownies. Maybe she'd intended to cover up whatever poison had been used? Could the mixer that Darcy discarded because Meg cut the cord be the one Meg used to make the shop hop brownies? It was still in her trunk. If Meg's brownies had something to do with Camille's death, Kevin would want to take it in as evidence.

But Meg was always helpful and pleasant at the shop. And she had been a model student. Grace couldn't imagine her hurting anyone. Then again, going off to college and living in the big city could change a person. How well did she know Meg since her return?

Kevin turned into a wide curved driveway, and Grace followed. Could this place really be where Bea lived? At the end of the drive, a massive stone and cedar shake house looked out toward the lake. It took a moment for Grace to take it all in. Kevin must have been thinking the same thing she was—never in a million years would either of them be able to afford a home like this.

While property on the shoreline was prime real estate and most homes were practically built on top of each other, this house must have been built on two lots. A large gardener's shed sat on one side of the curved driveway. What appeared to be an old carriage house, now a three stall garage with loft apartment, sat on the other, with the incredible house in between. The main house was built into the side of a hill that gently sloped toward the lake. The ground floor was level with the driveway and it looked like there was a lower level where you walked out into a back yard that extended to the lake shore and a dock.

A huge stone chimney rose from the center of the house and windows on either side filled the peak of the vaulted roof allowing natural light to flow into the interior. Double doors of hammered copper, gleaming in the large covered entry, invited them inside.

If this was the street side of the house, Grace couldn't imagine what the lakeside would look like. That was where Shoreline Drive homeowners spared no expense constructing multi-level landscaping, patios, fire pits, and illuminated docks for their boats and other water toys.

As Grace and Kevin walked toward the tall copper doors, they swung open, and Bea stood waving them to come inside. "About time you all got here. Can't wait to tell you both what I heard," Bea said with a gleeful voice and a mischievous look on her face. "Shall we go sit on the back deck? It's nice and sunny out there."

Grace looked at Kevin and wondered what he was thinking behind the dark lenses of his sunglasses. This should be interesting.

As beautiful as the outside was, the interior was even more spectacular. Grace thought she had walked into the pages of some upscale interior design magazine. The foyer had a polished wood side table with a huge arrangement of white and deep pink flowers which were reflected in the mirror hanging above it. Their sweet, soft scent flowed through the space.

They entered a huge great room with wood beams spanning the vaulted ceiling which rose two stories above them. A double-sided gas fireplace encased in subtle blue-veined white marble with custom walnut shelves and cabinets filled one wall.

Comfortable furniture in shades of ivory, cream, and aqua, with occasional pops of deep sea blue green, was choreographed around the room. Beyond, accordion glass doors provided access to an enormous deck with a mesmerizing view of the lake.

Although it was gorgeous, Grace didn't think it was Bea's style. Other than the pink flowers in the foyer, it was missing the bright, bold splashes of color that Grace had learned Bea loved. If she stayed, Grace was pretty sure changes would be made and Bea would make the place her own. Only time would tell.

"Where do you two want to sit? In here, or out on the deck and enjoy the lake breeze while we talk. It's up to you."

Grace couldn't pass up a chance to see the deck and enjoy the lake view from a home like this. "Let's sit outside. It's such a lovely day. We should enjoy it when we can."

Kevin nodded his agreement, and they walked out onto the deck.

The deck stretched across the entire rear of the house. Clear panel railings allowed an uninterrupted view of the lake. It was beautifully furnished according to function. They walked into the entertaining area with outdoor sofas, chairs, tables, and a fire pit. Near it was the bar and also an outdoor kitchen. Off what must be the master bedroom there was a hot tub and a mix of comfortable lounging furniture.

A table in the entertaining area held a pair of crystal pitchers, glasses and a tray of desserts easily recognizable as from the MainSail Deli. Anyone who had been to the MainSail recognized their amazing and impossible to resist sweets on sight.

Being the good hostess, Bea asked what they preferred to drink. She poured Grace a glass of tea and Kevin one of lemonade. He chose a toffee blondie from the tray and Grace couldn't stop herself from taking a lemon bar.

Grace marveled at the landscaping and patio extending from the walkout level beneath them. Large oak and maple trees edged the property, giving privacy and shade. Colorful beds of flowers, shrubs and ferns accented several areas like jewelry on a movie star. The grass yard, like lush green carpeting, sprawled down to a narrow band of sand and rocks with a lighted dock that reached out on the lake.

Sailboats floated across the lake and the soft sound of water lapping against the shore enticed them to sit and relax. As she sat in one of the thickly cushioned chairs, Grace wished she could stay and escape from it all forever. But that wasn't why they were there.

"Bea, this place is absolutely lovely. I'm speechless, trying to take it all in. You are so lucky to be staying here."

"Thank you, sweetie. It's pretty nice for a vacation home. I'm so glad you could come on over. I've been dying to tell you about last night. After you left those ladies at the dinner were something else. They came over and started being all nice and chummy, but I could tell they were after something."

"What ladies are you talking about?" Kevin asked.

"Well, those two high and mighty ones. What are their names? Julie and Eve or whatever."

That made sense. Julia and Elaine looked like they had a problem with Grace when they were at the Old Windmill Quilt Shop.

"Julia and Elaine. They were the ladies you talked to at the Lakeside Marketplace and Spa. Julia was the leader on the shop hop and she's president of the quilt guild. Elaine is her vice president." Grace clarified for Kevin.

"That's right. Anyway, after you left the dinner, the two of them came over to our table. Miss Julie started bragging about how she's president of the quilt guild and she leads these wonderful guild meetings that all the quilters in the area just love. She told me that even my new friend Grace comes to 'em."

Grace stopped chewing the delicious lemon bar. It surprised her that Julia would lower herself to talk to Bea after the way Bea had so blatantly ignored her when she'd won the grand prize. Julia must have wanted to know something quite badly to have swallowed her pride and approached Bea after being snubbed in front of everyone.

"Yes, I go to the guild meetings, but it's really only a club that the shop sponsors," Grace said.

"So after she mentions your name, I said sure, I'd been getting to know you on the bus and you were helping me do a little shopping. That's when she

161

started asking me about you and how you're such good friends with Deputy Kevin here."

"Why's she so interested in me being friends with Kevin?"

"I was wondering the same thing and figured I'd be real careful about what I said. I played dumb and said I'd just met you and him, so I really didn't know much. That I thought he was a friend of the family. I didn't tell her about the brownie he took for testing or anything. I think she was probably trying to find out what all you and Kevin talked about and if he'd told you anything about what happened to old Camille. Ya think they want to know if there's an investigation going on about Camille's death? They seemed kind of worried about something."

After the looks Julia and Elaine had given her at the Old Windmill, Grace agreed.

"Grace, does this Julia have some sort of problem with you?" Kevin looked concerned.

Grace wasn't sure how much she should say in front of Bea, so she tried to sidestep his question. "I'm still trying to figure it out." She took a sip of her drink and avoided looking at him.

"Well, her and her little minion wouldn't let it go," Bea continued without seeming to have noticed the exchange. "And I kept being blissfully ignorant. I'm pretty good at that when I want to be. I think those two School Marm Quilter gals who were sitting at the table with us thought Julia was being a royal pain, so they started pestering her with loads of questions about the agenda for the next quilt guild meeting. Julia didn't seem to want to talk with them quilt ladies about her amazing quilt meeting so she and her little buddy got frustrated and slithered off."

"I'm so glad Connie and Judy spoke up and helped you." Grace had forgotten they had sat at the same table at dinner.

"Oh boy, the way it sounds, none of them School Marm gals like Miss Julia much. They said they just let her call it a quilt guild because Julia thinks it's fancier and they don't really care what it's called. After teaching all day they're tired and don't want to be responsible for running the club or any meetings so they let her do it. Mostly, they come to the meetings to show and tell about their quilts. They like hearing Meg, Darcy, and even that Camille share about new projects and stuff. So they just let Julia think she's in charge. By the way, from what they said they may have liked Camille's quilt designs but otherwise didn't like her much."

Kevin spoke up then. "What did Connie and Judy say about Camille?"

Bea seemed excited to tell Kevin what she'd heard. "It was something about Camille causing trouble for one of those School Marm Quilters. When I asked, they just said Camille always blames things on everyone else."

Kevin seemed intrigued by what Bea was saying about the School Marm Quilters. Grace knew more information about the trouble Camille had caused, but didn't want to talk about it in front of Bea. She figured sooner or later Kevin would probably ask her if she knew anything about it. She'd have to think about how much she wanted to tell him when the time came.

"You really did get an earful after I left. Did you hear anything else?" Grace asked.

"No, not that I can think of right now. I am thinking I might like to check out that quilt guild meeting to see what it's like. I like those School Marm Quilters. Maybe they need someone like me at those guild meetings to shake things up a little bit with that Miss Julia."

The quilt meetings would be very different if Bea was a part of them. Having Bea join the guild might liven them up.

"Thanks for inviting Kevin and since he's here, he wanted to ask you a few questions."

Bea switched into her flirting mode. "Why sure Deputy Kevin, you can ask me anything."

QUILTING FACTOID: Using a home computer, personal photographs can be printed onto special photo fabrics and then pieced into blocks to make a unique memory quilt.

CHAPTER TWELVE

Once again, Kevin managed to maintain his professional manner after Bea's flirtatious comment. "Ma'am, I was wondering what happened when you sat with Mrs. Christianson at the start of the shop hop."

"Well sure, I was all out of breath from almost missing the bus and when I got to the top of the steps, I had to sit down right away before I passed out. I barely got sat down before that Mrs. Christianson started telling me the seat was unavailable. But I needed more time to catch my breath, so I kept sitting there. Besides, it was my chance to talk to a real professional quilt designer."

"That's understandable." Kevin was probably thinking back to when he compared quilt designers to rock stars.

"I told her I was going to be a quilt designer too and asked her if she could give me any tips. You would think she'd be flattered, but oh no, she started going on and on about how being a designer wasn't as easy as everyone thought it was. Next thing I know she pulled out this notebook and started drawing in it and wouldn't talk to me."

Grace wondered if it was the same notebook Meg had claimed belonged to her when they talked after the shop hop dinner.

"She wouldn't talk to me, but she's pretty famous, so I wanted her picture. And I got out my phone and tried taking some selfies with her. Well, she didn't want any part of that and started fanning herself with some white business envelope she pulled out of her purse. Then she got mad and told me to move or she'd have me kicked off the bus. So I got my stuff together and moved to the back and sat next to Grace."

Kevin looked very interested. "I'd like to see those photos."

"Do you really need to? It's just a few photos of Camille."

"Exactly why I would like to see them. They'll show her appearance and demeanor when the shop hop started."

"Well, okay. Let me get my phone and you can look at them." Bea went in the house and came back with her phone. After she sat back down, she began thumbing through it. She finally stopped and turned it for Kevin to see. "There, you see. There she is, scowling."

When Kevin reached for the phone, Bea pulled it back. Kevin's expression froze into a no nonsense stare which surprised Grace. She'd never been officially questioned by law enforcement but knew James could be plenty strong willed when he wanted to be. After a moment, under Kevin's unflinching stare, Bea handed the phone to him. "I guess, it's all right. I wasn't doing anything wrong. There." she pointed to the photo on the screen. "There she is taking a drink out of that there mug she kept flashing around."

Without saying anything, he studied the photo, then thumbed through the next several photos. "Mrs. Christianson doesn't appear in most of these. Did you intend to take several photos of these sketches she appears to be working on?"

A flush appeared on Bea's cheeks. "Well, maybe. I was just trying to get an idea of what a quilt designer does."

"Bea and I already talked about how inappropriate it was to take photos of someone else's work and consider using them herself. She would have deleted them already, but I told her she needed to save them to show to you." Grace explained to Kevin while giving Bea the look she gave her students who had made a poor choice, but who she hoped would try to make better ones in the future.

"Well, I was more like borrowing them, just having a look-see."

"And when Mrs. Christianson realized what you were doing…?"

"That's when she got all huffy and told me to get up and move or she'd have me kicked off the bus."

"Since she wouldn't talk to me about how to be a designer, I thought maybe I could learn about designing by looking at her sketches, but I couldn't figure out the numbers, kinda because the pictures ain't that good and kinda because I don't know what I'm doing as a quilt designer. Not yet anyway."

"And where is this design book now?"

Bea squinted and rumpled her eyebrows together. "She maybe put it in her bag?"

Kevin glanced at Grace. "Do you remember seeing it when you gathered her things?"

"No." Grace shrunk. She'd been so careful to get everything, and she had missed the design book.

Kevin looked back at Bea. "Did she have it when you left?"

"I'm pretty sure she did. I don't remember her shoving it in her tote bag or anything while I sat with her."

Grace thought this was good information, but it still didn't tell them what had happened to the design book.

"You said she had a bag. Did she also have a purse?"

Grace was glad Kevin had remembered to ask about Camille's purse. Maybe Bea knew more about it.

"Yep. She had a big leather purse that had all sorts of pockets inside and out. Seemed like there was a pocket for just about everything. Even ones on the sides for water bottles or shoes or whatever."

"Other than drinking from her travel cup, did Mrs. Christianson eat or drink anything else while you were sitting with her?"

"She was chowing down those brownies like nobody's business. I'm positive she ate two of them while I sat with her. I think she took a couple swallows from her water bottle, too."

"Could you tell what was in the cup?"

"Well, I'm not positive, but it smelled like coffee."

That made sense and confirmed what the School Marm Quilters said about Meg making a pot of decaf for Camille before they left the Quilters Playground.

"If you could forward these to the sheriff's office." Kevin gave Bea the email address and Bea's phone made a swooshing sound indicating the pictures had been sent.

"Grace, I'm hoping you'll still help me learn more about all this quilting stuff." Bea gazed over at Grace. "Could I tag along to that guild meeting with you?" Bea sounded unsure of herself and worried Grace might say no. She didn't want to disappoint Bea, and besides, Bea might rattle a few people there and make them nervous. Who knows what Grace might hear to help Kevin with his investigation?

"I think it would be nice. The meeting is tomorrow. Let's talk in the morning and work out the details." Grace saw Bea's face light up. It felt good to make someone a little happy by doing such a simple thing.

"I have everything I need for now. I'm sure Grace wants to get back to James, and I need to head back to the office. Thank you for your assistance." He got up from his chair and pulled out Grace's chair for her. Bea walked them to the door, and they said their goodbyes.

After the door closed and they were alone outside, Grace decided she better give Kevin the broken mixer. "Kevin, I have something in my trunk that might be evidence."

Kevin followed Grace to her car. She opened her trunk and pointed inside. She thought Kevin would be grateful and curious, but he barely looked inside and had a stern yet concerned look on his face.

"It's nice to have evidence found and delivered like this. But before we talk about it, you need to tell me about any problems this Julia has with you and also anything you might know about the teacher who got into trouble because of Camille. I think you've been withholding information."

"I'm sorry, Kevin. I was going to tell you, but we were interrupted by Bea's phone call and I just ran out of time. Believe me, I was going to tell you everything I know."

"So start by telling me why Julia and Elaine have an issue with you?"

"I guess it could be because they suspect that I overheard a phone call Julia made to her husband. At the Old Windmill Quilt Shop, I'd stayed on the bus when everyone else got off. I just needed a few minutes to myself. Julia must have stayed on the bus as well. I was toward the back, so she didn't know I was there. She was talking to her husband on her phone and I'm sure she thought that she was alone. It was very awkward at first, but when I heard her say Camille's name, I slouched down and listened. I don't think Julia ever saw me, but I think Elaine figured out I was still on the bus and had probably overheard Julia's phone call." Grace admitted.

"Why would that bother Julia so much?"

"It probably has something to do with her husband's reputation and her need for status. From the conversation I overheard, Julia's husband was Camille's lawyer and she wasn't pleased with his representation or his billing practices and was writing others complaining about him. Julia sounded really relieved Camille was dead and wouldn't be a threat to her husband's job or their social standing any more. She could be worried I have that damaging information now and might tell people about it."

"Is that everything?" Kevin asked. He looked at her with raised eyebrows and tilted his head a bit.

Grace guessed he was checking to be sure she didn't leave anything more out. "I don't know if it matters, but I also heard Julia call the quilters on the shop hop busybodies and say the shop hop was tedious. She's nice to everyone's face and insults people behind their backs. I think it shows she's putting up a pretty good facade around town and has some people fooled about the kind of person she really is." Grace felt like this was gossiping, but it was a relief to have told Kevin everything she'd heard during Julia's phone call.

"Watch yourself. We still don't know who is responsible for Camille's death. Let me know immediately if Julia or Elaine give you any kind of trouble."

From the lines creasing his forehead, Grace could tell Kevin was worried, but anyone who knew Grace would realize that she was too busy with James to gossip or spread rumors. Then again, here she was telling Kevin. But this was different.

"I will, absolutely. Now, if you'd like a potential piece of new evidence, it's right here and it's all yours." She pointed inside her trunk. Grace really didn't want to talk about the teacher who got in trouble because of Camille, so she hoped showing him new evidence would distract him. Kevin wasn't able to resist and peered into her trunk.

"A mixer? How is it pertinent to the investigation? I was hoping maybe you'd found that coffee cup Camille had on the bus." he asked.

"I wish I'd found the coffee cup, but I'm pretty sure this mixer is the one that Meg used to make the brownies for the shop hop."

Kevin looked at her and smiled. "How did it end up in your trunk?"

"I was at the shop the day before the shop hop and Darcy was going to throw it out after Meg accidentally damaged the cord on it. I asked if I could have it so some nice deputy I know could put a new cord on it for me and I'd have a newer mixer for practically free."

Kevin looked rather sheepish now. "Let me get my gloves and put it into an evidence bag." He got what he needed from his vehicle and then retrieved the mixer from her trunk.

"Thank you Grace. You've been very helpful."

She closed her trunk and smiled at him as she got ready to hop in her car and leave. "You're very welcome."

"However, I have one more question. Can you tell me anything about the teacher Camille got in trouble?"

Grace should have known Kevin wouldn't forget. She hesitated, thinking carefully, before answering his question. The privacy of the teacher involved and the School Marms' trust were important to her. But she wanted to help with Kevin's investigation too. "I heard rumors about something when I was still teaching, but nothing concrete. Then yesterday when we were at the Willow Grove Quilt Shop, a couple of the School Marm Quilters told me Camille had cost one of them her teaching job."

"Do you know who lost their job?"

Instead of naming who, Grace dodged the question. "They said Camille threatened to get a lawyer. And if it went to court, everyone would hear about it. The teacher felt her reputation would be damaged by Camille's lies about her. So the teacher retired instead."

Kevin shook his head.

Grace knew Kevin had always respected her teaching job and appreciated the work teachers did.

"What did this teacher do that upset Camille so much she wanted her fired?" Kevin asked. Grace hated hearing the word fired in connection with a fellow teacher.

"The rumor around school was that a teacher had failed Camille's daughter for plagiarism. Apparently it would have jeopardized her graduating on time. Camille claimed her daughter was innocent, and the teacher had no proof. She took the issue to the school board and when they did nothing, she threatened to call in her lawyer. I guess that's when the teacher decided rather than having their reputation dragged through the mud in a public court hearing they'd retire." Grace once again felt badly that a teacher who was trying to do the right thing had lost her job.

"It would be rough to lose your job for trying to teach a student right from wrong." Kevin said. "But this is a murder investigation, Grace. If you know who the teacher is, tell me. Camille might not be the only person they have a grudge against."

The sound of the copper doors opening interrupted them and Bea walked out hollering. "What are you two still doing here? I just noticed you on my security camera. Is everything okay? You could have stayed on the deck and talked there instead of standing out here in the hot driveway."

Grace felt like she'd been saved by the dismissal bell. "I had something in my car that I needed to give Kevin, but I think we're finished now. Thanks again, Bea."

She got in her car as Bea yelled after her and waved. "Bye now. I'll call you tomorrow about the quilt meeting."

In her rear-view mirror she saw Kevin politely thanking Bea and hurriedly leaving in his car. Grace hoped he wouldn't turn on his sirens and pull her over, or follow her to the care center to ask her the name of the teacher who felt forced to resign. She knew she would have to tell him at some point. Unless he found solid evidence pointing to someone else, and then she would never have to tell him. Otherwise, she was sure he would ask her again. Thankfully, she saw him turn the opposite direction toward the sheriff's office.

~ ~ ~

She spent a quiet afternoon with James. After he finished eating his supper, he settled in his recliner to watch evening game shows, so she decided to head home to find something to eat.

After such a full day, home seemed especially quiet. The coffee cup she'd gotten out the morning of the shop hop still sat on the kitchen counter. Grace put the unused cup back into the cupboard next to James' big thermos. She ran her hand down the smooth stainless steel.

Every morning she told herself she was going to get rid of it. What did she need a quart thermos for? And yet every night it was there, right next to her favorite travel cup from last year's shop hop. Her little turquoise cup reflected in the shiny silver thermos. The blue green color her favorite, nothing like the dull green and gold cup Camille had been flashing around.

Grace paused. They still didn't know what had happened to Camille's cup. Kevin knew Camille had eaten the brownie containing St. John's wort. Now he was asking about what she'd drank as well, and her coffee cup would help tell him. He must feel it was important to his investigation.

Grace wrinkled her brow, trying to remember when she'd last seen Camille's cup. It hadn't been with Camille's things on the bus or in the Hummingbird bathroom.

Closing the cupboard, Grace pondered what she would have done with it if she'd been Camille? The bus is going along and she's feeling sicker and sicker. She wants to throw up. The bus stops. The door opens. She wants to get to the bathroom before she disgraces herself and throws up in front of everyone. She drops the travel cup and she runs. Grace was sure of it. Camille wouldn't have set it down, she would have dropped it like she had all those brownie wrappers. Just dropped it and ran.

So where was it? Maybe when everyone was filing off the bus someone kicked it under the seat. It would have rolled and scooted along the floor every time the bus made a quick stop or sped up, just like everyone's packages and purses had.

Something nudged Grace's memory. Hadn't Bea picked something up off the floor? After Vi and Rose had gotten off the bus and before Kevin came to get Camille's things at the Lakeside Marketplace. Something dark green.

Grace glanced at the clock. It was getting late. But Bea struck her as a night owl.

"Why, Grace, it's so nice of you to call. I was just sitting here looking at all the pretty fabric I bought and wondering if you were figuring out what to do with all them fat quarter things."

Grace had forgotten to get them out of her trunk. "I haven't had a chance to yet. I was thinking about Camille's coffee cup and have a question for you. When we were on the bus yesterday morning, I noticed that you picked something up off the floor. Was it a dark green and gold travel cup?"

There was a long pause before Bea said. "Ya know, I seem to remember something like that."

"Do you still have it? Does the logo read Farmers Bounty Fabric?"

"I don't remember anything about a logo. It was just like the mug that Camille woman was gulping out of after eating those nasty brownies. They were dark chocolate brownies, and ya know, dark chocolate is the healthier chocolate, even if it's pretty high in caffeine."

Grace wanted to roll her eyes, couldn't Bea stay on topic? "Well, Kevin's been searching for Camille's cup and told me he hasn't found any sign of it. Maybe that's because you have it."

"Except I don't have it."

Grace felt deflated. "No?" She sighed, talking more to herself than Bea. "What could have happened to it?"

"Why, I gave it to the bus driver. I figured someone must have dropped it and would be looking for it."

"What did the driver do with it?"

"Well, he said that he was going to put it in the lost and found."

Grace knew the cup was important. She had to find it and help Kevin. "The lost and found? Where is that?"

"Probably at the bus garage. I thought the driver would announce it'd been found during the trip so the owner could claim it, but you know it was such a stressful day I guess he forgot. I sure did. Now let me think, he put it somewhere." After a long pause, Bea continued. "Oh, that's right, he turned and put it in the side dashboard under the driver's side window."

"In the side dashboard?" That didn't make any sense.

"You know, the dashboard or console thing to the left of the driver's seat. There's that little nylon net thing under it that you can put stuff in. My first husband used to drive truck, and he kept his maps and log book and stuff there. Made it handy. But if that was your coffee cup, we should go get it."

"No, it's not mine. It might have been Camille's."

"That would sure help your friend Kevin out, now won't it? Let's go."

"At this hour?"

"Oh, sure. There's always a dispatcher or somebody at places like that. The buses go in and out at all hours."

Grace wasn't sure. Maybe she should call Kevin.

"I'll be right over to pick you up."

"But you don't know where I live. And I don't know where the bus garage is."

"Oh, sweetie, you never heard of GPS? Just tell me your address and I'm there."

Grace waited by the front door, her porch light on. She'd found an address for the bus garage in the phone book, but when she'd called someone had picked up the line, then disconnected. So she called back and got a machine that said when office hours were. After seeing the address, she'd realized the garage was outside of town and somewhat isolated. Even in daylight she'd be uncomfortable going alone. It was smart to have someone going with her at this late hour.

When Grace got into Bea's car, she wasn't surprised at how luxurious it was. It had temperature controlled seats with dual controls.

"Maybe it's too late to go."

But Bea shook her head. "I hadn't thought about that designer woman's travel mug. We need to get it back before all the evidence is messed up. I was watching this cop show the other day and fingerprints on a spoon were destroyed when they put it in the dishwasher.

"You think the killer's fingerprints are on that mug?"

"They could be."

Grace hadn't thought about fingerprints. Would there be any after it rolled around on the bus floor? She'd only thought about Kevin asking about what Camille had eaten, so what she'd drank would be just as important. Hopefully, its contents wouldn't have been contaminated or lost.

Bea accelerated enough to push Grace back against the cushiony seat. "Are we meeting Deputy Kevin there? I sure do like looking at that stack of walking muscle. Makes me think of my husband, Orlando." Bea took her eyes off the road long enough to glance at Grace. "That man had a mighty fine butt, too."

Fortunately, they arrived at the bus garage before Bea went into further detail. They pulled onto a gravel parking lot, with potholes large enough to swallow Bea's convertible. At the end of the lot was a huge metal machine shed with two oversized garage doors. A third smaller door was labeled as the office, and an older model car was parked in front of it.

Bea parked diagonally across the handicap parking spot in front of the office door,.

"I don't think we're supposed to park here." Grace told her.

But Bea was already bounding toward the garage door. "Lights inside are still on."

While Bea knocked, Grace looked through the windows of the large overhead door. No one came into view. The bus they had ridden in was neatly parked in the front of the bus garage, its doors open.

"Let's check there first."

Grace followed Bea onto the bus. Using the light on Bea's phone, they searched the driver's area, the floor, and all the overhead bins, but found nothing.

"Let's see if the office is locked."

Grace hesitated, but she knew finding the cup would help Kevin, so she followed Bea back to the garage. Bea fiddled with the office door.

"What are you doing?" Was Bea forcing the lock? For the first time since she'd called Bea, Grace wondered about the wisdom of looking for the travel cup instead of telling Kevin where it might be.

"Hello, anybody home?" Bea called as she entered. Grace reluctantly followed behind.

She wanted to talk to the bus driver, but there didn't appear to be anyone there. From her years at the school she knew they most likely had a big box, or drawer where forgotten belongings were collected. After a quick glance around the place, they discovered a large cardboard box near the door overflowing with mittens, hats, and scarves. Obviously, the lost and found. The women began rummaging through the box until an enthusiastic Bea tipped it onto its side spilling its contents onto the floor.

"Doesn't look like it's here." Bea said.

Grace had to agree. "Where else could it be?"

Before Bea could answer, the door flew open. Kevin, gun drawn, burst into the room. Both women screamed.

"Grace?" He lowered the gun. "What are you doing here?"

QUILTING FACTOID: A rotary cutter is used to cut fabric. It is similar to a pizza cutter, but is smaller and has a razor sharp blade.

CHAPTER THIRTEEN

"Kevin. I was about to call you. When we were on the shop hop, Bea found Camille's travel cup and gave it to the bus driver to put in the lost and found."

Kevin didn't look at her as he holstered his gun. When he looked up, his face was frozen in a neutral expression, like a father finding his kids had snuck out after being grounded.

Before Grace could explain further, the driver from the shop hop meekly appeared in the doorway. "Aren't you ladies from that bus trip where the woman died?"

"Yes."

"If you lost something, you should have called and left a message. I saw a light in the bus and someone moving around in there, so I called the cops."

Grace hadn't thought about it appearing as if she and Bea were trying to steal something. "We were looking for a travel cup. Bea found it on the floor and gave it to you for the lost and found, but it's not here."

"I clean the bus up after every trip and I gave what I found to this deputy here. Mostly food wrappers and a few receipts. And then he went over the bus himself. I don't know what you're talking about."

Bea lowered her eyebrows and gave the driver a withering stare. "I handed it to you at the Willow Grove Quilt Shop. That shop in the big barn. And I told you I found it on the floor. You put it in that little catch-all under your side dashboard. I saw you put it there."

The driver looked embarrassed. "Well, now that you mention it, I do kinda remember something like that. Had some quilt logo on it. My wife's a quilter, so I thought she might like it."

"You kept it! So where is the cup now? Does your wife have it?" Grace tried to stay calm.

"Nah, I threw it in the back of my car when I got back here after that trip. I forgot all about it till now. It should still be in my car somewhere."

"I'm going to need to take that cup as evidence." Kevin informed him.

The bus driver led the way. After putting on latex gloves, Kevin dug through the collection of fast food wrappers and cups before he finally pulled out a travel cup from under the front seat. "Is this the same travel cup that Ms. Vargas gave you to put in the lost and found?"

"Yep, it's the one."

Kevin dropped the cup into an evidence bag. Although he didn't scowl, his face continued to convey his disapproval. "You'll need to stop by the sheriff's office in the morning and be fingerprinted."

"Whatever you say. Again, I'm real, real sorry I kept that cup, deputy. I would never want to interfere with your investigation. I will definitely stop by the office right away tomorrow morning, deputy, right away. Not a problem."

Kevin turned to Bea. "You as well."

"Yes, sir, Deputy Kevin. Will you be there?"

Kevin didn't answer, instead he turned to stare at the bus driver.

The driver rubbed his chin. "Uh-m, will I get the cup back? I wanted to give it to my wife."

Grace saw Bea roll her eyes.

"No, sir, not at this time. We need to retain it as evidence for any legal proceedings that should occur, after which it will be released to Mrs. Christianson's family."

"Okay, that's fine. I understand."

The bus driver drove off. Kevin gave the two women a stern look. "Grace, I'm not sure what to think about you being here."

"I knew finding every piece of evidence was important and when I remembered Bea picking something up off the floor, I realized it might have been Camille's travel cup."

"Deputy Kevin, we weren't interfering. We were just trying to help. Grace called me so we could safely check into it together." Bea added.

"That's right. And as soon as we found the coffee cup we were going to call you to come get it."

"I know you think you were helping, but it could have jeopardized evidence. This can't happen again. If you think you know something, you call me first and let me do the investigating. That's my job." He gave each of them a severe look, his jaw clenching and unclenching.

Grace felt like a student who had been chastised by the principal. She knew Kevin was right, but she had wanted to help.

"Now please, go straight home and stay out of trouble." Kevin took the evidence bag to his vehicle and drove off.

"Well, do you think finding the mug will help?" Bea asked her.

"I hope so. He'll need to get it tested to see if anything Camille drank from it led to her death and to see whose fingerprints are on it."

"You think she got herself poisoned?"

Grace couldn't help but wonder. Flushing and hot flashes didn't match the signs of a heart attack. Camille's skin hadn't gone gray, and she didn't seem to have been in any pain. Rather, she'd acted like someone experiencing poisoning. Her stomach had certainly wanted to get rid of whatever was in it.

"It's sure going to be hard to wait while he figures out what happened." Bea said.

"Yes, it will be, but you heard him. We need to let him do the investigating.

Bea chuckled. "That bus driver fella sure doesn't know much about romance. Does he really think bringing his wife-y a travel mug from the lost and found impresses her much?"

"Who knows? It does make me appreciate good guys like James and Kevin."

"I know what ya mean. Who wouldn't appreciate a feller like Deputy Kevin or your James? My last husband was one of them kind of fellas too." Bea sighed.

~ ~ ~

The next day, Grace woke early. In the gray of predawn a clock ticked and the refrigerator whirred, but the sound of James' gentle breathing beside her was missing. After a few tears, she forced herself to get out of bed. She had to remind herself there was always someone who had to face things worse than what she and James were going through.

She thought again of Meg leaving her big city career and moving back in with her parents. As pretty and personable as Meg was, she'd certainly had someone in her life. Had Grace heard something about a fiancé dying right before the wedding? She wasn't sure.

If Grace wanted breakfast, she needed milk and eggs and coffee, which meant making a quick run to the grocery store. When she got home, she wasn't hungry and only ate a piece of toast with her coffee. She didn't like to visit James too early; it upset his morning routine. Instead, she sat and watched the clock until she realized that her coffee was cold. Forcing herself to get up and move, she went to her car and retrieved her forgotten shop hop purchases from the trunk.

Pulling out the fat quarters she'd gathered with Bea's help, she thought of James' room and using them for a wall hanging to give it a touch of home. Setting aside the project she'd been working on, Grace sorted out a blue and then a brown. Then she started cutting out the pieces she needed for the center blocks. When she began straightening the fabric's edge and cutting the first couple of strips, the blade of her rotary cutter made a ripping sound.

As she moved the strip off to the side, the fabric caught and stretched from threads of uncut fabric the dull blade hadn't cut cleanly. Frustrated with the blade cutting hit and miss across the fabric edge, she finally gave up and decided she'd visit James for a quick hour and then pick up a new blade at the Quilters Playground.

Her visit with James went well. They watched his favorite morning game show together, and he slapped the arm of his recliner when a lucky player unexpectedly won the grand prize. When the show ended, she told him she had some errands to run and would come back in the afternoon.

She arrived at the quilt shop just as it was opening. She was a little surprised to see Kevin's patrol SUV in the parking lot as she pulled in. When she went inside, she saw Kevin talking to Meg and Darcy. On the counter in front of them was Camille's purse. Grace wandered over to a display of fabrics located close enough to overhear their conversation.

"And you ladies are sure this belonged to the deceased?"

Darcy didn't say anything, but Meg confirmed the purse belonged to Camille.

"And where did you find it?"

Darcy tipped her head toward Meg, a look of interest on her face.

"In the bathroom trash." Tripping over her tongue, Meg explained. "You see, we normally empty the trash after we close, but it was so busy yesterday and I was tired last night, so I left it until this morning."

"Meg, you know that's not how we do things. If you were tired, you should have said so and I would have helped." From the expression on Meg's face, Grace doubted that Darcy ever helped.

"Was there anything else in the trash?"

"Just the usual, paper towels, tissues, and, at the bottom, Camille's purse." She noticed Darcy seemed to be watching Kevin closely. He was looking intently at Meg as she talked. Grace didn't know if it was because of the conversation or if it was the light from the window highlighting Meg's golden red blonde hair and her blue-green eyes.

Darcy waved at Grace. "It will be just a moment." Then turned to Kevin. "If you're done here, my employee needs to get back to work." She motioned for Meg to go help Grace.

Kevin's steely expression stopped Meg from leaving. "I have a few more questions."

Meg twisted her hands, unsure if she should stay and answer Kevin's questions or go help Grace as Darcy had directed her.

"It's all right," Grace reassured her. "I just need a new blade for my rotary cutter."

"Blades and rotary cutters are at the back of the shop." Darcy loudly told her. "I think you know where to find them."

"Yes, thanks, I don't need any help." Grace walked to the back of the shop near the hallway to the offices and back room. Kevin, Meg and Darcy spoke in low voices for several minutes. Then Meg returned to the cutting table.

As Grace looked for the right size blade, she heard Kevin's calm voice. "I need to inspect Camille's office."

"Oh. You'll need a key." Darcy told him.

"I have the key you gave the deputy."

"I'll show you where her office is. Was." Darcy said. "Meg, you'll need to stay up front while I help Deputy Oleson."

Grace had heard the School Marm Quilters say Camille and Darcy ordered Meg around. She thought someone with Darcy's work experience running a fabric shop in the big city would know to treat her employees with consideration and respect. But maybe Darcy knew Meg didn't have any other employment options, so she didn't think she had to. Or had something happened between Meg and Darcy that had affected their relationship?

Grace found the blade she needed and pulled the package off the hanger. She was curious about what was happening in Camille's office. She thought she could say hi and maybe listen in, but worried Kevin would try to pin her down on the teacher's name again. Surely he wouldn't do it when there were others around. She had to know what was going on, so she walked down the hallway. Just inside the office doorway, she found Kevin holding an evidence bag containing Camille's purse and Darcy looking around in disbelief.

Darcy's voice lifted in distress. "I'm sorry but the door has been locked since that deputy left with the key."

Kevin stood, his broad shoulders blocking Grace's view of the room. "Could this have happened before he locked the door?"

Grace eased past him and stepped into the room.

"I don't know who could have disturbed things or when it happened." Darcy told Kevin.

Without thinking, Grace spoke up. "Maybe they were looking for something."

Darcy and Kevin turned to look at her. And if Grace hadn't known Kevin as well as she did, his face would have appeared to be a calm mask, but the set of his lips and slight knit in his brow told her he was upset. "Why do you say that?"

Grace bit her lower lip before answering. Why did she think that? "Because they took Camille's purse, so they had to be looking for something in it. When they didn't find it they must have decided to look for whatever it was in Camille's office."

"But no one could have gotten in here. That deputy locked the door and took the key with him." Darcy reminded Grace.

"Are there any other keys to this office?" Kevin asked.

"I have a spare in my desk." Darcy opened her hands in a gesture of not understanding. "My office wasn't locked so I guess anyone at the dinner could have taken the key from it."

"We were just so busy. We had customers all day, then with serving dinner and keeping the food trays filled. I couldn't keep track of everyone. Meg was helping me most of the time, but she was also at the front of the shop passing out patterns. She might have seen someone. Check with her."

"What about you, Grace? Did you see anyone in Camille's office that night?"

"I ate quickly and left early. While I was here I didn't notice anyone in her office." Grace responded honestly wishing she had seen someone so she could help Kevin. "But wouldn't Camille have had a key? Is that what they were looking for in her purse?"

"I need to get back to work." Darcy tried to excuse herself, but Grace knew that Darcy seldom helped customers and was probably trying to avoid more of Kevin's questions.

As Darcy turned to leave, Kevin called her back. "Ms. Duncan, were you aware that Mrs. Christianson had signed with a national fabric company?"

Darcy gasped. Her eyes widened. "Why no. What do you mean? Camille and I had an agreement. A written contract."

"So, she hadn't approached you with the possibility of designing for someone else?"

"No, no, of course not. It would be a breach of contract."

Kevin glanced around the room. "Is this how Mrs. Christianson's office normally looks?"

Darcy's gaze followed his. "I really couldn't tell you. I don't have any reason to come in here. She usually kept her door closed. Too many people would just wander in thinking they could stand around and talk. Hoping to see the newest design before it was ready. And when she was out, she would usually lock the door."

Darcy paused, as if just thinking of something. "You might ask Meg. She's been back here a lot the last couple of weeks. Why, you'd think she and Camille were best friends." Darcy gave Grace a bright smile before glancing at Kevin. "Will that be all, deputy?"

"What can you tell me about the travel thermos Ms. Christianson had that day?"

Darcy tipped her head as if she didn't understand. "Do you mean that free promo cup she got at quilt market?" Darcy glanced around, then shrugged. "I don't see it. She must have tired of the joke and thrown it away."

"Joke?"

"Yes, you see we don't carry Farmers Bounty Fabrics—or FBF, funny-backward-frump as she liked to call them."

"Any idea where the cup is now?"

"Like I said, she must have thrown it away. The joke was getting stale."

"All right. I need you to check your desk and bring me that spare key." While he waited for Darcy to return with the key, he used his cell phone to take pictures of the office.

After a few minutes, Darcy returned with the key and handed it to him. "Now, may I get back to work?" Darcy asked.

"That's all for now." Kevin replied, locking the door and keeping the key. He motioned for Grace to walk with him back to the shop area where Meg was taking down the shop hop displays.

"I can ring up your purchase whenever you're ready." Darcy informed Grace.

"I think I'll look around a bit first." Grace answered.

Grace stopped to look at some of the new fabrics. She'd avoided looking at them during the shop hop and knew she wasn't going to buy any of them now, but it was a good way to stall so she could hang around and hear Kevin question Meg.

Behind the checkout counter, Darcy straightened baskets and bins on the back shelves, appearing to wait for Grace, but also close enough to overhear Kevin and Meg's conversation.

"Excuse me, Meg, uh, Ms. Reynolds, did you see anyone in Ms. Duncan's or Mrs. Christianson's offices on Saturday?"

"No, I don't think so." Meg glanced at Kevin and then looked down to finish placing the little Lego figurines into a storage container. "We were so busy with the buffet dinner. Then I handed out shop hop patterns over by the cutting table, and I can't see the offices from there."

"Things have been disturbed, and it appears that someone was searching for something."

Meg's hand shook as she stacked some tiny charm packs. "I'm sorry, but I don't know anything."

"Thank you. If I have any other questions, I'll contact you later."

Kevin studied Meg a moment before turning and speaking to Darcy. "Ms. Duncan, I locked Camille's office and kept the key. Thank you for your time today."

He turned back to Grace. "Grace, if you're done shopping, do you have a few minutes? I'll wait outside for you."

Grace paid for her rotary blade and rushed to join Kevin outside.

QUILTING FACTOID: Binding is the finished band of fabric that covers the raw edges of a quilt. Some people decorate the outer edge with prairie points or folded triangles.

CHAPTER FOURTEEN

"How's James this morning?"

Grace was surprised Kevin asked about James, instead of the episode at the bus garage or the School Marm Quilter's identity.

"He's having a good morning. We watched his favorite game show together." She shared. "But don't you have more important things to worry about than what kind of day James is having?"

"I do, but I wanted to be sure you were okay after scaring you and your friend last night." He paused, shaking his head. "You know you were lucky I caught that call. It could have turned out differently if another deputy had taken it."

Grace hadn't thought of that. "I should have called you, but I didn't want to waste your time on a wild goose chase." She knew it was a lame excuse, but it was the truth.

"I understand that, but you put yourself and your friend in an unsafe situation. You could have jeopardized evidence."

"We were just trying to help."

"I know, but worrying about what you're doing wasn't helpful." He looked her square in the eye. "You have good insights on this murder, Grace. But you need to call me when you have these ideas or information. Let me look into it."

She saw the tense look on his face and realized that rather than helping, she had probably caused him more stress. "I will Kevin. I'm sorry. I don't want to worry you. I'm going to head home for a quick lunch, and then spend the rest of the day with James. I'll be safe and away from trouble there."

"That sounds like an excellent idea. Tell James that I said hi. You two have a nice day."

~ ~ ~

Grace was trying to decide what to eat for lunch when her phone rang. Bea's distinctive voice burst over the line. "Hope I'm not interrupting anything important. I wanted to be sure to get a hold of ya before you went to visit your hubby. Didn't want to interrupt your time with him."

Grace was noticing Bea could be rather thoughtful at times. The more time she spent with her, the more there was to like about her. "Your timing is good. I was trying to decide what to have for lunch before I visit him."

"I'm glad I caught you then. That quilt guild meeting thing is tonight, isn't it?"

Grace had forgotten. "Why yes, it's tonight at 7:00. Did you still want to go?"

"For sure, that's why I'm calling. You said I could tag along with you and I'm hoping that's still okay. I also wanted to take you to dinner before the meeting as a thank you for all of your help during the shop hop."

"Bea, you don't have to take me to dinner for helping you. Besides, you already gave me those fat quarters, so let's call it even." Grace hoped Bea wouldn't press her to have dinner. She wanted to spend as much time as she could with James before the quilt meeting.

"We're not even close to even. I hogged your whole day making you find things to help me be a quilt designer. You barely got a chance to shop for anything and enjoy yourself, so I'm taking you to dinner. I won't take no for an answer. Then, afterwards, we'll go to the quilt meeting together."

She missed having meals with James, cooking or reheating a meal for him after a late shift. Fixing a meal for just herself was not the same as spending mealtime with someone. Since there was no denying Bea, she might as well go and not eat alone. "If you insist. I accept."

"Great!."

"Where shall we eat?" Grace asked.

"How about we eat at that restaurant across the street from the quilt shop?"

Grace knew the place. They had delicious sandwiches and wraps, along with burgers and fries. "It's called The SandBar and Grill. I will meet you there at 5:00?"

"Works for me. We can eat and visit until that quilt meeting starts. See ya then."

Bea clicked her phone off before Grace could change her mind.

Grace ate a light lunch and then spent a quiet afternoon with James. They took a walk around the hallways and then watched TV until he dozed off for a nap before supper. That left her just enough time to head home and get ready to meet Bea.

Grace found Bea sitting at one of the outdoor tables in the side alley next to the restaurant. Bea waved at her and she joined her at the table.

"Hey there. Hope you like sitting outside. I thought it was more private than indoors and besides, fresh air is always nice."

Grace sat down under the umbrella covering the table and picked up her menu. "Outdoors is good. I like the fresh air too." There was a soft breeze and the shade of the umbrella to keep them cool while they ate.

"I got ya some ice water. The gal will be back shortly to take our orders."

"It will give me a little time to decide what I want. Do you know what you want yet?"

"Yep, I'm thinking of having the summer chicken salad." Bea read aloud from the menu. "Grilled chicken breast on a bed of lettuce with feta cheese, candied walnuts, dried cranberries, and raspberry walnut vinaigrette sounds light and tasty. I do try to look after my girlish figure every once in a while."

Grace smiled slightly and nodded agreement. She couldn't tell if Bea was serious or not.

"I think I'll have the pork tenderloin. They're enormous. But I can save part of it for lunch tomorrow." Whenever Grace ate out, she usually had something left over to take home, so she kept a small cooler in her car for her leftovers.

"With my appetite I rarely have anything left to take home." Bea laughed at herself.

"Wait till you see this pork tenderloin. Then you'll see why I can't finish it in one meal."

After they placed their orders, they sat for a minute awkwardly waiting for the other one to say something. Making small talk wasn't easy for Grace and she was surprised Bea was struggling, too. Then Bea broke the silence. "I'm glad that you and Deputy Kevin came over on Sunday. It was nice to have some visitors in that big place." Bea said.

"Thanks for inviting us. Your home is beautiful and being on the lake has to be so relaxing. The view and the sound of the water are so soothing and calm. If I lived there, I'd probably sit watching the water and never leave or get anything done."

"It is nice, but it's plenty big for little ol' me. There's times it can feel mighty empty." She sounded a little lonely. "I do hope Deputy Kevin got what he needed from our talk."

"I think he did and if he didn't, he'll contact you. I'm glad you decided to be honest about the photos on your phone. You know I would have had to tell him the truth about them if you hadn't. That would have been pretty uncomfortable for all of us." Grace remembered explaining to some of her students that it's better to tell the truth right away even if you think you're going to get in trouble. It only gets harder and the consequences are worse if you wait.

"You were right to nudge me along. And I hope you know I had your back when that snobby Miss Julia and her little buddy Elaine were asking about you at the shop hop dinner." Bea looked a little ashamed about not being open and honest about the photos right away and chose to highlight how she'd helped Grace at the dinner.

"I'm glad that you listened and told Kevin the whole story of the photos. The way you handled Julia and Elaine after I left was pretty impressive. It was very nice Connie and Judy stepped in and helped you too. That gives you a taste of what small town life is like. It has its good and bad sides like most everything does." Grace was grateful for how Bea had been so protective and also that Bea had told her what happened after she left the dinner.

"I don't like those two high and mighty ladies much. That's for sure. But the School Marm Quilters, they're my kind of gals. I like 'em."

"I'm sure Kevin appreciated how you handled things and used your discretion too." As soon as Grace said discretion, she remembered Bea not telling Julia and Elaine about Grace giving Kevin her brownie. It made Grace think back to Bea flushing the toilet at the Hummingbird after they found Camille. Aaliyah said having its contents for testing would have helped the police, but Bea flushed them away. Did Bea have her own reasons for flushing the toilet so quickly?

"Bea, I know this isn't proper dinner conversation, but I've been wondering why you flushed the toilet right away when we found Camille at the Hummingbird? Is there some reason that you wanted Camille's stomach contents to be flushed away?" Grace saw Bea frown and wrinkle up her nose.

"Why honey, I flushed that toilet because of the horrible smell. Some of those ladies standing by that bathroom were turning a little green and looked like they might get sick themselves. Reminded me of the time on my third husband's yacht when the seas got so rough his guests got seasick all over the place. Phew, I didn't want something like that to happen at that sweet little quilt shop."

"That would have been awful." Grace agreed, but she still had her doubts and Bea must have been able to read it in her face.

"Besides, why would I tell Deputy Kevin about the St. John's wort being in those brownies if I was trying to hurt Camille? And I just met the woman. Even so, I admit that I didn't like her much, and she sure didn't like me. But I still wouldn't want to do anything bad to her. I've got plenty of money and I'm a smart cookie. I'll learn to be a quilt designer without her help. Plus, I've got you to help me learn the quilting biz."

Grace thought Bea had some good points. She had shared the information about St. John's wort. She had only just meet Camille on the bus so really didn't know her. As far as Grace knew Bea didn't have much, if any, reason to kill Camille. Grace wasn't sure what she could teach Bea about quilt design, but she could help her learn about quilting.

"I was just worried that Camille's stomach contents had been destroyed when you flushed the toilet. I'm guessing they found spatters of it on her clothes or body when they did her autopsy and luckily, I still had my brownie for testing."

Bea didn't have much of a motive. And from the things Grace had heard, there were others who had much bigger issues with Camille.

Their food came and Bea was wowed by the size of Grace's tenderloin. It was bigger than Grace's plate and she had to cut it in two so she could hold it and eat it. They fell quiet as they started eating so they could finish their food before the club meeting.

Then Grace felt Bea poke her elbow and nod her head toward an outdoor table further down the alley.

Kevin was pulling out a chair for Julia. He sat down and placed a large manila envelope on the table.

"That's pretty interesting, don't ya think?" Bea asked.

"It certainly is."

With all of Julia's committees and social obligations, tracking the woman down to talk with her must not have been an easy thing. Maybe this was the only way he could find her and question her.

Grace, and Bea continued eating while watching what was happening with Kevin and Julia. At first the conversation looked cordial, but when Kevin pulled out what looked like an 8 x 10 photo from the manila envelope, things changed. Julia's perfect facade disappeared into a look of disdain and anger. The conversation continued a few minutes longer. Then Julia shoved her chair away from the table and stormed off to her vehicle. She drove away with a squeal of her tires.

QUILTING FACTOID: Quilts can be hand tied rather than quilted. A stitch is taken through all three layers of the quilt and knotted on the surface. Yarn or a thicker cotton thread is used. The tying makes a loftier quilt. It's a quicker way to complete a quilt and works well for quilts that will be handled with less care.

CHAPTER FIFTEEN

"Sure hope she's not going to miss the guild meeting." Bea quipped, a smirk on her face.

Kevin put the photo back inside the envelope and walked over to their table. "Hello, ladies."

Before Grace could say a word. Bea spoke up. "Why, hello, Deputy Kevin, fancy seeing you here. I asked Grace to dinner before the meeting at the quilt shop tonight. My way of thanking her for helping me out on the shop hop."

"Grace could use a night out. She spends a lot of time at the care center or alone at home so it's nice of you to invite her out for a meal together."

Grace was a little bothered by what Kevin said, but maybe there was a grain of truth to it. Other than visiting James, she didn't get out much, except to buy groceries and go to the quilt shop every now and then. "I manage to keep myself pretty busy. I'm very happy with my retirement and spending time with James."

Bea batted her eyelashes. "So, Deputy Kevin, what'd you say to Miss Julia to get her so riled up? I'm surprised a handsome fella like you had that sort of effect on such a fine lady."

Kevin looked at Bea and then at Grace, obviously trying to decide how much to say to them. "Sorry, I can't disclose that information."

Grace wondered if he would tell her more if Bea wasn't there. As if reading Grace's mind, Bea excused herself and got up from the table. "You two probably want to talk privately about James and such. So I'm going to take care of our bill and head over to the quilt shop. Darcy might need a little warning that Miss Julia hightailed it out of here and is possibly a no-show at the meeting tonight."

Bea nodded first to Kevin and then to Grace. "Good to see you, Deputy Kevin. Grace, thanks for having dinner with me. I'll save ya a seat at the meeting." Bea picked up her bright pink designer bag and headed to the cash register.

Once Bea had left, Kevin relaxed. "Nice seeing you. I've been busy trying to catch up with Julia." He smiled, showing his dimple. "But then I remembered you ladies had a quilt meeting tonight. I called Meg, umm, the shop and asked what time the meeting was so I could catch Julia before she went in."

"I'm glad you didn't let Julia off the hook. She looked awfully upset when she blew out of here. What happened just now?" Grace asked.

"I told her forensics is checking Camille's purse for fingerprints and that I suspect they will find either hers or Elaine's. Since I don't have copies of her fingerprints yet, she didn't seem worried. But when I showed her what was in this envelope, she knew I had her backed into a corner."

"I can't wait to find out what's in the envelope, but why'd they hang on to the purse? Why not search it on the bus and leave it there with Camille's things?"

Kevin kept glancing at the uneaten half of Grace's sandwich. "Because they didn't have time. They took it, but couldn't put it back before I came and got Camille's things, so they hung onto it." He tightened his lips. "Are you going to finish that? I haven't had time to eat much today."

"Please, help yourself."

Before she answered him, Kevin grabbed the remaining half of her sandwich and bit into it. After he'd swallowed, he took a leftover fry. He chewed the fry and then continued. "Julia figured they would leave it in Camille's office after the shop hop, but by the time the bus got there we were already thinking things weren't adding up, and the office had been locked."

"So they hid the purse in the bathroom."

"Probably thought it would get thrown away. Like the travel cup." He took another bite of pork tenderloin.

"But why would they take her purse?"

"Julia wanted the letter Camille was fanning herself with on the bus. Thanks to your friend Bea's photo, when we saw the address on that letter, we realized why." Kevin pulled a photo out of the envelope he'd shown Julia. Although it was blurry, Grace could make out the address to the State Bar Association in Camille's large, flowing handwriting, with Camille's return address in the corner.

"I showed her the photo, and told her I had a witness who had overheard her talking about Mrs. Christianson sending letters of complaint to her husband's partners about his alleged mishandling of Mrs. Christianson's divorce and possible fraudulent billing practices. She tried to deny it. That's when I requested a copy of her fingerprints for the lab. I guess she felt backed into a corner and confessed what she and Elaine had done."

"So, what exactly did those two do?" Grace was eager to hear.

"Tried to steal the letter. Julia was panicked that the letter to the bar association would ruin her husband's career. While on the bus, Mrs. Christianson was waving it around in Julia's face. According to Julia, Mrs. Christianson did it on purpose so she would get upset. Elaine noticed Mrs. Christianson had more letters in her purse. When Mrs. Christianson rushed off the bus, she left her purse behind which gave them the opportunity to take it."

Grace knew reputation and status in the community was all important to Julia so she would want to avoid any hint of a scandal. Grace wouldn't have been surprised if Julia had political ambitions for her husband. "I guess Julia thought her problems were solved when Camille's dead body was found at the Hummingbird."

"How would that solve her problems?" Kevin asked between bites.

"With Camille dead, she wouldn't be around to write any more letters. When Rose ran to the bus to get Aaliyah, everyone, including the bus driver, left the bus and ran inside the quilt shop to see what was going on. Julia sent Elaine outside to call 911 and watch for the EMTs. I remember Julia and Elaine having a whispered conversation and then Elaine said the oddest thing—'I'll take care of things.' So Elaine called 911, but then she must have gotten onto the bus to search through Camille's things. Unfortunately for her, people started coming out of the quilt shop when they heard EMTs arriving, so Elaine shoved the purse in her own tote bag to search later."

"That's a good assumption, but how would you prove it?" Kevin asked.

"When I was getting back on the bus, I thought I saw Julia slide something under the things on her seat. I bet it was those letters." Grace said.

"Probably. Julia claimed that Elaine found letters addressed to newspapers and television stations."

"I thought I was the only one who still mailed letters to people. It seems like most everyone uses email or texts or some sort of social media these days." Grace hadn't thought someone as accomplished as Camille would be as out of step with the times as she was.

Kevin shrugged. "Maybe she was old school too or she might have thought those places get tons of emails and hers would get overlooked or deleted easily from someone's inbox. What you're suggesting is once they found and destroyed the letters and with Camille dead, Julia figured she wouldn't have to worry about Camille ruining her husband's reputation."

"Did they find the one to the bar association that's in Bea's picture?" Grace asked.

"Funny thing. They didn't find that one. Julia didn't think Elaine found the design notebook when she searched Camille's things, but she was positive Camille put that letter in it. She's still very concerned that they didn't find it and get rid of it."

"That is strange. If they didn't find or take the design notebook, where could it and the letter be?"

Kevin didn't have an answer.

"So how did the purse end up back at the Quilters Playground?"

"With me visiting you ladies at the Lakeside Marketplace and again at the Willow Grove Shop, they didn't know when I might show up again. They didn't want to take the chance of being caught with the purse. They didn't want to dispose of it at any of the other shops because Camille was already deceased and couldn't have forgotten it at any of them. They decided it would be safer to go through the purse and dispose of it when they got back to the Quilters Playground. Once they got there, they took it to the restroom and searched all the pockets for anything else that might be damaging to Julia's husband. But when they went to put the purse in Camille's office, it was already locked."

"That makes sense. I remember seeing Julia and Elaine coming out of the hallway to the restroom when we got back to the Quilters Playground. It was while you were talking to Darcy by the cutting table." Grace had thought they looked like they were up to something, but at the time she figured she was being paranoid because of the way they'd acted at the Old Windmill Quilt Shop.

"I told Julia we needed her fingerprints and that she needed to bring Camille's letters to the sheriff's office as soon as possible or I'd get a search warrant for her house. And if she didn't bring them by early tomorrow morning, I would pick her up in a marked squad car and give her a ride to the sheriff's office myself. That's when she got really upset. She told me she would never murder anyone and I should talk to people like Meg who was arguing with Camille the morning of the murder."

Of course, Julia would be worried about how deputies searching her house would look to the neighbors. And being taken away in a sheriff's vehicle would destroy her standing in the community. It was no surprise Julia would try to deflect blame on someone else–like Meg. "Did you ask Julia if anyone else knew about Camille's heart condition?"

"Yes, Julia said she told Elaine. She also said Meg and Darcy knew about it because whenever they needed to set up chairs or tables, Camille would say she couldn't help because it was too much stress for her heart. Camille wouldn't even put up the ironing boards for the classes she taught."

"Did Julia say what Meg and Camille were arguing about that morning?" Grace hated to ask about it again when it made things look bad for Meg.

Kevin looked like it bothered him to tell her. "She said it was something to the effect that Meg told Camille that she was done being pushed around and that she wanted what belonged to her. Or else."

"Or else what?" Grace asked, her heart pounding in her throat.

"Meg never finished. She must have heard Julia in the hall and stopped talking. Instead, she went to the kitchen."

Oh dear, Grace thought. Now Kevin knew for sure Meg had knowledge of Camille's heart condition, and the two of them had been arguing that morning. That didn't sound good for Meg.

"So, are you going to talk to Meg again?"

Kevin sighed. "It looks like I'll have to. I really want to talk to Elaine before she talks to Julia."

"Do you remember that Elaine is vice president of the quilt guild? She should show up for the guild meeting any time now."

"You don't say. I just might have to catch her before the meeting starts."

When Grace and Kevin crossed the street to go to the Quilters Playground, Elaine's vehicle pulled into a parking spot. While Grace continued to the quilt shop, Kevin walked over and opened Elaine's car door. Elaine smiled thanks, then her face filled with panic when she saw it was Kevin. Julia must not have called to warn her Kevin would be looking for her and that he knew about their activities on the shop hop. Instead, Julia probably called her husband and left her dear friend hanging high and dry. Grace stepped inside the shop and went to the front window to watch what happened next. She felt someone come over and stand next to her.

"What ya looking at?" Bea asked her.

Grace lowered her voice, "Kevin's talking to Elaine."

"About what?" Bea whispered. Until now, Grace wasn't sure Bea was capable of a whisper.

"I'm not sure, but I want to see how she reacts to whatever it is he says."

They pretended they were browsing the new displays while they kept checking out the window. Kevin and Elaine walked across the street and sat on a bench outside one of the shops that had already closed for the day. He appeared to be politely talking to Elaine.

Without Julia, Elaine looked small and insecure. She kept touching her pearl necklace, rubbing the pearls between her fingers either to calm herself or make a wish to disappear into thin air. She looked like she wanted to sink into a hole in the sidewalk beneath her. Kevin must have been telling her what he had learned from Julia. Then he showed Elaine the photo from the manila envelope, and she shook her head. When she looked at her hands, Grace reasoned he must have told Elaine he needed her fingerprints. She nodded agreement before dashing off to her car and scrambling into the driver's seat.

Grace could see her chest heaving in and out as she sobbed uncontrollably. Her hands shook as she frantically tried to start her vehicle. At last, it started, and she drove away.

"Now that looked rather dramatic, didn't it?" Bea said.

"It sure did. I wonder what they talked about." Grace hoped Kevin would find the time to fill her in on his conversation with Elaine.

"Oh, I'm sure you'll find out." Bea said with a knowing voice.

QUILTING FACTOID: Novelty or conversation prints are fabrics designed with a theme such as holiday symbols, hobbies, sports, or pets. Quilt panels include a theme or novelty prints and are 24-36 inches wide and 36-40 inches long. Blocks and borders can be added around the panel to create a quick and easy quilt.

CHAPTER SIXTEEN

When the phone rang the next morning, Grace was still in bed. Her caller id said it wasn't the care center, so she let it go to voicemail. Wishing James was there to wake her with a morning kiss, she stayed there a few moments longer before getting up to check her voicemail. Vi's familiar voice said she had something important to tell her and to please call back as soon as possible.

Grace wondered what that was all about. What sort of information would Vi have? Vi had been at the guild meeting the night before, but without Rose. She'd arrived late and left early, so Grace didn't get a chance to talk to her. There was a lot of chatter about Camille. Most of the ladies mentioned Deputy Oleson had already contacted them about what they had seen on the shop hop. As Bea had predicted, neither Julia nor Elaine showed up for the meeting, so Meg had filled in. She'd put the stress of Camille's death aside and kept the meeting light and enjoyable.

Grace made a quick cup of coffee, hoping the caffeine would jumpstart her thinking, and then dialed Vi's number. Before the first ring had finished, Vi answered. "Oh, Grace, thank you so much for returning my call. I didn't know who else to talk to about this."

"Of course, Vi. I'll try to help however I can."

"Well, I don't know where to begin. It's so upsetting, all this stuff about Camille."

"Yes, I know how you feel. Just start at the beginning."

"You know that Deputy Oleson has been talking with everyone who was on the shop hop. When he came over to talk with Rose and me he was very polite and kind, but having a deputy question you is pretty scary for adults so you can imagine how nervous Rose was."

"I'm sure she was frightened and knowing Rose she was probably pretty quiet."

"Exactly. I answered all of his questions and tried to get Rose to share anything she'd seen. She didn't say a word. After talking to some of the gals at quilt guild last night, I got to thinking Rose might know something and not realize it. Since a couple days have gone by, I thought she might be less worried and talk to me. So I left the meeting as soon as I could to get home and talk with her."

"That makes sense. How did it go?"

"Grace, I couldn't believe it. Rose showed me Camille's design book. That purple one Camille had on the bus. That's why she wouldn't talk to Deputy Oleson. She thought he would arrest her for stealing it. When I asked her where she'd found it, she said she just picked it up out of the box of garbage when we got off the bus."

"Oh, poor girl. Kevin would never think taking something out of the garbage was stealing. He's been looking for Camille's book. He will be so grateful that she found it."

"That's what I told her. I've tried to reassure her, but she's still afraid to talk to him and turn it in." Vi paused, and Grace could hear her take a ragged breath. "I know how close you and Deputy Oleson are, and you have a way with kids. Would you mind being there when Rose gives the design book to him?"

"I would be happy to be there for Rose. Were you going to take her to the sheriff's office to turn it in?"

"No, I talked with my daughter Lily, Rose's mom, about it. We think that'd be even more terrifying for her than when Deputy Kevin came here and questioned us. Rose was so scared and we don't want her to feel like that in my home again. Grandma's house needs to be a safe, happy place for her. I was thinking someplace different, maybe the quilt shop. Rose enjoys going there. And I think if you're there to help me reassure her, she'll be less tense and hopefully will talk about things."

Even though Vi couldn't see her, Grace nodded her head in understanding. "We all want to do what's best for Rose." She reassured her anxious friend. "It sounds like a good plan to me. When do you want to do this? If you'd like, I can call Deputy Oleson for you and make the arrangements with him."

"I think the sooner the better. The shop opens at 10:00, so how about today at 10:30?"

"I'll call Kevin. If you don't hear back from me, that means he's available and will meet us there at 10:30. Tell Rose not to worry, she's doing the right thing."

"I'll tell her. Thank you, Grace. Thank you so much."

As soon as Grace hung up, she rang Kevin's number. She couldn't wait to tell him Camille's design book had been found.

"Deputy Oleson. How are you today, Grace?"

"I'm doing well and you will be too when you hear my news." Grace was finding it hard to contain herself. "I just got off the phone with Violet and she told me that Rose has Camille's design notebook." Maybe something inside would tell them if it was indeed Camille's notebook, or if it belonged to Meg, like she claimed.

"That's fantastic." Grace could hear the excitement in his voice. "When I talked to them the other day Rose barely said a word."

"Vi said Rose was too frightened to tell you about it because she thought you might think she stole it. She asked if I could be there when you talk to her this time. I hope that's okay. They'll meet us at the quilt shop at 10:30 this morning, if that works for you."

"I'm available then. But why the quilt shop?"

"Several reasons. Vi was worried that going to your office might be scary and possibly traumatizing for Rose. She's thinking the quilt shop is a place Rose likes and with me there maybe I can help her feel more comfortable talking with you."

"If that will help her share what she knows, I don't have a problem with it."

"I think talking there and keeping things low key will help Rose."

Since Rose was already so frightened about having the book, Grace hoped Kevin could contain his natural energy and drive to solve this case when questioning the young girl.

"I'll meet you at the Quilters Playground at 10:30."

Ending the call, Grace finished her coffee. The day was off to a good start. She had just enough time for a quick visit with James before leaving for the quilt shop at 10. She wanted to be sure and be there before Vi and Rose arrived.

~ ~ ~

Grace waited by a display of nickel packs. The coordinating 5 inch fabric squares had always appealed to her and the accompanying patterns seemed quick and easy. But did she want to start yet another project?

When she and Vi had spoken, she hadn't considered anyone else would be in the quilt shop. Fortunately, Meg was busy putting out new fabric and Darcy had disappeared into the back the moment Grace had arrived. Grace sighed with relief when the only other early shopper paid for her purchase and left at ten-twenty.

At 10:25, the bell on the shop door rang and Grace turned at the sound. Vi walked in. Rose trailed behind her, a purple backpack over her hunched shoulder. "Come on, Rose. It will be alright. My friend Grace is meeting us. You remember her from the bus. The nice lady you took the magazine to." Rose shrugged and stared at her feet.

Grace left the display she had been studying and walked toward them.

From where she was putting fabric on the shelves, Meg smiled at the young girl. "Hey, Rose. Good to see you, and you too, Vi. Can I help you ladies with something?"

Vi looked at Grace, then back at Meg. "Oh, hello, Meg. No, we don't need any help, we're just meeting Grace here."

Evidently Vi hadn't considered they wouldn't be alone in the shop either.

"That's nice. Grace is a great teacher. I had her in school. You ladies let me know if you need anything from me."

Grace smiled at the shy girl. "Hi, Rose. How are you doing today?" When Rose didn't respond, Grace led Vi and Rose to the far side of the room where a small table held several baskets of fabric panels featuring whimsical animals. "Look at these cute fabrics. They make me smile, especially the ones with the llamas wearing clothes and jewelry. What do you think?"

Rose hung behind her grandmother. Then Rose pointed at a panel with dogs romping around on it. "This one is funny, but it's too baby for me."

"You're right. It is too baby-ish, but there are others here. What do you think of the unicorns and rainbows?" Grace smiled.

Rose gave her a shy smile in return. "I like them." She stepped away from her grandmother and touched the soft fabric.

"Have you gotten any fabric for the quilt you showed me in that magazine the other day?" Grace asked.

Rose pulled back behind her grandmother. Perhaps mentioning the quilt magazine reminded Rose of the shop hop.

Vi tried to distract Rose. "We're still trying to find just the right fabrics for it, aren't we, honey?" Vi straightened the barrette in Rose's hair. "I told her she could pick out some fabric today after we talked with Deputy Oleson."

"Picking out fabric is about the fun-est part of quilting to me. I bet you'll find something perfect for that quilt with your grandma's help."

"I told her Meg would help us if we needed it. She always likes what Meg picks out for her, don't you?" Vi tried to encourage Rose to speak.

Rose nodded her head while watching her fingers outline the shape of the unicorn on the fabric. The door chimed, and Kevin walked in.

Meg greeted him, a look of worry on her face. "Deputy Oleson. Is there something I can do for you?"

"I'm meeting these ladies. If you could give us a little privacy."

"Of course. I'll let you all take care of your business and stay out of your way." She went back to the cutting table.

Grace greeted Kevin. "Hi, Deputy Oleson. You remember Vi and her granddaughter Rose, don't you?"

He smiled at Rose who stood trembling behind her grandmother. Kevin bent at his knees to lower himself to her eye level. "Why, yes, Grace, I certainly do. I met with them the other day. They gave me some of the tastiest cookies and Vi told me Rose had baked them herself. She can bake cookies for me anytime." Rose peeked at him when he talked about her baking, and her shaking seemed to lessen.

"Meg gave Grandma and me the recipe." Rose told him in a quiet, timid voice.

He smiled at her again, showing his dimple this time. "You'll have to tell her you baked them perfectly, and I thought they were delicious." He paused before continuing. "Rose, I heard you found something that could help me. I hope you brought it with you today. I would really appreciate looking at it."

A hesitant smile replaced her trembling. She seemed to be falling for Kevin's dimples and charm. She took her backpack off her shoulder, opened it, and pulled out a purple notebook. She held the notebook close to her chest for a moment before reluctantly handing it to him. Grace could see her hand shaking.

"Can you tell me where you found it?"

Rose looked at her grandma and Vi nodded her head okay. "When we got off the bus to ride home with Grandpa, I saw it in the box of garbage by the top of the steps." Rose's voice was soft and timid. "Grandma was talking to the bus driver, and the trash was right there. I thought someone threw it away because they didn't want it anymore, and I liked the cover. Purple's my favorite color. So I picked it up."

"I think when Camille raced off the bus the way she did her things must have flown all over the place." Vi explained. "Her notebook must have fallen into that box for the trash by the bus driver's seat. I told Rose she wasn't in trouble for taking it out of there."

Grace tried to help reassure Rose. "You did a good thing telling your grandma about the notebook and bringing it to Deputy Oleson." Grace remembered the damaged mixer she'd taken from the quilt shop trash. "Your grandma is right. We've all seen or taken things from the garbage that were trash to whoever threw them away, but looked like a treasure to us."

Kevin agreed. "Rose, this could be important evidence that you found for me. Nice work." Rose's face lit up.

Kevin began flipping through the pages of the book. Grace was sure he was looking for the letter to the State Bar Association that could be seen in Bea's selfies with Camille. Elaine and Julia said they hadn't found the letter in Camille's purse and they thought Camille had stuck it in the notebook. Or perhaps the letter had fallen out at some point.

"Rose, did you find a letter in the trash as well?" Grace asked.

Rose slowly shook her head.

"There was one in the book." Rose added helpfully. "It had a stamp on it, so I mailed it." The girl looked up at her grandmother. "That's okay, isn't it? That's what you do with letters."

Vi smiled down at her grandchild. "That was the right thing to do. I'm sure whoever wrote the letter appreciates it."

Grace doubted Julia would appreciate Camille's letter to the bar association complaining about her husband being mailed, especially when she thought it was gone for good. Her plan to stop the letters and protect his reputation hadn't worked.

"That's okay, Rose. I know who the letter was to and now that I know it was mailed I can call them and see if it mentioned anything that would pertain to my investigation." Kevin explained to her.

Although Grace wasn't sure Rose understood all the words Kevin used, the girl nodded her head like she did and leaned into her grandmother. Slower this time, Kevin thumbed through the notebook, allowing Grace to sneak a peek over his shoulder.

Except for the pages she'd seen in Bea's photos, most of the book appeared to be blank. Her hands itched to take the book and study the designs closer. But Kevin would need to process it, and even then he might not be allowed to share it with her.

After she had finished shelving fabric, Meg walked toward the cutting table. She stopped. "My design book." Her face lit up with a mixture of happiness and relief. She hurried over. "You've found it. Oh, thank you."

Kevin slowly stood. "Your design book?" His voice held a firmer tone than the one he'd used with Rose.

"Yes. Camille had it, but it is mine."

He looked at the purple embossed cover and the tight stitching. "And why did Camille have it?"

Grace thought Meg looked more anxious than Rose had been. But why would she be so nervous? Meg seemed intent on getting her notebook back. Did she know about Darcy's key to Camille's office? Could she have taken it and searched the office for her design notebook?

"I'd been helping her with fabric selections for her designs, and with my art background I thought it might be interesting to try designing myself. So I drew up a few sketches and asked Camille for feedback. She told me the designs showed promise and offered to take them to market and show some publishers."

"You didn't take them yourself?"

A bead of sweat formed on Meg's upper lip. "Darcy wouldn't let me off. She said someone had to keep the store open."

"I see."

"When Camille came back from market, she said Farmers Bounty was interested in them but they needed to see the design book to prove they were my original designs. So I gave her the book to show them."

Kevin maintained a professional stance giving Grace no clue if he believed Meg.

"Look inside." Grace told him. "Is there a name in the front? On the first page." Even Bea, who was a beginner, put her name in the front.

Kevin opened the cover. The first page had a simple checkerboard pattern.

Meg gasped. "My name, it's gone."

Kevin ran his hand along the binding. Grace guessed he was trying to feel if the pages were loose, something she'd done many times with test booklets that seemed a little thin. Since the book was bound, it would be easy to feel if there was any ease in the spine.

He knelt down next to Rose. "Did you tear any pages out of this book?"

Rose shook her head.

Before Kevin could ask another question, Darcy came from the back carrying several papers. She stopped and stared at the group. Her gaze focused on the book Kevin was holding. "You found Camille's design book."

Kevin stood. "Camille's?"

Grace didn't know what to think. The missing front page made her suspicious. It was a little too convenient that it had been torn out. But who had torn it out?

"Yes, I know it is. Camille carried it with her everywhere." Darcy reached for the book. "If you don't mind, according to our contract, everything Camille designed belongs to Quilters Playground."

Kevin didn't move, letting Darcy's hand hang in mid-air. "Sorry, I'll need to keep this until the case is closed."

Trying to retain her composure after being rebuffed, Darcy tossed her hair back. "Of course." She turned to give Meg a piercing look as she handed the papers she was carrying to Kevin. "I was just coming out here to talk to Meg. It seems we have a whole unit of caffeine pills missing from inventory."

QUILTING FACTOID: Children as young as three would be given thread, needle, and fabric scraps to make what were at first thought to be doll quilts but were actually determined to be quilts for younger siblings.

CHAPTER SEVENTEEN

Trying to process what was going on, Grace looked from Vi to Rose to Darcy to Meg to Kevin.

Rose's small voice spoke up. "Deputy Oleson, I have something else to show you. On our way here, I reminded Grandma I took lots of pictures on my new phone that day. She'd forgot. We thought maybe you'd want to look at them. You can even see Grace, Meg, and Darcy in some of them."

Grace could see Rose enjoyed telling them she had reminded her grandmother about her pictures. Kids always seemed to enjoy showing up adults whenever they got the chance.

Vi chuckled at her own forgetfulness. "You know youngsters. There are some things that they just don't forget, unlike older folks like me."

Kevin's dimple reappeared as he grinned. "You're a smart girl, Rose. Those pictures could be very helpful. Could I look at your phone and scroll through them?"

Kevin set the papers Darcy had handed him on the table while Rose took her phone out of her pocket and opened it up to her photos from the shop hop. She held it out to him, and he gently took it from her hand.

They all watched as Kevin scrolled through the pictures. He stopped at one to zoom in on something and study it more closely. "Rose, can you tell me about this picture here?"

Grace peeked over Rose's shoulder to see a picture of Vi with Connie. In the background Meg was taking something from under the counter. Could it be the box of caffeine tablets?

"Well, I was taking a picture of Grandma and one of her quilter friends when we had breakfast here that morning."

Darcy jabbed her finger at the papers on the table. "That's what I've been trying to tell you. I always do inventory before a shop hop. These ladies get busy and forgetful, and they walk out without paying for those fat quarters and charm packs they've picked up and carried around. After the hop I do a second inventory to document the shrinkage. It all has to be accounted for in the cost of putting on a hop. And the count for the caffeine pills was off. An entire box is missing. That's twenty-four packages of two pills each." Darcy arched an eyebrow and stared at Meg.

"Could you have sold them on Saturday and not recorded the sale?" Kevin asked.

"Not likely, not that many. That's why I came out here to ask Meg about it."

Meg shook her head, trying to speak, but no words came out.

Darcy pressed on. "But now you have proof that she was handling the packets on Saturday."

She scowled at Meg. "What did you do? Did you put them in Camille's coffee?"

Darcy turned to Kevin. "When the first pot of decaf got cold, Meg made another — just for Camille."

The store was suddenly quiet. Meg's chin quivered. "Camille and I had our differences, but I—"

Darcy stepped away from Meg. "I can't have you here. People won't feel safe coming in. You need to get your things and go. And I'll need my shop keys back immediately."

"Ms. Reynolds, I think we should finish this discussion at the station." Kevin informed Meg. A battered Meg stood like a lone tree beaten and broken after a storm. Grace couldn't believe what was happening to her former student.

Kevin gave Rose instructions to email her shop hop pictures to the sheriff's office. The girl seemed to enjoy being helpful, but had a sad look on her face whenever she looked at Meg. After checking the pictures had been delivered, Kevin bagged the notebook and papers. Then he followed Meg to get her purse and shop keys. When they went past on their way out, Darcy held out her hand for Meg to return her keys. As if she was sleepwalking, Meg handed them to Darcy. Grace and the other ladies watched out the window as Kevin put Meg in his patrol car and drove off.

When they turned from the window, Grace saw looks of shock and dismay on Vi's and Rose's faces.

"Grace, Rose is worried about Meg. Would you mind walking us to our car and talking a little more?" Vi seemed worried herself.

"We're all shaken by this, Vi. I'll try to help." Grace imagined Violet and Rose must feel somewhat responsible for Meg being taken to the sheriff's office. "Darcy, I'll be right back to find that fabric."

"No worries, Grace. I'll be here." Darcy was already behind the cash register where she dropped Meg's keys into a drawer under the counter.

Firing Meg, and watching Kevin take her former employee in for questioning, didn't seem to have bothered Darcy much, if at all. Grace left the shop alongside Vi and Rose.

"Rose, why don't you go sit on that bench on the corner and do something on that fancy phone while I talk to Grace."

"Oh, Grandma. I know what you're going to talk about. I hope it's not my fault Meg got fired, and Deputy Oleson took her away. I like her and besides she's the nicest, smartest one in the shop." Rose wrinkled her brow and lowered her head.

"Rose, it's not your fault." Rose looked like she didn't believe her grandmother.

Grace didn't want the young girl to feel like Meg's situation was her fault. "Don't worry, Rose.

Deputy Oleson is questioning Meg like he questioned all of us. You did the right thing and it will help Meg, but it's going to take time. He'll use the evidence that you gave him to figure out what really happened. We like Meg too and we'll help her however we can.

"It will be okay. Please let us talk now. Sit on the bench for just a little bit, honey."

Vi pulled Rose to her side and gave her a brief hug.

"Okay, Grandma. As long as you're going to help Meg." Rose went to the bench and dug her phone out of her pocket.

Once Rose was busy, Violet opened up. "You know I hate to talk about people in a negative way, but things have changed at the quilt shop. In the beginning Darcy and Camille started out as friends and worked real well together." She thought back a moment. "But as Camille became more and more successful, it seemed like things between them soured. Camille wasn't very grateful for the support Darcy gave her or the things that Darcy did for her."

"I've heard a few other people say that Camille could be rather self-centered and rude." Grace shared.

"I'm glad I'm not the only one who thought so. Then when Meg started working at the shop, it got worse. I think Darcy might have taken some of her frustrations with Camille out on Meg. Camille and Meg seemed to get along well until around quilt market time. Meg even helped Camille with fabric selection, not that Camille would ever give her any credit for helping her. Lately, it felt like Darcy and

Camille were jealous of Meg because of the way everyone goes to her for help, especially with picking out their fabrics."

"I didn't realize they were having difficulties getting along." How could she have missed that the relationships at the shop had deteriorated to such a degree?

"I feel so badly about poor Meg getting fired. Do you think Kevin is going to arrest her?"

"I'm sure he just wants to ask her more questions in private and on the record." At least that's what Grace thought would happen.

"I hope you're right. And where does this leave Darcy? I mean, what's going to happen to the shop after all of this?" Vi shrugged her shoulders and deeply sighed.

Grace felt bad for Darcy. Without Camille, where was her business? Lots of ladies shopped there and would miss the shop if it closed, and an empty storefront on Main Street wasn't good for the town either.

Vi motioned to Rose it was time to leave. "Thanks for your help and for being here for Rose today." As they walked to the car, Rose turned and waved.

Grace returned to the shop and found a substitute fabric. Thankfully, another customer came in so she could pay Darcy and leave without any further conversation. Once home, she spread her quilting project out on her worktable. She didn't want to think about the morning's events, but her mind kept replaying them, especially the look on Meg's face when Darcy accused her of putting caffeine pills in Camille's coffee. After making two wrong cuts, she put her rotary tool down. Maybe having lunch with James would take her mind off Camille's death, Meg, and the surrounding investigation.

Thinking of James made her heart heavy. She used to tell him her worries. He'd listen and then put his arm around her and kiss away the worry lines on her forehead. Maybe today when she went to see him, he would be himself again and she would feel the warmth and strength of those arms around her. Feel his lips on her forehead again. There was only one way to find out.

Grace tossed leftover pasta salad, a stale breadstick, a paper plate, plastic silverware, and a bottle of water in her little cooler and took what she thought of as the scenic route. The sun's rays melted into the lake, giving it a warm glow. The beauty and calm of the view quieted her thoughts. Her shoulders and neck relaxed.

Once at the care center, she found herself both impatient and reluctant to enter. Would James be more like the man she loved? Or would he be a stranger? His failing mind making him unrecognizable even to himself.

She found James in his room, watching the television. "Hey, Deputy. Would you like a date for lunch?" Grace held her breath, waiting to hear his response.

"Well, little lady. If you mean a lunch date with you, then I'm your fella." He grinned and winked.

"Why, who else would I have a lunch date with? You know you're my one and only." Grace winked back at him.

She cleared off the little side table, and they pulled up a couple of chairs. An aide brought in James' lunch tray.

James peeked inside Grace's cooler, and shook his head. "Hope you aren't thinking of sharing my meal. You know how big my appetite is."

Grace laughed. "Some things don't change, do they? Of course not, I brought enough for me." She looked up from unpacking her light lunch and saw James was already halfway through his ham and cheese sandwich. After spending years working a job where he had to eat quickly in case he was called away at a moment's notice, slowing down and enjoying a meal was still hard for him.

As she nibbled at her pasta salad, her mind returned to Camille's murder and Meg's situation. James seemed to be in good form today. Maybe he would understand and be able to help her. It was worth a try. "You remember that shop hop I told you about?"

"Sure I remember. That lady died in the bathroom…." James told her.

Grace was excited, he'd remembered. "Yes, she did. Kevin is still investigating. I guess they think someone poisoned her."

"Poison?" He thought a moment. "Probably a woman did it. Women are more likely to use poison."

"I guess they think her heart medicine reacted with a large amount of caffeine that had been added to her coffee."

James nodded as if he understood, so Grace continued telling him what she knew. "The shop owner, Darcy, thinks Meg did it because she made coffee for Camille. That gave Meg the opportunity to put caffeine pills in it."

"Sounds pretty convincing. But why would Meg want this Camille person dead? What would Meg gain from her death?"

James was thinking more clearly this morning, and he was making her think about things, too. "That's a good question. I'm not sure. Meg claims Camille took her design book, but Darcy said she saw Camille carrying the book around all the time. When the design notebook was found there wasn't a name in it so we don't know for sure who the owner is. Plus no one even knew that Meg was designing, except for, I guess, Meg and Camille."

"Is the notebook worth something? Money makes people do crazy things. Ya gotta follow the money. I always told Kevin that." James finished his sandwich and took a spoonful of his baked beans before tasting his coleslaw.

Follow the money. Grace had heard James say that before. How much money can someone make from quilt designs? If the design book was Meg's, were the designs in it worth killing Camille for? Even if they were valuable, Grace couldn't imagine Meg doing something like that. Meg was not that kind of person. So who else would gain from Camille's death?

"Everyone was thinking that the quilt shop would close if Camille left to design for someone else. But today Darcy said she had a contract with Camille. Something about her owning all of Camille's designs."

"Contracts lock people into things. Always read the fine print." James cut his dessert in two and put half of the rhubarb crisp on Grace's plate. Touched that he had remembered it was her favorite, Grace patted his hand.

"Kevin asked Darcy about her contract with Camille. I wonder if he's looked into it more closely. You know how contracts and that legal stuff confuse me. I never have understood that kind of stuff. You always took care of those things for us." Times were changing and she knew she needed to learn about them now that James couldn't manage, but she kept putting it off.

"Contracts...read the fine print. Lawyers write contracts, contracts make money for people. Check for insurance, life insurance, insurance pays money. Who gets the money?"

He was starting to ramble, but somehow his ideas made some sort of sense and were helping her. After all his years as a deputy, this information must be so embedded in his mind that it bobbed to the surface when triggered by certain words he heard. Luckily, in the context of this conversation, his comments made sense and seemed helpful. Her phone rang, but things were going so well with James she just couldn't interrupt their conversation right now.

"Insurance." she hadn't thought of that. "Who would have life insurance on Camille? Wouldn't her children be the beneficiaries?" Insurance was another thing that she didn't like to think about and had let James handle.

"The money. Follow it." James repeated as he took the last bite of his dessert and pushed back his chair. "How's your rhubarb crisp, Gracie?"

"Tart yet sweet. Just perfect. Using just the right amount of sugar is the key to good rhubarb crisp."

He looked over and smiled at her. "The keyman makes it sweet. But not as sweet as you."

Grace felt her heart flutter. This was the James she knew, but just as quickly as the smile had appeared, it disappeared. He blinked in confusion before shuffling to his recliner and picking up the television remote. Leaning back, he switched on the TV and put up his feet.

He was gone to her again. Slowly, she cleared the little table. But what was all his insurance talk about? She knew people could get rich from collecting on life insurance, but what did a keyman have to do with insurance? And what did being sweet have to do with it? Understanding insurance and legal matters was definitely not her strength. James would tease her that for someone so good with numbers, she sure didn't have a mind for business. And she would reply she just liked him to take care of those things so she didn't have to. She'd have to ask Kevin if he knew what James meant by keyman. But would he think she was interfering or grasping at straws trying to help Meg?

Quiet snoring came from the chair, just like used to happen after so many lunches when he was still at home. Although she'd known eventually his thoughts would become less coherent and he'd tire out from thinking so hard she had to look on the bright side. He'd done really well, following along and offering good suggestions, helping her think about things differently. And talking together like old times had made lunch special. Her gaze ran across his features, the jaw still strong, and the graying hair at his temples. She wished he would come back to her, but wishing wouldn't make it so. After clearing the table, she gave him a kiss goodbye before she slipped out of the room.

As she strolled to her car, she remembered her phone ringing during lunch and hoped they'd left a voicemail. Once settled in her car, she checked. Sure enough, there was a message from Kevin. What could this be about?

She quickly called Kevin. "Grace, I was getting concerned when you didn't answer or call back right away."

"I'm sorry, Kevin. I was having lunch with James and we were having a real conversation. It felt so good, I just couldn't interrupt it to answer my phone. Has something happened?" She bit her lower lip.

"Maybe you've already heard. I hate to tell you this, Grace, but we're arresting Ms. Reynolds for Mrs. Christianson's murder."

QUILTING FACTOID: Borders are the fabric pieces surrounding the center blocks. They frame in the design and give the eye boundaries.

CHAPTER EIGHTEEN

Grace blinked her eyes and took a deep breath. She couldn't have heard Kevin right. "What?"

"Ms. Reynolds has been arrested. The DA thought we had enough evidence."

"But Meg couldn't have murdered Camille. She's just not that kind of person." Grace stared at the phone in disbelief.

"We got the lab work back and it tells a different story. That's about all I can say. You know the rules. I wanted you to hear it from me first." His voice sounded discouraged.

"I understand. But no matter what the evidence is telling you right now, I don't think she did this. And I don't think you believe she did it either. I know how these things work, but please do what you can to help Meg."

"I have to handle this by the book, and I have orders to follow. But you know I want to be sure we have the right person too." Kevin was letting her know he agreed with her, but there was only so much he could do.

"I understand, Kevin. Thank you for doing what you can." She sat in her car, trying to absorb what Kevin had just told her. As if losing her job wasn't bad enough, now poor Meg was in a jail cell. Grace had to help Meg, especially since she'd promised Rose she would. But she'd also promised Kevin she wouldn't interfere in his investigation. She had to do something. After talking with James, she realized there were business and legal things she needed to learn more about before she could find Camille's actual killer. Kevin was duty bound to his job, so she couldn't go to him for help, so that left only one person.

"Bea, I need your help. Have you heard the news?" Grace struggled to get the words out.

"Ya mean that Meg got fired and was taken in for questioning about Camille's murder." Bea blurted out.

"No, I mean yes, those terrible things happened, but there's more. I just got off the phone with Kevin and he said they've arrested Meg." Grace sighed. "I hate thinking about her being in jail for something that she didn't do."

"That's unbelievable. That girl is too sweet to kill anyone."

"I know. Even though she has been arrested, I think Kevin will keep on investigating to be sure that they have the right person. But he has rules to follow and superiors to answer to."

"Deputy Kevin must feel awful."

"He was doing his job, but I agree it had to have been hard for him to arrest her." Her voice caught in her throat.

"Grace? Grace, are you going to be okay? You need someone to be with you."

"I'm fine. Meg is the one who needs our help. I think the only way to help her is to figure out who really killed Camille. Will you help me?"

"Of course I'll help you. Count me in for whatever you need."

"Right now, I'm in the care center parking lot. I saw Kevin's message, so I called him and he filled me in. Can you meet me at my house and we'll come up with a plan?"

"You got it. I'm on my way. I'll be there before ya know it." Bea disconnected without saying goodbye. Grace stared at the phone. She should trust Kevin would figure things out, but his hands might be tied by his superior officers or the district attorney's office. Now that she had drafted Bea to help Meg, she knew there was no stopping her. She hoped and prayed together they could figure things out and get Meg out of jail.

Grace pulled into her garage. Before the garage door closed, she saw the front of Bea's red convertible turning into her driveway. Bea slammed on her brakes, jumped out of her car, and rushed through the garage walk-in door. She grabbed Grace's arm and charged into the house and kitchen. "I bet you ain't been eating like you should." Only then did Grace notice Bea was carrying a takeout sack from the MainSail Deli. She didn't have the heart to tell her she'd just eaten lunch with James. "You start some coffee and I'll get some plates. Then we can start figuring out how to help Meg and find the actual killer."

After banging through several cabinets, Bea found the everyday stoneware that Grace used and set the table. Taking thick deli sandwiches out of the bag, Bea put one on each plate along with little containers of salad and finally two pecan pie bars.

After two cups were done running through the pod coffee maker, Grace set the cups on the table.

"There's no way Meg did this." Grace couldn't stand the thought of Mcg being in jail overnight. "I think the first thing we try to do is get her out of jail. Do you know how we can help her get bail and be released?"

"I can call my attorneys. They'll know what to do to get Meg out of that place." Bea declared, taking a huge bite of her sandwich and starting the call.

Grace listened to Bea give her attorney Meg's name and helped her with other information they requested. She wasn't hungry after eating with James, but knew Bea would make a fuss if she didn't eat and the sandwich looked much tastier than her leftovers.

"That's taken care of. My attorneys have contacted the sheriff's office and one of them is on his way there. When bail is set, I told him I would post it, whatever the amount. If bail isn't set today, then she might end up staying overnight. There's nothing he can do about that. Unfortunately, it all depends on when the court is in session for her bail hearing. He'll contact us once he knows."

"Thank you for calling your lawyer, and for paying her bail. I'm sure Meg and her parents can't afford bail and she would never want to burden them with something like that."

"That's for sure. Meg is the kind of daughter any parents would love and be proud of." Bea shared wishfully.

"Maybe we should go to the jail to visit Meg and wait with her while they're working on getting her released?" Grace asked.

"That's a great idea. I'm sure Meg could use the moral support and I want to be sure my lawyer is doing everything he can to help her."

"I could try calling Kevin and see if we can be there for her."

"Do that. Give Deputy Kevin a call." Bea watched as Grace made the call.

"Deputy Oleson." Kevin's voice sounded dejected.

"I'm with Bea and she's contacted her lawyer about posting bail for Meg." Bea nodded her head as Grace spoke.

"So that's who called the lawyers in to help Ms. Reynolds. That was generous and kind of your friend. Once her bail is set and her paperwork is processed, she should be able to leave, hopefully sometime later this afternoon."

"That's good news. We want to pick her up when she's released. Can we come there and visit her while she's waiting?"

"I believe that would be fine, as long as Ms. Reynolds agrees to your visit." Kevin's voice seemed less strained.

"We're on our way. Thank you."

She waited for him to say goodbye. He didn't speak for a moment and then simply said. "Thank you, ladies. See you shortly." He sounded like he wanted to say more, but as a law enforcement officer knew he shouldn't.

Bea had heard Grace say they were on their way and was already headed out the door. Grace shoved their sandwiches and salads into the refrigerator, grabbed her purse, and raced out behind her. They climbed into Bea's car, tires squealing as they sped out the driveway.

"Don't you get a ticket or arrested on our way to help Meg." Grace warned.

"Don't worry, I'll take it easy the rest of the way. I sure don't want to make more work for them pricey lawyers either. How did you find out about Meg getting fired?"

"I was there when it happened. Bea, it was so unfair."

"So why was she fired?" Bea asked.

"It had something to do with those caffeine pills that Darcy sells the ladies when the shop has late night or extra-long quilting sessions. Darcy said when she did her inventory after the shop hop, there were some missing. And Rose had pictures on her cell phone of Meg getting a box from a shelf under the counter."

"Rose was there? She had pictures of Meg from the shop hop?" Bea sounded surprised.

"Well, yes. Vi, Rose, and I met Kevin at the quilt shop so Rose could give Kevin Camille's notebook."

"What in tarnation? How did Rose end up with Camille's notebook?"

"Rose saw it in the box of garbage when she and Vi got off the bus early that day. She thought someone had thrown it away. She liked the purple color and plucked it out of the trash for herself. You know, one man's junk is another's treasure."

"Why sure. That makes sense. I suppose the notebook fell in the garbage when Camille dropped everything and scrambled off the bus." Bea theorized.

"That's what Vi thought too. Anyway, Rose took lots of pictures on her new phone while she was on the shop hop and showed them to Kevin. He scrolled through them and noticed a photo of Meg taking something from under the counter. Then Darcy gave him her inventory papers showing caffeine pills were missing and accused Meg of taking the pills and putting them in the fresh pot of coffee that she'd made just for Camille. It all happened so fast. It was unbelievable."

"Whooey, that is unbelievable." Bea took a few seconds, absorbing what Grace had said. "So did Darcy fire Meg first, or did Kevin say he was bringing her in for questioning first?"

"Does it matter?"

"Sure it matters. When Darcy fired Meg, according to her little theory, it made Meg look pretty guilty." Bea pointed out.

"Sort of like the power of suggestion? Darcy could have been trying to suggest to Kevin that Meg had something to do with killing Camille." Grace blinked, realizing the implication. She bit her lip, trying to remember exactly what had been said. "Darcy accused Meg of poisoning Camille's coffee. And then she fired her. Only she didn't use the word fire — she said that she couldn't have Meg working at the shop because it would make people feel unsafe. Then Kevin asked Meg to go with him to the station."

"Yep. Firing Meg might have influenced Deputy Kevin to take Meg in for questioning. Do you get what I mean?"

"I think I do. I hadn't thought of that before. I think Kevin would realize that Darcy was trying to influence him by doing something like that. But he still needs to cover his bases and check on what she said. I bet he took Meg in so he could get her side of the story without Darcy around. Meg was so devastated after Darcy's accusations and being fired that she could barely talk. Then, on top of that, Meg claimed the purple notebook was hers. That's a whole other story." Grace shook her head.

"That surely is and I do want to hear about it, but we're here now so we need to focus on getting Meg out of this place." Bea's convertible jerked to a stop in front of the sheriff's office and they rushed through the entryway.

~ ~ ~

The deputy behind the counter let Deputy Oleson know they were there. A few moments later, Kevin appeared. "Hello, ladies. I checked with Ms. Reynolds and she's agreed to see you." He led them to a room in the back and then left to get Meg.

Meg entered the room, followed closely by Kevin. Stray wisps of her golden red hair had escaped from her ponytail and fallen onto her pale face. When she saw them, she managed a wan smile.

"Oh, sweetie, we're here for ya." Bea reached out to hug Meg, but Kevin stepped between them.

"I'm sorry. No physical contact allowed." Kevin pulled out a chair for Meg to sit down. "I want to remind you since you are not her legal counsel you have no expectation of privacy or confidentiality while you're visiting. Someone will be posted outside the door."

"Understood, Deputy Kevin. I believe my lawyer should be wrapping things up and letting us know when Ms. Reynolds will be released." Bea stated.

"That's correct. It shouldn't be much longer. I'll bring him here when he's finished with arrangements."

"Thank you, Deputy Oleson." Bea was all business now, no flirting to be seen or heard.

Kevin walked out of the room, but left the door open. They could hear his voice as he spoke to the deputy posted outside, and then heard footsteps down the hallway.

Bea pointed up at a camera in the corner. Grace and Meg nodded at the reminder to be careful what they said or did. After all her years married to James, Grace had never experienced this side of his work.

"How are you doing?" Grace looked at Meg and saw a shell of the friendly, energetic young woman who was so helpful to everyone at the shop. "Bea called her lawyer, and he's here now making arrangements to pay your bail and get you released as soon as possible."

"This is all so surreal. I'm feeling lost and numb." Meg rubbed her fingers against her temple. "Thank you for your help, ladies. Bea, thanks especially for getting me a lawyer. I don't quite understand why you're doing this. You hardly know me. I never thought I'd be in this place...like this…." Her voice trailed off.

"Why, of course I'd want to help you. You're a good person and I can't stand to see good people wrongly accused. We know you didn't do this. My lawyers and Grace and I are going to help you. We're going to get to the bottom of this." Bea sounded like she spoke from experience and it made Grace wonder more about Bea's life before coming to Lake City.

"Thank you for believing in me. I didn't do this, but it looks like the sheriff's office and the DA are pretty positive I did." Meg's shoulders dropped, wilting under the weight of being wrongfully accused.

Grace didn't want Meg to give up on herself. "Meg, I know it looks that way right now, but there are things we can look into and find out who really did this. Don't give up. We believe in you and we're going to help you."

Kevin appeared in the doorway. "Ms. Reynolds, your lawyer is here." Kevin's eyes focused on Meg. "Your bail has been posted. You ladies can wait outside while she's processed for release."

While waiting for Meg, Grace and Bea leaned against the side of Bea's convertible. It wasn't long before a tall, distinguished gentleman wearing an expensive suit exited the building, pausing to hold the door open for Meg before joining them near Bea's convertible.

He shook Bea's hand. "Good to see you again, Beatrice. I'm glad that you called."

After Bea made introductions, she turned to him. "So what do we do now?"

Mr. Gilbert acknowledged Bea with a nod of his head and then turned to Meg. "As your legal representative, I must caution you, don't talk to anyone about your case, especially law enforcement. If you have any questions or worries, please don't hesitate to call me."

"Well, of course, she won't talk to anyone. But Gilbert, my friend Grace and I would like to help figure out who really committed this crime. We were on the shop hop when the murder happened so we're witnesses. Can Meg talk to us and can we get information about her case to help us find the actual murderer?" Bea's stern gaze moved from the lawyer and then back to Meg who nodded her approval.

"Well, typically I don't allow that type of communication, as it can put my client at risk. However, if she wishes to assume that risk I can't stop her."

Grace thought it sounded like the man knew Bea well and realized she was a hard woman to stop from doing what she wanted.

Meg straightened her shoulders and brushed her hair from her face. "Sir, I appreciate Bea hiring you to help me and am so very thankful for your representation. I have no problem with Bea and Grace knowing any information related to my case. I think they may be my best chance at proving my innocence."

"Ms. Reynolds, from what you just stated, am I to understand that you have requested that Mrs. Vargas and, err, Mrs. Meadows, be informed of any information that pertains to your arrest and the charges that have been filed against you? Is that correct?"

"Yes, sir, that is correct. I am giving you permission to do exactly that." Meg agreed.

"If that is your directive, I think we can use Mrs. Vargas and Mrs. Meadows as, shall we say, investigators on your case." Everyone nodded. "I believe we're all in agreement on this arrangement so let's leave and get you on your way home."

QUILTING FACTOID: A signature block has an open or blank area where a signature can be written with permanent ink or embroidery.

CHAPTER NINETEEN

Grace and Meg climbed into Bea's car while she thanked Mr. Gilbert. He handed her a file folder before leaving in his shiny black Mercedes. Bea joined Grace and Meg in her car and handed the folder to Grace in the back seat. Grace peeked at the official-looking papers inside and wanted to read them, but decided against it while riding in a convertible.

"Meg, let's get you home so you can eat something and spend some time with your folks, then get some rest. You have to be exhausted after everything that happened today." Bea pulled out onto the street without squealing her tires.

It was a quiet ride to Meg's parents' house. Grace watched Meg close her eyes, feeling the wind on her face and through the escaped wisps of her hair as they drove around the lake and then off into a tidy residential neighborhood. Her face had regained some color and looked less drawn. Bea pulled up in front of a little yellow house several blocks from the school.

"Bea, words aren't enough to thank you for what you're doing." Meg said.

"Honey, don't you worry about thanking me. Grace and I will talk to you tomorrow. Right now you try to get some rest and tell your folks not to worry. We've got this covered."

"I hope Mom and Dad can handle this. Their health isn't the greatest and they worry so about everything." Meg's eyes teared as she spoke. "Bea, Grace, I have to tell you something and I know you'll be very disappointed in me and probably regret helping me. I can't keep it from you after everything you're doing for me. I hope you'll understand and forgive me."

"Why, Meg, whatever are you talking about? Honey, we're here for you and you can tell us anything." Bea tried to reassure her. Grace wondered what Meg could have done that was so serious.

"Please understand I was desperate to get my design notebook back from Camille and she refused to return it. I needed that notebook to have a chance at getting a contract with Farmers Bounty. It hasn't been easy trying to support my folks and myself on what I make at the quilt shop." Meg took a deep breath and then blurted out. "I'm the one who searched Camille's office. I wanted to see if my notebook was there and get it back before it became evidence." She glanced at Bea and then turned to look at Grace in the back. "I'm so sorry. You'll never believe anything I say or trust me now."

"Oh, Meg, I think we understand how important it was for you to get your designs back. But how did you get in the office after the deputy locked it and took the key? Did you use Darcy's key?" Grace asked.

"I didn't have to. There was a key to Camille's office on the keyring that Darcy gave me. I didn't even know that I had one to her office until a few weeks ago when Darcy needed to get into it and couldn't find her key. She asked for my keyring and used a key on it to get inside." Meg told them.

"So you didn't know that Camille took the design notebook with her on the bus that day?" Grace worried that this information gave Meg even more motive to want Camille dead.

"I wasn't sure. I didn't think it would hurt anything to look around and see if it was there. Now I realize how guilty it makes me look, especially since I didn't tell Deputy Oleson about what I did." Meg's voice quavered.

"Ya know, some of them other people might think that, but we're your friends and we know that just because you made a mistake or two it doesn't mean that you killed Camille. In fact, if I was in your shoes I probably would have done the same thing to get back what belonged to me." Bea tried to be supportive.

"Bea is right. We're just glad that you told us now." Grace was glad to know the truth, but knew it made proving Meg's innocence harder. "And if there is anything else that you haven't told us you need to tell us."

"That's everything. I promise you I was upset with Camille but I would never kill her. I can't go to prison. My parents need me and I would never want to disappoint them after all they've done for me."

"We're going to get to the bottom of this, Meg. We're still on your side and are going to find the actual killer. Don't you worry now. You spend some time with your parents while we get to work." Bea told her.

"If you or your folks need anything, you call me anytime. We're here for you." Grace offered. They watched the slim young woman climb the steps to her front door and stop to take a deep breath before going inside.

"Poor thing. She has a lot to stress about: her arrest, her parents, no job, evidence piling up against her, you name it. We need to get to the bottom of this ASAP." Bea said as she pulled away.

"That's for sure. Especially now that she's admitted to searching Camille's office and given herself a probable motive." Grace shook her head. "By the way, I didn't know we were going to be designated investigators on her case. It's an unexpected surprise, but the important thing is that being investigators will help us help Meg." Grace only hoped that Kevin would feel the same way. "After all, we were on the shop hop and saw everything that went down that day, and we found Camille's mug, too."

"I knew you would like it. Like you said, we've already been doing some investigating. And you know we couldn't just sit around when we think the sheriff's office has prematurely closed the case by charging Meg. Now we're official and it'll help us get access to more info. Let's go back to your house and get started going through that file Gilbert gave me. I'm getting hungry and we still have those sandwiches to finish at your place. I always think better on a full stomach."

~ ~ ~

Grace pulled the sandwiches and salads out of her refrigerator while Bea started reading through the papers in the file. "So what's in there?" she asked.

Bea took a huge bite of her sandwich and chewed for a few seconds before finally swallowing. She waved her hand. "Ol' Gilbert did what he does best. He got these reports or charges or whatever they are. It sure doesn't look good for Meg."

"What do you mean?" Grace asked.

"Well, it's worse than we thought. Meg's fingerprints are all over that travel mug, and the lab found caffeine residue in the bottom. Not a little bit like you might get from not washing out your cup, but from a partially undissolved pill."

Grace put down her sandwich and stopped chewing. "We knew that Meg's prints would be on the cup since she made Camille's coffee. But that caffeine pill residue is not good news."

"The missing caffeine pills and the big argument everyone heard before we all got to the Quilters Playground that morning, along with Meg searching Camille's office and claiming that Camille's notebook and the designs in it are hers, makes it look pretty bad for her."

"Oh, Bea, I know she didn't do it. I just know it. Vi and especially Rose are worried about Meg and I told them we would help her. I think we can figure this out if we go back over the clues. James gave me some advice, too."

"How is James doing?" Bea's voice softened as she spoke about him. "When you talked with James about the murder, did he understand what you were telling him?"

"What do you mean?" Grace hadn't told Bea much about James' condition, so why would she be asking such a thing?

"Grace, I know why James is in the care center." Bea gently told Grace. "At the dinner after the shop hop, I mentioned to them School Marm gals that you worried all day about being away from him. I asked them if he was in the care center for some sort of recovery or rehab after a surgery or serious illness or on the job injury. They told me why he's there. They just said that he's in the memory care unit and they admire how you're handling a very sad, difficult situation. I'm so sorry Grace."

Grace felt blindsided and upset the ladies had been talking about James and her, but she also knew it was the nature of small town life. At least now she didn't have to tell Bea about James herself. It was so difficult to talk about and to know when or how to tell people. Most found it hard to believe such a capable, physically healthy man had developed his condition at his age. There were days she still couldn't believe it herself.

"Thank you. I guess I should have told you myself, but it's still hard for me to say the words out loud."

"I understand. I had a hard time myself telling people about losing my Orlando. There's no pressure from me to talk about James, unless you want to." Bea patted her arm. "I just wanted to be sure about the advice James gave you so we can do our best to help Meg."

"I know we need to get to the bottom of things quickly for Meg's sake. James was having a good afternoon and understood most of what I told him. His suggestions seemed to connect with what I was saying, but I need help to understand how." Grace explained.

"If you believe and trust the advice that James gave you, then I trust you, and him, too. Besides, you know everything about everyone in town, and we're both pretty smart. I know together we can figure this out." Bea said. "So what clue do ya want to start with?"

Grace took a bite of her sandwich as she thought. "James said to follow the money so let's make a list of people who didn't like Camille and who have some sort of money connection with her."

"People who didn't like Camille. I think that could be a mighty long list, like most anyone who met her. But if we follow the money like James said that should help narrow it down. We can start with that Miss Julia lady, that's for sure." Bea said.

Grace swallowed. "Exactly. Camille was writing all those awful letters about Julia's husband to his partners and even to the Bar Association." She put her sandwich back on her plate. "We should write this down."

Grace got a pad and pencil and made two columns. One column for the suspect and the other for their motive. Bea read along as she started writing information. In the first column she wrote Julia's name and then why Julia didn't like Camille, then drew a line under it.

After a moment's hesitation, she wrote SMQ for School Marm Quilter. She didn't want to put down Judy's name. Sharing that information with Bea didn't seem right, especially since she hadn't told Kevin. Across from the initials she wrote forced her to retire. Then Grace crossed the entry out. If Judy was going to kill Camille, wouldn't she have done back when she had retired? Why would she have waited so long? After all this time, Judy had nothing to gain from killing Camille.

While staring at Julia's name, Grace took another bite of sandwich. Although Julia was upset about Camille's letters, this hadn't been the first one Camille had sent. If she followed the money, like James had told her, Julia's husband had overcharged Camille. But was that money worth killing her over? Her husband was actually a decent lawyer, he'd gotten Camille's health insurance covered by her ex, despite Camille having a heart condition. That was worth a lot of money.

During the phone call on the bus, didn't Julia say something about him checking on some contract for Camille? So whatever her reasons, Camille was still using him as her lawyer, but probably on her terms. It was another example of Camille always placing blame for her problems on others or using someone to benefit herself.

Reluctantly, Grace crossed out Julia's name. That left no one except Meg. Wishing she didn't have to, she wrote Meg's name on the list.

Bea frowned. "So you think Julia's in the clear. What about that other lady? You know, that mini-Julia."

"Elaine?" Grace nearly choked on her sandwich. "Why would she kill Camille?"

"To please her friend." Bea narrowed her eyes and nodded, a knowing smile on her face. "You know, like in them movies—I'll kill the person you want dead and you kill the person I want dead."

"But who does Elaine want dead?"

"I don't know. Maybe she hasn't decided yet. Maybe she killed Camille as a pay it forward kind of thing."

Now Bea was acting like a student reaching for any explanation, whether or not it made sense. Without realizing it, Grace must have given Bea one of her teacher looks, letting her know it was a bit of a stretch.

"Okay, maybe it was a bad idea." Bea said. "How about we write down all the clues?"

Grace wrote CLUES on the top of the next page. They could come back to their list of suspects later.

"Those nasty brownies full of them weeds that interacted with Camille's heart medicines. That St. Johns wort can really mess with some medications. I know it did a doozy on me. I can only imagine what it would do to someone on heart meds. Especially if ya kept inhaling them brownies like a vacuum the way Camille was. How many do ya think she ate?" Bea made a disgusted face, probably remembering the one she'd tasted and spit out.

"I'm not sure." Grace tried to think back and count. "She had one or two at the shop and you saw her eat a couple on the bus. So I'd guess she had four or five of them."

"And them brownies were dark chocolate. That would add to her caffeine levels too, don't ya think?"

"Possibly." After Grace wrote down brownies, she squinted at the word. "Does it seem odd that Meg made them at the shop, the day before the trip?"

"What do ya mean?"

"With everything Meg had to do: cut and fold fat quarters, make kits, organize the meals and snacks for the different buses, why was she making brownies? That was a lot of extra work, especially with the mixer out of commission."

"But Darcy was Meg's boss, and she was just following orders." Bea stopped shoveling salad into her mouth. "I thought you said that she makes them brownies all the time."

"Yes, for quilt guild, but didn't Darcy say they were a special treat just for the hop? I heard her say that she had Meg put one in every shop hop tote to be sure everyone got one."

"Why, yes, she did. You write Darcy down next to that clue."

"Then there are the caffeine pills that are missing from inventory." Grace wrote down pills.

"And that sweet girl Rose has a picture of Meg taking them." Bea shoved the last of her pecan pie bar into her mouth.

"No, she has a picture of Meg taking something from under the counter, but you can't see exactly what's in her hand." At least Grace didn't think you could. Maybe if she asked Kevin he would enlarge the picture and they could tell. She reached for her sandwich, only to realize it was gone. Had she eaten the whole thing?

"Well, if you think about it that way. Anybody could have taken them. Or it could be a miscount in inventory. I remember once, one of my husbands thought he'd lost a case of wine. Blamed the cook, but someone had shoved it behind the door of the storage room and somebody else had put it up on a shelf. When they went to get napkins, there was the missing wine. Had to hire the cook back and give him a raise."

"So we really could use a better look at that picture, but I don't know if that's likely to happen. Unless we get your lawyer to request a copy of it for us, but that will take time. So what else do we have?" She added Rose's photo to the list as a reminder to ask Mr. Gilbert about getting a copy.

"That there design book. Was it Meg's like she says? Or did it belong to Camille like Darcy says?" Bea polished off her pecan pie bar.

"It must be Meg's, otherwise why would she admit to searching Camille's office for it? Then again, that's only Meg's word and doesn't prove it's her book. Do you still have those pictures on your phone? The ones you took of the design book?"

"I surely do." After licking the last of the pecan pie filling off her fingers, Bea began scrolling through her phone.

Grace took several bites of her salad while she waited.

"Not that I was going to keep them. I was going to get rid of them, just like you told me to, but I thought I should hang onto them a while longer. Ya know, just in case."

Bea stopped and turned the phone toward Grace. "Here they are. But they're pretty fuzzy."

Grace enlarged the picture as much as she could. The checkerboard quilt was neatly drawn, the dimensions labeled with tight, precisely written numbers. "Didn't you have a picture of Camille fanning herself with something on the bus?"

Bea reached over and scrolled back to the first picture she'd taken of Camille. "Yep, there she is."

Grace enlarged the part of the picture, showing the envelope Camille was holding. "Look, you can see the address. It's not typed, it's handwritten. See how it sprawls out to the edge of the envelope."

"Uh, huh?"

"But look at the book, see how small and neat the letters are." Grace swiftly flicked through the photos until she got back to the hazy book page. "I don't think they were written by the same person." After years of students trying to hand in someone else's work as their own, she was sure of it. "And look at how the ends of the last letters curl like a pig's tail. But in the design book…" Grace squinted, carefully checking the ends of words and letters. "They do in some but not in others. As if someone added them but missed a few."

"By golly, you're right. They teach you that in teacher school?"

No, it was just something Grace had picked up on her own checking papers. Inconsistencies in handwriting were often indicators a student wasn't doing the work themselves and needed extra help, or they were cheating. "So we know the writing on the envelope is Camille's, and it's not hers in the design book. But whose is it?"

Bea knit her eyebrows together. "What do you mean? If it ain't Camille's, then it's Meg's."

"No, we can't prove that. We don't have Meg's handwriting to compare it to." Grace hesitated. Should they call Meg and ask for a writing sample? She hated to bother her and get her hopes up before they knew something definite.

"Ya know. I think I saw some handwriting on the papers Gilbert gave me. Maybe Meg wrote on them or signed something." Bea started flipping through the papers and waved a sheet of paper in Grace's face. "Look, here's one with her handwriting on it."

Grace took the paper from Bea's hand. Meg's handwriting was on it, but it was just her signature and the date. "You're right, it's Meg's handwriting, but it's such a small sample that it's hard to tell."

"Well, it looks pretty neat and tidy to me. Not much of that big, fancy, flowy stuff like on the envelope."

"I agree about the size, but this form has a small box to write things in so that could have affected the size and flow of Meg's handwriting. We need to find more of her handwriting to look at, to be sure. I wonder if we could find something with Meg's handwriting on it at the quilt shop."

"I bet we could. Didn't she make them pretty signs for the window?" Grace looked at Bea. She was right, Meg had been making all the signs.

"Let's go." Bea stood.

But Grace kept staring at the list she'd started. "Slow down a minute. Remember, we were going to follow the money. When I visited James today he said to look at who had a reason to kill Camille and to follow the money." She tapped her pencil next to Meg's name. "How does Meg benefit from Camille's death?"

Bea sat back down. "Well, she'd get her notebook back."

"If she can prove it's hers." Grace wrote: notebook onto the page. "Why did Camille take the notebook?"

"Because she was being mean. Like she was being mean to that Julia, saying that her husband was a poor lawyer and stuff like that."

Grace made a doodle on the side of the paper. "At the shop this morning Meg said that she gave Camille the notebook."

Bea gave Grace a perplexed look. "Now why would Meg do that?"

"For the same reason, you wanted to look at Camille's design book. Well, almost. You wanted to see how a designer worked. Camille saw one of Meg's designs and liked it, so she asked Meg if she had any more. Meg showed more to her because she wanted Camille to tell her if her patterns were good enough. Camille told Meg they showed promise, and she took them to market for her."

Bea narrowed her eyes in disagreement. "Why didn't Meg just take them designs to market herself? I looked on the internet and there's all these quilt markets where you can sell your patterns. I was thinking of getting myself a booth–once I got a few patterns done."

"Darcy wouldn't let her go. She said Meg needed to stay back and run the shop. Camille went. In fact, she'd just come back from a big show in Chicago. That's where she got the Farmers Bounty travel cup." Grace motioned toward Bea, "May I look at your phone again? Those designs in the notebook, simple, old fashioned blocks, with charming applique, not Camille's style at all."

"Yep, don't ya think that's why the design book's got to be Meg's?" Bea asked her.

Grace held back a sigh. They didn't know that yet. "They are just the kind of patterns that look good in Farmers Bounty Fabrics." Even though she wasn't a designer, Grace could tell that. "What if Camille used Meg's patterns to get a contract with Farmers Bounty?"

"So Meg wouldn't get any money from Farmers Bounty publishing her patterns and Camille would get the money because she told them they were hers. Hold on there, doesn't that give Meg a money reason to kill Camille?"

Bea was right. Camille claiming Meg's patterns as her own to push her own career forward might have made Meg angry enough to kill Camille. "Maybe." Grace didn't, couldn't, believe Meg would kill anyone. But after hearing Camille's daughter had committed plagiarism and gotten away with it, she could believe Camille wouldn't have any qualms about doing the same thing herself.

"But with Camille gone, and if Meg can prove she's a designer, doesn't that make Meg the best choice to become shop designer?" Bea asked.

"Yes, you're right." Grace put down the pencil. Maybe she should leave the detecting to Kevin. "That means Meg didn't have to kill Camille over the design book." Grace picked the pencil back up. "If Camille had signed on with Farmers Bounty, she would be leaving the shop anyway. Camille didn't have to be dead for Meg to take over and become shop designer. But Meg still wouldn't get the money from Farmers Bounty."

"Unless she got a good attorney and with that notebook I bet Meg could have proved those designs were hers. My husband had to prove intellectual property on one of his little inventions. Costs money to sue like that, had to hock my wedding ring to pay for it, but in the end it was worth it. He got me an even bigger rock. That new diamond was a whopper."

Grace wondered if that was where Bea's money had come from. Maybe one of her late husbands was an inventor and entrepreneur.

"So, if Meg benefited from Camille leaving, but not necessarily from her dying, who did benefit from her death?" Grace asked herself, not expecting Bea to answer.

"What about Darcy? She said that the book was Camille's."

"She said she saw Camille carrying it around and thought it was hers. But maybe that's what Camille wanted her to think." Grace said.

"Or maybe Camille's contract was for any and all works."

"What does that mean? James said something about contracts lock people in and told me to read the fine print." Grace stared at Bea in a new light. Where had the woman learned such things?

"See my husband, the same one that invented things, did some work at a company that tried to claim everything he did was their property. That's what any and all works means, everything that Camille did would be the property of the Quilters Playground. Is that the kind of contract Camille had with Darcy?"

"I don't know." Grace was glad Bea understood about contracts. She wondered what exactly the contract said and who had the most to gain, or lose, now that Camille was dead. "Wait, when Kevin was talking to Rose, Darcy demanded the notebook. She said that everything in it belonged to the Quilters Playground. That could be what James meant by locking people in. Camille didn't want her designs to belong to Darcy. She wanted control of them. Could that be what Julia's husband was looking at for Camille? How Camille could break her contract with Darcy? If Camille left and took all her patterns with her, where would that have left Darcy?"

"Sounds to me like she'd lose the store. At least with Camille dying, she'll get a settlement."

"Like an insurance settlement? Would Darcy have life insurance on Camille? James mentioned insurance and said something about a keyman. But what's a keyman?"

QUILTING FACTOID: Quilters use an iron, but they don't "iron." Instead of sliding the iron across the fabric, they press the patchwork by lifting the iron off the fabric and then placing it back down in another location.

CHAPTER TWENTY

"It's a special kind of life insurance. I bet there was a keyman policy on Camille."

"A what? Keyman policy? James told me the keyman makes it sweet. Do you know what that means?" Grace was relieved Bea might be able to make sense of what James had told her.

"Why, sure. And James is right. A keyman is someone who is vital to a business. If you lose them, you could lose the whole business. Sometimes a business will take out a policy to pay them if a keyman dies, so they have an opportunity to find a replacement."

"So Darcy is going to get money now that Camille is dead? Is that what James meant by the keyman makes it sweet? Keyman insurance pays you money and makes you richer?"

"Sometimes. My late husband had that kind of policy on one of his executives—poor man got shot by his girlfriend's ex-boyfriend. We'd have gone under if it hadn't been for that keyman policy. Kept us afloat for the eight months it took to find somebody who could run things."

There was so much about Bea that Grace didn't know. Maybe she had lived a much different, more complicated life than the carefree one Grace had pictured.

"But Kevin would know about this keyman policy. James said that he taught Kevin to follow the money." She was sure James said they always asked about insurance policies and who would benefit from a death. Grace stopped and thought about what she'd just said. "But what if Darcy didn't tell him? Is there any way he would know?"

"That Darcy could have lied to Deputy Kevin about it. Maybe he doesn't know what to look for. Business ledgers can be pretty hard to understand if ya don't know what you're looking for. That's why they have auditors and accountants. If she's been making payments for over a year, nothing new, nothing would look suspicious. But if someone knows what to look for and takes a peek at her books, they could find out."

"We can't just go in and demand to look at her books." Grace stared at her empty cup of coffee. "If Camille was leaving the store, and it looks like she was, would Darcy still get something?"

"Nope, not from a keyman policy." Bea sounded disappointed. "I guess it wasn't a good idea."

"Wait a second. Maybe Darcy didn't know when Camille was leaving, but the way Camille was taunting her with that travel cup, Darcy must have known Camille wasn't going to stay." Grace chewed on her bottom lip. For a moment she thought she heard James tease her—keep biting on that lip and pretty soon I'm going to have to kiss it and make it all better.

Grace got up and put their empty dishes into the dishwasher. "So if Camille left to design for Farmers Bounty, Darcy wouldn't get anything from the keyman insurance? But if something happened to Camille…."

"Then Darcy would get a payout. They only pay if the keyman dies, or is incapacitated." Bea finished for her.

"That's what I thought." Like James had told her, the keyman pays out money and takes you to the sweet life."

There wasn't enough in the dishwasher to start it, so Grace closed the door and stared at Bea. Was she making up leads because she wanted Meg to be innocent? "But Kevin would have asked Darcy about insurance policies and he would be looking into it."

"Just because you're honest don't mean everyone else is. Maybe she didn't tell him. Maybe she lied. Ya know one of them lies of omission."

"If you looked at her books, could you tell if she had this, this keyman thing?"

"Give me twenty minutes and I'll tell you if her pigs could fly. Like I said I got an eye for numbers and know my way around a business ledger."

~ ~ ~

It was a few minutes before closing when Grace hurried through the door of the Quilters Playground.

Darcy scowled at her. "Can I help?"

Grace froze. Why hadn't she thought of a reason to be at the shop before she'd walked in? She couldn't just blurt out: did you know Camille was leaving? "I started a quilt. Yes, I started to cut a quilt and ran short of fabric."

"A miss cut?" Darcy clicked her tongue like you would to a child who should have been more careful.

"Actually, the pattern didn't call for enough fabric."

Darcy did an eye roll. No wonder people preferred Meg's help. "Well, what are you looking for?"

"Background. Something white on white or a tonal white and beige."

"Never anything too exciting for you." Darcy led her over to a shelf of jumbled bolts of light fabrics.

The chime over the front door sounded and Bea came in. She waved at them. "Don't mind me. Just a potty emergency."

Although Darcy glared at Bea's back as she went down the hallway, she didn't stop her. "What does she think this is? A public restroom."

Grace tried to get Darcy's attention back on her. "There are so many. Meg always helped me. What would you recommend?"

"Well, I don't know, Grace. How much are you going to need?"

"Oh, not too much."

"Just pick something. If you don't like it, come back and get another half yard of something else." Darcy glanced down at her watch.

"That seems wasteful. What would I do with what I didn't like?"

"Make another quilt. What else?" Darcy turned toward the checkout counter.

Grace nodded her head, as if she'd never thought about that. "It must be hard for you running the shop all by yourself. I feel so bad for you, what with Camille's death and Meg being arrested. I hope that doesn't mean you're going to close."

Darcy turned back to stare at Grace. "Why do you say that?"

"Oh, just a rumor. But I'm sure you have a keyman policy to tide you over." Oh, my, she'd said it before she could stop herself. She wished she could reel her words back in.

Darcy's eyes narrowed. "That's none of your business, Grace. Just because that deputy is a friend of yours doesn't mean you can just come in here and ask a lot of questions." She turned to stare down the hallway. "Isn't that Bea woman a friend of yours as well?"

"We just met on the shop hop. We barely know each other."

Grace randomly pulled a bolt of fabric off the display. "I think this one will do."

"Just in time to help me close up." Darcy locked the front door and turned off the lights. She grabbed Grace's arm, jolting the bolt of fabric along with her purse out of Grace's hands. "Let's go to the bathroom and see what's taking your friend so long."

Grace tried to jerk her arm free. But Darcy was younger and stronger, easily propelling Grace down the hallway. There was nothing Grace could do.

When they came to Darcy's office door, it stood wide open. Darcy stopped to stare inside. Hearing the backdoor click shut, they both spun around to look through the empty classroom at the closed back door. Grace took a deep breath. That hadn't been the plan.

"I guess she abandoned you." With a shove, Darcy sent Grace skidding into her windowless office. Before Grace could find her feet, the door slammed closed, and the lock snapped in place.

Horrified, Grace stared at the door. "What are you doing?"

"What I should have done months ago when Camille started threatening to leave—burn this place to the ground."

"Darcy, you can't."

"I'll say that I thought you went to the bathroom to check on your friend while I locked up. Then I heard you go out the back. How was I to know you hadn't left and were still here? Why would I think you'd be in my office?"

"Kevin will figure it out."

"Will he? So far he hasn't figured out anything. Why, he even arrested poor Meg." Darcy laughed. "All you have to do is look at her sternly and she goes running."

"But a fire, those are hard to fake. I know; James has investigated them before."

"Yet you were the one who gave me the idea. Talking about the cut cord on that mixer and how it was such a safety hazard. Accidents happen, especially when, as you just said, someone is short on help and stressed and overworked. After having to fire my best employee and watch her taken in for questioning about the murder of another employee, I'm surprised I can even think straight. Those irons are old and get awfully hot when someone forgets to unplug them. If a can of spray starch happens to be left next to them, it might even explode. How unfortunate for you that an exhausted shop owner forgot to unplug the irons."

Her voice broiled with sarcasm. "Goodbye, Grace."

As Darcy's footsteps faded away, Grace pounded on the door for help. Where was Bea? Why had she left? Grace's purse was still in the quilt shop with her phone in it, so she couldn't call for help. She grabbed the phone on Darcy's desk only to find the line dead.

What now? Would Bea come back and help her? Would Bea think to call Kevin?

The room grew hotter. Grace could hear the crackle of flames in the adjoining room. A wisp of smoke appeared beneath the door. The smell choked her sinuses. She pounded on the door. "Help! Help! Anyone, help!" The smoke filled her lungs and she coughed. It was hotter. The smoke blacker. What would James do without her? Who would look after him?

"Grace!" A voice called down the hallway.

"Kevin. Please help me out of here."

He tried to turn the door handle. "Stand back." The loud thud of something solid hitting the door bounced around the room.

Smoke choked Grace. Please hurry, she wordlessly begged. Kevin slammed against the door a second time. The frame splintered and wood flew across the room. Grace couldn't hold back a scream.

Kevin grabbed Grace and shielded her from the smoke and flames with his body. He rushed her away from the blazing fire in the classroom and out the front door.

Fire truck sirens sounded down Main Street, and people lined the sidewalks. A frantic Bea paced back and forth next to Kevin's patrol car.

When she saw Grace, she stopped and let out a "Thank heavens."

QUILTING FACTOID: A quilt that held special value to pioneer women was a Friendship Quilt. It was often done in secret and then given to the woman as a going away gift. A group effort, each block was sewn by a friend or relative with their signature in the center. Today a friendship quilt is a gift to honor relationships among friends, classmates, relatives, or co-workers.

CHAPTER TWENTY-ONE

After the fire and Darcy's arrest, Grace gave a statement at the sheriff's office. By the time she'd finished, visiting hours at the care center were over so she couldn't be with James and had nowhere to go but home. Her house felt empty and dark, like the black smoke that had almost suffocated her. Too uneasy to sleep, she drove down to the seawall and gazed at the sun's first rays breaking over the lake. The dawn of a new day and the gentle sound of the water on the beach settled her. When an acceptable hour arrived, she hurried to the care center to find refuge with James.

Grace sat at the table and watched James butter his waffle and drizzle syrup across it. She was thankful to be alive and be there with him. If Kevin hadn't arrived, Grace hated to think what might have happened to her. A sharp rap on the doorframe interrupted her gloomy thoughts.

"Morning, James. Morning, Grace." Kevin's face looked exhausted, but his voice was upbeat. "I thought you'd be here. I wanted to be sure you were okay."

"Okay? Gracie's doing fine." James informed Kevin between bites of fluffy waffle.

"I haven't told him about what happened last night." Grace didn't know how much to tell James about her evening adventure.

"Last night. You were here last night. You're here every night," James told them.

"I try to be, but there was a situation last night, and I didn't make it." Grace's explanation stalled, and she looked at Kevin for help.

"James, did you hear the sirens last night? There was a fire downtown at the quilt shop." Kevin explained.

"Sirens. I missed the call. I need to report for duty." James put down his fork and pushed his tray away.

Kevin kept his voice calm. "At ease, James, it's all taken care of. Fire trucks, law enforcement, and an ambulance were all at the fire. Grace was there at the quilt shop when the fire started."

"Gracie started a fire?" James gave Grace a quizzical look.

"No, Grace was in the shop when the fire happened, but she got out completely unharmed." Kevin kept his explanation simple and didn't take any credit for being a hero and saving her.

James sat frozen in his chair. Then he reached

across the table to touch her hand.

Grace smiled at him with tears in her eyes, thinking how close she'd come to losing this time with him. She grabbed his hand and held it tight, feeling protected by the warmth of his grip. "See James, I'm just fine."

"That's good, Gracie. Be a good girl. Don't mess with fire again." James gave her hand a squeeze before pulling away. Grace longed for James to hold her in his arms and keep her safe, but the clasp of his hand would have to be enough for today.

Grace didn't want to continue discussing the fire. She decided to see if Kevin would tell her more about Darcy's arrest. Talking about the arrest might also keep James interested and participating in the conversation.

"Kevin, you must be excited after making that arrest last night." Grace praised the young deputy.

James' eyes lit up and he straightened in his chair when he heard the word arrest. "An arrest? Who? For what?"

"Kevin arrested the person who killed the lady on that shop hop I went on." Grace explained.

"I had some help. Grace was a good witness and she helped us catch the killer." Kevin was so modest about his accomplishments. James had always said Kevin was a team player and believed any credit given on a case didn't belong to one individual.

Grace watched James to see how he would react.

"Gracie shouldn't be catching killers." James

looked bothered.

Kevin gave Grace an 'I told you so' look. "No, she shouldn't be catching killers, but she and her friend Bea put the pieces together and figured it out."

Grace wanted to give James credit for helping them. "James, when you told me to follow the money and look into the keyman, it helped us identify the killer. We couldn't have done it without your advice."

"See James, you're still the best at solving crimes." Kevin smiled at James trying to keep him talking with them.

James puffed up his chest. "Glad I could help you two. Hope you lock this perpetrator up and throw away the key."

"I think we have all the evidence we need for the DA to do just that." Kevin nodded his head.

"Does that mean the charges against Meg have been dropped?" Grace hoped Meg would be exonerated.

Kevin grinned at Grace and his dimple appeared. "Yes, it does."

"Meg, Meg who? What evidence?" James asked. Grace wondered if James was echoing phrases or really understood.

"We charged Meg Reynolds with the murder based on our initial investigation. I can't give you any specifics, but following a later interview with Darcy Duncan, the quilt shop owner, we looked into the shop's finances and discovered Darcy was having money problems. By murdering Camille, Darcy would collect the keyman insurance payout and get enough money to keep her shop in business."

"Money, follow the money." James wiped syrup off his chin.

"So Darcy framed poor Meg to take the fall for her." Grace thought it was an evil thing to do.

Kevin pursed his lips. "Darcy did her best to make Meg look guilty. But after we told Darcy about all the evidence we had found, she confessed."

Grace sat forward, ready to hear more. "Tell me about it."

"You had already discovered most of it. Darcy admitted to lying about Camille's coffee cup and the missing caffeine pills. As you suspected, Darcy used the design notebook controversy to give Meg a motive for killing Camille. And you also knew Darcy put Camille's office key on Meg's shop keyring to implicate Meg with lies about Meg stealing the notebook from Camille's office."

"I'm so glad you kept looking into things. Bea and I knew Meg would never kill someone. I think you knew she wouldn't, too." From the beginning, Grace and Bea had known Meg was innocent, and this proved they were right.

Kevin smiled in agreement. "Well, I need to be heading out. It's been good seeing you two alive and well this morning. James, I'll stop by again soon."

James held his hand out to Kevin. "Deputy, you did some good investigative work. Congratulations on solving your case."

Grace watched the two men in her life shake

hands and it made her heart happy. "James, I'm going to walk out with Kevin. I'll be right back."

Grace and Kevin strolled down the hallway together. "Kevin, words aren't enough, but I wanted to thank you for rescuing me last night. If you hadn't gotten to the shop when you did, I wouldn't be here with James."

"I'm glad I got there in time and got you out safely. Now maybe you understand why I asked you not to get involved in the investigation. Even James said you shouldn't be involved in finding killers." Kevin spoke firmly, trying to make his point.

"Bea and I took a huge risk. I won't take a chance like that again. No more murder investigations for me. I'm going to lay low and spend more time with James."

"It's a relief to hear that. Hopefully, Lake City won't have any more murders so we won't have to worry about it." Kevin stifled a yawn. "I've gotta go, but you know I'll be in touch."

After being up most of the night interrogating Darcy and writing his reports, Grace thought he was overdue for some sleep. She wondered if the only thing keeping him going was the adrenaline from Darcy's arrest and Meg being cleared.

Grace patted his shoulder. "Thank you, Kevin. Thanks for everything."

~ ~ ~

Grace was relieved they'd helped prove Meg's innocence, but now she needed calm and quiet. She was true to her word and stayed close to home, except for spending as much time as possible with James and taking walks by the lake to soak up the soothing view. She'd seen Kevin several times when he'd come to visit James at the care center. And Bea had called her a few times to chat, but Grace hadn't seen Bea or helped her with any of the quilt projects she'd bought on the shop hop. It might sound lonely to some, but Grace was enjoying the return to her peaceful routines.

A month after the fire, Bea called. "Sorry I haven't talked to you lately. How are you and James doing?"

"Things are back to normal." As normal as life was going to be for James.

"Well, I was wondering if you'd meet me at the quilt shop today."

"But isn't it closed?" Grace inwardly shuddered. She could still feel the dense smoke filling her lungs with every breath she'd struggled to take.

"Yep, the fire did quite a number on it."

"How about we meet for lunch?" Grace had been counting her pennies and had set aside enough to treat herself to a nice lunch at the MainSail. After all that had happened, she'd intended to ask Bea, or maybe Meg to go with her and reconnect.

"I'd really like you to meet me at the quilt shop. We can go for lunch after."

Grace could tell by the tone in Bea's voice that she wasn't going to take no for an answer.

"All right. What time?"

They made arrangements and Grace steeled herself to go back to the shop. At least she wouldn't have to go inside. But why would Bea want to meet there?

When she arrived at the shop, she noticed the Quilters Playground sign on the building was covered by heavy canvas with a long rope dangling to the ground. Meg and Bea were sitting on one of the benches in front of the shop. Grace was relieved they were already there. Thoughts of the fire flickered through her mind and she didn't know if she could have waited for them alone.

"Why are we here?" Grace was surprised at the quiver in her voice. She took a moment to steady herself. "The shop is still closed, isn't it? And what's going on with the shop sign?"

"You'll have to ask Bea." Meg gave Bea a mischievous look.

"Well, ladies. All of your questions will be answered shortly. But first Meg needs to tell you something, Grace."

"No, Bea. You need to tell her your news first." Meg prompted Bea.

"Sure thing. I've decided to stay here in Lake City a while longer." Bea's face beamed.

"That's wonderful news. I'm so happy you're staying. You're going to love settling down here." Grace was excited that her new friend felt like she'd found a place where she belonged and could make a home for herself. "So what's Meg's news, then?"

"Bea and I were talking about how sad it is that the quilt shop is closed. I told her about some things that I'd wanted to try to make it more profitable but never got the chance. Then Bea told me that she'd bought the shop. Can you believe it?"

Bea interrupted. "I got to wondering what was going to happen to the quilt shop, what with Darcy going to jail and all. I'm pretty good at business stuff, if I do say so myself, and I got to thinking owning a quilt shop is probably a better fit for me than being a designer. So I had Mr. Gilbert make some phone calls and what do you know, but it was up for sale. Cheap. I snapped it up. Then all I had to do was fork over some cash and sign my name on the dotted line. Now the place is all mine."

"Isn't that fantastic? Bea has asked me to run the shop and she's going to be a silent partner. Or owner, I should say. I get to try some designing, too." Meg waited to see Grace's reaction.

Grace was thrilled for Meg. All the other quilters in the area would be delighted as well. But she knew there was no way Bea was going to be a silent owner. Grace was sure Meg knew it too and would welcome Bea's financial backing and business background. With the two of them working together, the shop was sure to be successful. "Oh, Meg, I'm so glad that you'll be running the shop and designing, too. You and Bea make a perfect team and are going to do great."

Meg smiled at Grace. "Thank you Grace. In spite of everything that happened here, I'm looking forward to it." Meg looked at Bea who was grinning from ear to ear.

"Now can you tell me what's going on with

the sign and why we're sitting out here instead of going inside your shop?" Grace was surprised she wanted to go inside after the fire.

Bea stood up and motioned for Grace and Meg to stand by the curb. She walked over to the rope and pulled on it. The canvas fell to the ground revealing a new name. "I'd like to welcome you to the Sew Happy Quilt Shop."

Bea pointed to the bright pink and green lettering on the huge sign over the storefront. A new shop logo was painted on it, a sailboat named the Sew Happy with a quilt design on its sails. "What do ya think?"

Meg exclaimed, "It's perfect. I love it."

Grace nodded her agreement. "It's incredible. This will be like starting with a clean slate."

"That's what I was thinking. Speaking of a clean slate. I have more surprises inside. I sent out an SOS to some people I know who work in construction and design. They've been working 24/7 to clean up this place and work their magic on it. Come on in and check it out." Bea unlocked the doors and led them inside. She turned on the lights and twirled around in the newly remodeled shop.

Meg was speechless. "Bea! This is awesome. How did you do this? In such a short time?"

"Well girl, knowing the right people and having a little money always helps get things done quick. This place was a stinky mess after that fire and I was worried about you coming back here and being reminded of what happened. So I figured as the new owner I should freshen up the place. Make it feel new and different. Make it a happy place for you and all the quilters who come in."

"Oh Bea! You are too good to be true. I can't believe this. Thank you, it's wonderful. Everyone will love it."

"You're so welcome, sweetie. You think this is good. Wait till you see the classroom, kitchenette, and offices." Bea led them through the refreshed and reorganized shop area and down the hallway to the back of the shop.

Everything had been updated. New appliances, cupboards, and countertops in the kitchenette. The classroom had a large design wall and a smaller one so ladies wouldn't have to lay out their quilts or blocks on the floor. Ironing boards were in one area along with a couple of taller work islands for ladies to stand at when cutting out their projects. Or sit at during meetings and classes.

With new tables and wheeled, cushioned chairs that could be adjusted to different heights there would be fewer backaches from long hours of quilting. Every detail was well thought out and beautiful.

"I can't wait to show ya the offices." Bea took them back down the hallway and opened the door to what was now Meg's office. New cabinetry and countertops along one wall provided storage, a work area with a design wall, and a little coffee bar.

Meg scampered over to her new desk, sat in the chair, and spun around. "Bea, how will I ever repay you for everything that you've done for me?"

"No repayment necessary, just enjoy running

the shop and doing some designing here. I thought we needed a fresh start and a happy place to work together. If you're happy here, that's what's important to me."

Grace hated to ask. "What did you do with Camille's office?"

"Let's go check it out." Bea strutted down the hall and swung the door open. Grace hesitated, remembering being trapped in that smoke-filled room. She slowly followed her friend.

The office was similar to Meg's with new flooring and cabinetry, but instead of one desk there were two. One was gleaming white and chrome with a bright pink flowered chair behind it. That could only be Bea's.

The second desk reminded Grace of the heavy wooden teacher desks from the old school building. Grace remembered having a scratched and worn one like it when she started her teaching career years ago. This desk had been cleaned up and painted the serene aqua color that Grace favored. Behind it a plaid chair in shades of aqua, turquoise, and soft greens on a sandy cream background coordinated with the desk perfectly. She loved the desk and chair and wished she could try them out, but they weren't hers.

She noticed Meg watching her. "Bea and I have a problem that we could use your help with."

"Oh?" Not more problems. Grace had had enough of problems. She liked her life being normal again and wanted it to stay that way. Visiting James, sewing, reading, gardening, walking by the lake, those things were plenty enough for her.

"I need some help in the shop. Do you think we could work something out?" Meg pleaded.

Work at the quilt shop? Grace had thought of getting a part-time job, but in a small town there weren't many opportunities. Look at all the difficulty Meg had had finding something. And Grace needed a flexible schedule so she could spend time with James or get to the care center at a moment's notice.

"You already know quilting and work well with all kinds of people. With Bea's backing, we can pay you a little more than minimum wage. Maybe you'd be willing to teach a few classes too?" Meg asked.

Grace couldn't believe it. Teaching was something she missed.

Bea looked at Grace hopefully. "It seems to me, you're exactly what we need. This pretty aqua desk is just right for you, isn't it?"

Before Grace could answer, they heard the door chime and footsteps coming toward them. Bea smiled at Meg when Kevin entered the office. Out of uniform, you couldn't help but notice his tall, muscular physique and striking blue eyes. Now that the investigation was over, he looked relaxed.

"Hello, ladies. Bea asked me to stop by to check out the changes here at the shop. It looks pretty fancy to me."

Kevin's attention focused on Meg. When Meg noticed, her cheeks took on a pink glow.

Of course, Bea spoke up without hesitation. "What do ya think? I bought the shop as an investment. I've asked Meg to run it and we're working on adding a new employee."

"I'm sure Meg will do a great job running the shop for you." He smiled at Meg before he turned to look at Bea. "But who's the new employee you want to add?"

"We asked Grace if she would be willing to work here part time and maybe teach a few classes. Don't you think working here would be perfect for her?"

Grace knew Kevin was thinking she wouldn't want to work and give up spending time with James.

"It might be fun for you to work here, Grace. I know you miss teaching and would enjoy doing that again." He paused and thoughtfully added. "I think James would want you to try it. These gals won't ask you to work hours that interfere with your time with him. Give it a try and if it doesn't work out, I'm sure they'll understand."

"Of course, we'll understand. We know how important James is to you. Please, just give it a try." Meg pleaded.

Grace looked at their hopeful faces waiting for her answer. She walked over to the plaid chair and twirled it around. "You've twisted my arm. Yes, I'll give it a try. On a trial basis." Grace smiled and sat down at her new desk. She ran her hand across the smooth surface. In all her years of teaching, she'd never had anything this nice.

"Hallelujah! I was starting to worry I might have to have this desk delivered to your house, and I didn't know if you had a spot for it. I can't wait to share an office with ya and watch you and Meg in action running the place. We're going to make this the best quilt shop for miles around."

Grace laughed. It wouldn't be dull or boring.

Bea lifted her eyebrows and nodded toward Kevin. "Now, Deputy Kevin, why don't you help Meg celebrate her new job running the shop?"

Kevin glanced at Bea and then turned to smile at Meg. "Well, Meg, I'd be happy to help you with that. Are you available for lunch?"

"Now?"

"Now."

Meg turned to the two women. "Ladies, I don't know how to thank you for giving me this fresh start. I just hope you're as excited about working together as I am. How about we meet here tomorrow and figure out how we want this place to run? Then we can hopefully have a grand opening soon."

"That sounds peachy to me. You two go ahead and scoot on out of here." Bea waved Meg on. "We can take care of things. First thing we're going to do is give little Rose a call and tell her she won the shop hop grand prize. Now that I'm the shop owner it wouldn't be right for me to keep it."

"Sounds like a great idea to me. You two go and enjoy your lunch." Grace shooed Kevin and Meg on their way.

As they left the shop, Kevin gently placed his hand on the small of Meg's back. Grace remembered the warm, safe feeling of James' arm guiding her in the same way. She could hear his rich deep voice saying sometimes things happen for a reason. Maybe he was right.

THE END

The Authors

Barbara and Diane have known each other since the nineties, when they were both designing quilts. They currently live in neighboring small towns in the northern Midwest.

After teaching elementary special education for nearly forty years, Diane now spends her time quilting, crocheting, writing and walking along the lakeshore with her little dog, Lennie.

Barbara stays active with quilting, reading, writing, and going to the movies with her husband. Although she has published other stories, this is her first venture as a co-author.

Acknowledgements

Those who have helped and encouraged me as I tried writing an actual book with Barb for the first time are like the thread used to piece a quilt. The pieces of fabric would be nothing without the thread holding them together. A special thanks to Barb for taking a chance asking a novice like me to write this book with her; and for being such a wise leader and patient partner. Thanks also to her talented husband, Henry, for reading the book and designing its cover. To Elin and my mom for reading, sharing their feedback, and even requesting a sequel. To Greg for answering my random questions and being so understanding as I wrote for long hours. And thanks to all of my friends who kept me writing as they asked when do we get to read it?

~ Diane

Every book has its own challenges and rewards. The story of murder on a quilt shop hop has haunted me for years, but I could never pin it down. Thanks to Diane, who accepted my suggestion that we try writing together, that elusive idea became this book. Fearless, she accepted my guidance and edits. It was a joy to watch her grow as a writer.

~ Barbara

www.ingramcontent.com/pod-product-compliance
Lightning Source LLC
Chambersburg PA
CBHW071249250626
47163CB00002B/385